RENDITION

CHRISTOPHER J WILLIAMS

ISBN-13: 978-0-6481438-2-6

Cover design by Teodora Chinde
https://teodorachinde.carbonmade.com/
http://www.coversought.com/

"Thieves must sit in prison."

Vladimir Putin

Prologue

May 2012, Portorož, Slovenia

It is close to midnight, but being a Friday, reasonably busy in Portorož, a small holiday destination in Slovenia on the coast of the Adriatic. A number of restaurants and bars remain open and it will be several hours before the last of the revelers make their way to their homes and to bed.

Two men emerge from a bar and, between them, they support a woman. Her hair is disheveled and, as her high heels drag across the pavement, it seems obvious to passersby that she is very drunk. The two men keep her on her feet and slowly weave between the few people still on the street at this hour. Some of the people notice, but the scene is not out of the ordinary and they move to the side to allow the threesome to pass. None of their business.

In a side street, one of the men remotely unlocks his car, a black Mercedes SUV, the newest model, and opens the rear door. The woman has passed out and they spend a few minutes getting her onto the back seat. They get into the front seats and take some time getting their breath.

'This is getting out of control, Marko,' says the older man in Italian. 'Sooner or later, someone is going to wake up to this.'

The man named Marko presses the starter button on the dash board and the car comes to life. 'Nonsense, just some fun. You know

1

you like it and what a prize, no?'

'I guess. She is a stunner, I must admit. But, we could have taken both of them home anyway.'

'No, the other one was getting nervous and this way, we get to have some fun together.'

Marko checks his mirrors and heads down the side street.

An hour or so passes and the woman slowly became awake. She is feeling very odd indeed. Her head is woozy, not drunk, something else and it takes her thirty seconds to gain any sense of where she is. She is lying down in a bedroom and slowly becomes aware that there is a man on top of her, vaguely sensing his penis as it slides in and out of her vagina. She tries to shout out and raise herself up, but her body doesn't respond. The man continues to ride her and she can see another man to her right who is fondling himself. She passes out.

She opens her eyes and sees one of the men over by a window which is curtained. She closes them and remembers being in a bar with her friend. They were having fun, some time off. A number of men had propositioned them during the evening, but two in particular had persisted. They were well dressed and spoke passable English. Her friend had expressed her wariness during a break in the toilet, something about the two that wasn't quite right, and she had calmed her friend and said that nothing would happen.

She tries but can't remember leaving the toilet or the events since.

She is feeling cold and knows that she is naked, is lying on her side. Her mouth is very dry and she tries to swallow. Nothing seems to work.

She is turned over onto her back and hands press down onto her shoulders. She opens her eyes and can see the older man is behind her head, still naked. They speak to each other in a foreign language and she does not understand. She tries to speak, but her body remains frozen. The other man, the good looking one, approaches and sits on the side of the bed. He is carrying a hypodermic needle and she is reminded of her work and of the children lining up to be vaccinated against tuberculosis. She closes her eyes, a happier time. She feels the needle enter her flesh and the warmth of the liquid as it enters her bloodstream.

She manages a word. 'No,' but it is barely audible. Blackness descends.

Chapter 1

Somewhere over Washington State, August

Jake Walker sat in a comfortable club chair on the Cessna Citation and figured that at least three cows had sacrificed their skin to provide the soft, tanned leather beneath him. He was nursing a very good single malt on ice that had been served to him by the co-pilot, a man who introduced himself as Paul. Jake comprised the only passenger onboard the LA to Seattle flight and Jake thought back to his last ride on a private jet and its crash landing in the rain forest which borders Panama and Colombia.

It had been an experience he did not wish to revisit, and his survival of the crash had been due as much to luck as it had been to the skill of the pilot, his former friend Mick Rogers, who died that day. Following the crash, his fellow survivors, the ex-President's daughter, Emily Parker, and a US Secret Service agent, Karen Duffy, were kidnapped by Colombians. There followed a roller coaster forty-eight hours as Jake pursued the gang, eventually rescuing the women from the clutches of the Colombian FARC.

On that day, Parker's Gulfstream had been travelling from La Paz in Bolivia to Houston, and the only reason Jake boarded the jet in the first place was because his Father had suffered a stroke and Mick Rogers asked Emily Parker if they could give Jake a lift home. The entire episode occurred due to a random confluence of events.

Jake's Father pulled through and was now being cared for by his older brother, Dan. Instead of heading back to work, Jake needed time to recuperate and think and he rented a beach property south of LA, where he spent several lazy weeks thinking about his future. In the end, he succumbed to pressure from his boss at Jerico Security. Jake's fame in rescuing the ex-President's daughter led to new work for his employer and Jake spent a couple of weeks back in LA responding to media requests and talking up the capabilities of Jerico and its personnel.

Earlier on his leave, Jake received a call from an Iain Fisher and it was Fisher's jet he was flying in. He'd resigned from Jerico, but still wasn't sure why. Something changed him in the rain forests of Colombia. Did he miss being a soldier? Sure, he missed the camaraderie, the sense of belonging, of being tested in battle. But, the reason he left the Army in the first place was the fear of losing more friends, of being responsible yet not being able to fix everything that went wrong.

In Panama and Colombia, he felt his honor, courage, tenacity and reputation were compelling forces within him, a fresh drive to prove himself and to help others. With the whole series of events now behind him, Jake realized that he still possessed the skills to outwit opponents in combat. He no longer felt fear, only a strong conviction that he could do what was necessary.

So why was he here on his way to Fisher's property near Everett in Washington State? Partly, he knew that he no longer wished to be working as a security consultant. The job had filled a gap for him and had got him back into the workforce when he had been contemplating working for Halliburton and heading back into the Middle East. He also had Jerico to thank for his ownership of a house in LA and a small share portfolio.

Fisher had offered him five million dollars. This intrigued him more than it had provided a push to come up here. All would become clear soon.

The jet commenced its descent into Paine Field Airport.

Chapter 2

Granite Falls, Washington State

Jake was still thinking about his forthcoming meeting as he sat in the back of a black BMW sedan on its approach to Fisher's house. He was unfamiliar with this part of the world and had enjoyed the new sights on the drive over from the airport at Everett. Upon his arrival at Paine Field, the car had been waiting for him and the driver had introduced himself as Bill Palmer, Mr. Fisher's personal assistant. For the entire journey, Jake had been content with his own thoughts and Bill had respected this.

'This is it,' said Bill as he operated an electric gate by remote control. 'Will you be staying the night, Mr. Walker?'

'I don't think so. I'm really not sure...'

'That's a shame, I'm not only Mr. Fisher's driver, I'm also his chef and I have some nice venison on the menu for this evening.'

The BMW swept along a gravel drive toward a large and imposing modern home with sharp angular shapes and lots of glass. The grounds were immaculate and Jake estimated that the house occupied several acres in a very opulent area of the small town of Granite Falls.

Jake checked his Seamaster, which had been a gift to himself on his retirement from the Special Forces. It showed the local time as 16:10. It was late summer, yet there was already a hint of a chill in the air at this latitude.

'How long have you worked for Mr. Fisher?' asked Jake.

Bill operated another remote and they descended down a ramp and into a large garage.

'About twenty years or thereabouts,' replied Bill. 'He's been a great employer, the best.'

Jake didn't wait for Bill to open his door and got out of the sedan. Bill opened the trunk and took out Jake's overnight case, set it on the floor and extended the handle.

'I'll take that,' said Jake.

'Wouldn't hear of it Mr. Walker. Follow me, the lift is over there.'

The interior of the elevator was paneled in wood with intricate patterns using several different types of veneers. Jake noted three floor levels and they stopped at level two. The doors opened onto a large entrance hall with parquetry flooring and dominated by a large ornate vase in the center.

Bill went out first and Jake followed him across the foyer into a drawing room which was full of light and had a great view down the valley from large plate glass windows which extended from the floor to the ceiling.

'Please take a seat, Mr. Walker and I'll tell Mr. Fisher you are here.'

There were two large leather sofas opposite each other and adjacent to a high tech fire place covered with a plate of glass. Jake took a seat. The room was masculine but well decorated and furnished. It was set on the corner of the house and there were bookshelves, full of books on either side of the stone fireplace, which dominated the room. Jake could see no pictures or photographs, which seemed odd.

Only a minute or two passed and a man entered the room. Jake stood and saw a man in his fifties, slight gray at the temples, dressed in beige chinos with a button down shirt. 'Mr. Walker, I am so pleased you agreed to come and are now here.'

Jake extended his hand and Fisher shook it warmly standing close and assessing his guest. For his part, Jake was wearing black wool trousers, new Timberland boots, a blue polo shirt and a navy jacket. 'Likewise, Mr. Fisher. Do you mind if I call you Iain?'

'Of course not, please take a seat. Can I get you anything to drink, coffee, tea, a cola, beer, anything?'

Jake sat down again and removed his jacket. 'A black coffee would be great, thanks Iain.'

Bill suddenly appeared. 'Anything for you sir?'

'Two coffees Bill, thanks.'

Iain sat down opposite Jake. 'Again Jake, thanks for coming up. Your exploits in Panama and Colombia have made you quite famous.'

'The kind of famous I don't really enjoy.'

'No, quite. Asking you to come and see me was difficult. I am well aware that I what I am about to ask of you will be dangerous, difficult to achieve… Moreover, it is a personal matter for me. Anyway, you came and that's a beginning.

'I know you know nothing of me. Would you mind if I start there and we can move onto the reason you are here?'

'Sure.'

'Okay. I'm in, or rather was in, IT. When I went to college in the late 70s, computers were still a new thing and the programs or code that we created were loaded into large mainframe computers using sheets with holes cut into them. It was a different era. No-one had a desktop computer, let alone a laptop. I undertook courses in programming and computing science as it was then called and, later, landed a job with IBM when IBM was a powerhouse in computing and the employer of choice for young graduates. I worked for them for about eight years before leaving to start my own company. At IBM, I had been dealing with a number of banks selling and implementing mainframe solutions. It was during this period, that I noted a need for systems which would help traders in the investment banks.

'I hired a couple of young programmers and worked out of my own house for the first two years developing a proprietary financial trading system which, briefly, allowed banks that were trading their own money to monitor financial risk in real time. In 1992, I sold the business for just under $10m.

'I was married by then to a wonderful woman, Victoria, and we were living not far from here in Seattle. Oh yes, we had a beautiful daughter, Danielle, who was born in… 1984. Yes, 1984. So, she would have been only eight or so when I sold my business. Sorry, I am not being very coherent.'

'That's okay, Iain. I'm following you fine.'

Bill appeared with a tray containing a coffee pot and two cups. He poured two black coffees and left them in peace.

'After my business sold, I took some time off and it was during this time that my wife was involved in a car crash.'

Iain paused and looked out of the window. Jake gave him time.

'Sorry, Jake. My wife died at the scene and it was a painful year for me. And for Danielle – I'll come to my daughter shortly. It was an accident. No one to blame…

'Anyway, after a period, I got back to work and I put my cash towards IT start ups. You've heard of venture capital?'

'Yes.'

'Well, it's a very hit and miss business, more miss than hit I can tell you. But, I just happened to get a call from a friend who was thinking of putting some money into some young guys from Stanford. The World Wide Web was still very new back then. I had some reservations, but when I heard the pitch, I offered up some of my capital and we got a percentage of the company. Best investment I ever made. The company was called Yahoo.

'I sold out in 1999, saw the writing on the wall, the crazy money that was being poured into companies that had no revenue and no idea how they could make some. I've made and lost money since, but that is where my wealth was started.'

Iain drank some coffee. 'So, I have a business proposition for you Jake, in due course, a personal proposition as I said. And, I wanted you to know that my money has been honestly earned. It's important to me.'

'What are you into now, Iain?'

'I sit on some boards and I trade on-line, nothing much, just to keep my hand in. I play golf with friends. To tell the truth though, I am lonely, but not so lonely that I want to find another partner. That part of my life cannot be replaced, particularly now that Danielle has gone too.'

'I see.'

'It was hard raising a daughter alone, particularly for single father. Sure, I had enough money. But I took the easy way out and sent her to boarding school. We spent time during school holidays, but it was hard for us both. In many ways, boarding school was a bad idea, I now realize that.

'Even so, Danielle was a smart kid. I would have been happy whatever she did, but was thrilled when she went to med school. She got into John Hopkins and excelled, became a woman, made heaps of friends. It was good to see her happy, in the prime of her life....'

'What happened after she graduated?'

'Well, like many med school grads, she took up a position in a hospital. She was working in Virginia Mason in Seattle. I bought her an apartment near her work; you know to give her some independence. And, she still found time to come and see her Father every month or so.

'She was a doctor, slim, young and beautiful. So, there were plenty of men in her life, but she became keen on one guy in particular. Used to bring him over on weekends. Their relationship lasted for almost two years. They never lived together, but I could see them getting married. Anyway, he – Todd MacAllum was his name – worked for the State Governor and I was happy for them. Out of nowhere, Todd and Danielle broke up. It was very unexpected. She never told me the detail, but I suspected it was something to do with a third person. I'll never know now.

'She came over one night, it would have been November or so last year. Told me she was quitting the hospital and had signed up with *Medicine Sans Frontiers* – a French organization, Doctors without Borders is the translation. You have heard of them?'

'I have.'

'I'm protective, like any father. I didn't want to see her out of my life. I didn't know much about MSF, but I knew that they worked in refugee camps and close to areas of conflict. I tried to talk her out of it. Was willing to send her on a round the world trip, but she was determined, forceful. Much like me, I guess.

'She flew to Armenia in January.'

'What happened, Iain?'

Bill appeared. 'Excuse me Sir, Mr. Davis has arrived.'

Iain stood. 'Jake, this tale is going to take some time to reveal. Would you please stay for dinner? There is also a guest room. Mr. Davis is a private detective that I hired to find out what happened to Danielle. Much of what I need you to hear will come from him. Is this okay with you?'

Jake had come a long way. The least he could do was hear the story. 'Alright. Bill told me there's venison on the menu. I've never tried it.'

'I'll take your bag to your room, Mr. Walker.'

The doorbell rang. 'Thanks Bill. I'll let Pat in.'

Jake stood and watched as Iain went into the foyer, greeted Davis and brought him over. Jake saw a man in his forties, brown hair and eyes, about six one or thereabouts. He held himself well and he was well dressed in a charcoal suit, white shirt and conservative tie. Jake saw someone in law enforcement or military, the way he moved and held himself erect gave this impression.

Jake moved forward. 'Hi, Jake Walker.'

Davis returned a firm handshake. 'Good to meet you, Jake. Pat Davis. Call me Pat.'

'Pat, thanks for coming,' said Iain, heading for the door. 'Get to know one another. I'm just going to see how Bill is going with dinner, okay?'

Pat sat on the other end of Jake's couch. 'Some view isn't it?'

'Yes, although I prefer warmer climates. How do you know Iain?' asked Jake.

'I've really only known him professionally, but over the course of the last three months, our relationship has changed. He's a good man and I've grown to like him enormously. You were in the forces, Jake?'

'Most of my life. You could say I was born in the Army. My Dad was an officer in the Marines and I was born in an Army hospital in the Philippines. I spent the first fourteen years of my life on military bases. Okinawa, Berlin and many more. I think I went to ten schools before my father sent me to military school in Virginia. He wanted me to complete school and follow in his footsteps. You can imagine his reaction when I went to grunt school when I turned seventeen. What about you?'

'Can't you guess?'

'Former cop?'

Pat smiled. 'Twenty five years in the Boston PD.'

'You'd get less for murder,' chuckled Jake.

'Loved the life, Jake. Had wanted to serve since I was this high. I was a beat cop for about five years and then went to detective school. Spent the balance of my time in homicide. Never a dull moment.'

'You married?'

'Nope. Only to the force. Saw too many buddies go through hell when their marriages failed. Being a homicide detective was full on. It never allowed enough time for families. I have a partner now, Jenny's her name.'

Iain came back in. 'Let's eat guys.'

Chapter 3

Betanja, Slovenia

Zoran Kovak was in a foul mood. One of his shipments hadn't arrived at its destination and he'd just received news of his truck, hijacked no less, here in Slovenia. A hijack that Zoran did not believe for a second. He sat at his desk in his study, his favorite space in the sprawling forty room mansion which stood proud on a hill and ten acres about five miles to the south of the small town of Betanya in Slovenia. He felt a sharp pain in his stomach and reached into the drawer of his desk for his pills. At fifty four, Zoran looked it and more, and his doctor had told him the ulcer would not go away unless his lifestyle changed. *Some chance.*

Born Vladimir Alekseev in a small rural community in the west of the Soviet Union called Molodoshkovo, Zoran never attended school. His family was poor and worked hard on one of the many State-run, collective farms so as to feed their five children. Vladimir and his younger siblings went to bed hungry every night. The state took most of what they produced and the land was poor and limited in size. Shortly after his eleventh birthday, his father gave him a battered suitcase, fifteen Rubles, some black bread and wished him luck.

The nearest big city for Vladimir was Petrograd (later given its original name, St Petersburg, in the 1990s) and he hitched whatever transport he could and walked when he couldn't. The young boy had never stepped out of the small hamlet that had been his home, so the sights and sounds of a big city overwhelmed him, sights and sounds he'd never experienced before.

For some reason, the dockland area of the city drew him in and Vladimir quickly saw there were opportunities for someone small and light on their feet. Corruption on the waterfront was a fact of life. Officials and the police were all on the pay of criminal gangs and the shipping companies accepted a 'natural' level of spoilage, goods that were 'written off'. It was a cost of doing business throughout the Soviet Union, just another input cost in the final prices consumers paid.

Two days after he arrived on the waterfront, Vladimir was sitting on the steps of a warehouse across from the dock enjoying the warmth of the morning sun and watching the large ships in the port. He was hungry, having not eaten for more that twenty-four hours, and wondered how he was going to get a meal. An older boy, whom Vladimir guessed to be about fifteen or so, walked up to him and leaned against the railing. The boy's fair hair covered his eyes and he had the same ragged, hungry look and appearance that many people, young and old alike, seemed to have in this part of the city.

'Hey,' said the boy. 'What's your name?'

Vladimir squinted up at his questioner, the first person to speak to him since he arrived. He thought quickly. 'Zoran,' was his reply, somehow recalling a comic book character from an earlier time.

'I am Petr.' The boy pointed behind him. 'You see that man in the black hat, behind me?'

Zoran peered through the railings at a man in a suit and wearing a black hat about fifty yards away. 'What of him?'

'I want you to follow him, where he goes, who he sees. Come back here tonight and tell me.'

'What's in it for me?'

'When did you last eat?'

'Yesterday,' he lied.

'There's your answer then.'

Zoran followed the man that day and watched as he visited a number of places and people. That night, he came back to the same warehouse and reported what he'd seen during the day and Petr took him to a house where he was given some bread and soup and he slept in a room with seven other boys, all older than him. The next day, he followed the same man and it wasn't long before he'd reported that the man made payments to various officials and people of importance. Two weeks later, Petr, Zoran and two of the other boys lay in wait for the man, beat him with lengths of pipe and robbed him.

From then on, Zoran found himself at the fringes, the lowest level, of a gang that regularly skimmed and thieved from the waterfront and one that also provided 'protection' to a number of businesses in the area. By the time he was eighteen, Zoran ran his own group of boys, organizing raids from warehouses, regularly taking payments from those in protection and passing a cut to higher levels in the hierarchy, men that permitted him to do what he did and paid the officials and police to look the other way.

Zoran somehow grew to be six foot tall and, with a generous smile and fashionably long black hair, he found plenty of female suitors and always had a new girl on the go, often several. Unfortunately, he met and soon bedded the wife of the assistant police chief who did not appreciate being made a cuckold. When confronted in a bar, Zoran pulled out his knife, stabbed the man several times and might have killed him had some of the man's police colleagues not been present.

The nature of Zoran's attack was such that his protectors vanished. This was 1975 and, within a day, Zoran found himself in front of judge and in receipt of a twenty year sentence. Two weeks later, and he passed through the gates of a prison called Perm-36, about one-thousand miles east of Petrograd. Originally built in 1946 as one of Stalin's Gulags, the prison housed mostly political prisoners – dissidents, artists, human rights activists and other enemies of the State. The prison's population also included a number of common criminals, as well as a few former police officers that had been convicted of corruption.

Many of the politicals were held in isolation, twenty-four hours a day in a high security area of the camp and the sounds of torture by the KGB was a constant sound, particularly when new prisoners arrived and the potential for new information existed. Given the violent nature of Zoran's offense, he was a 'true criminal', giving him status in the prison community, and he naturally associated with the prisoners who'd had similar gang backgrounds to his own. It was here that Zoran was first introduced to the *vory* (thieves in law) and inducted into their brotherhood as a *vor* (thief). The *vory* controlled all the illegal activities in the prison enabling them to pay off some of the officials in camp administration and received financial support from elements of their own *vory* who lived on the outside.

Zoran's induction as a *vor* involved making a solemn pledge to the members of the *vory*, which comprised about twenty-five men of a total criminal population of over three-hundred. He pledged allegiance to the *vory* and promised never to take a wife and to only work for the *vory*, effectively committing himself to being a criminal for the rest of his life.

He did not a pledge to a 'chapter' of a wider brotherhood. Other *vorys* existed, both inside prisons and Gulags throughout the Soviet Union, but they also operated criminal activities outside and in many countries. Zoran gave his oath to the *vory* which formed in Perm-36, and some of its members had been incarcerated for over ten years by the time Zoran arrived. So as to recognize one another and as a mark of initiation, Zoran took on a number of tattoos and he spent several weeks, two hours per day, having his right shoulder, his chest, hands and arms adorned by an elaborate array of demons, religious symbols, pirates and stars. This effectively marked Zoran for what he had been and showed his position in the *vory* hierarchy.

Although the *vory* didn't work in the prison, they were still incarcerated and many, including Zoran, longed for the day when freedom would come. In 1985 and ten years into his sentence, an ambitious Mikhail Gorbachev took the office of the General Secretary of the Communist party and slowly began to introduce reforms starting with *Perestroika* (restructuring) in 1986 and later *Glasnost* (openness) in 1988. The first reform aimed to introduce some market like reforms and multi-candidate elections which Gorbachev hoped would rejuvenate the party and also consolidate his authority. The latter reform gave new freedoms to the Soviet people, including freedom of speech. These provided the prelude to Gorbachev's rise to the Presidency and the eventual dissolution of the USSR in 1991.

In 1987, thousands of political prisoners were released throughout the country and Zoran and many of his fellow *vory* were also released. Outside, the reforms within the country offered opportunities for criminal gangs throughout the USSR to consolidate their power, wealth and influence. Billions of dollars were made overnight as the country's assets were privatized and stockpiles of military and other public assets simply disappeared. Zoran's *vory* was no different and they took good advantage through a multi-country network, their contacts and the ability to launder huge amounts of money.

In 1989, Zoran lived in Moscow and managed several 'projects' to help those in power to steal from their beloved Mother Russia. Their *vory* was strong and influential and moving into arms, prostitution and the wholesaling of drugs. He kept several women in apartments throughout the city and one in particular, a former gymnast, Tatyana, bore him a son, whom he called Marko.

The next ten years cemented Zoran within his *vory* and they lived well despite the real turmoil within Russia and its former States. Marko lived with his father in a modern penthouse apartment and a tutor came in every day to teach the young boy.

In 2000, one of the *vory's* senior men died of natural causes and Zoran was asked to take over his role in Slovenia. Marko commenced boarding school in Italy and Zoran strengthened the *vory's* roots within the former Yugoslavia and the brotherhood prospered through the huge amounts of money they made distributing and selling drugs throughout Russia and Europe.

Zoran thought back to his beginnings and the hard work and years he'd put in to create the criminal network which he now oversaw in Slovenia. He hadn't lost a shipment in over ten years and the safe passage of cocaine, marijuana and heroin from the port of Koper and up through Slovenia to Europe and Russia was guaranteed through a complex, but necessary, series of payoffs. Moreover, no competitor dared to touch him. Everyone respected Zoran's power and connections. He was a major player in a Russian international crime syndicate and when you stole from Zoran, you stole from the brotherhood, the *vory*, to which he belonged.

A phone call came in the morning just after breakfast from his lieutenant, Valery Petrov, a good, loyal man he'd inherited from his predecessor. *Five hundred fucking kilos. Gone.*

The trip from the port of Koper on the Adriatic up through Slovenia and through to various points in France, Germany and Spain was normally undertaken by a shift of drivers under Zoran's direct employ. When the driver did not change over at Graz, word came back and Valery made a number of calls, finally finding that the truck had been pulled over around 11pm the previous night about ninety kilometers north of Maribor.

The driver, a Serb, had only been working for Zoran for seven months and Zoran suspected an inside job. He would find out soon enough and had sent his son, Marko, to pick him up and bring the man back for a 'debrief'.

Chapter 4

Granite Falls, Washington State

Iain led the way to the opposite side of the house and a formal dining room, with a beautiful, solid timber table that could sit a dozen people. The table had three settings, one at the head and two nearby on opposite sides, and Jake saw that the room, on the front corner of the house, had floor to ceiling windows on two sides and oak paneling on the others.

Iain pointed to the place on one side of the table which looked out to the views down the valley. 'Why don't you take that place there, Jake?'

Pat took the opposite place and, once they were all seated, Bill entered the room and offered the three men some red wine, which he poured into cut glass goblets. He then stood formally and said, 'Dinner will be ready in five minutes, Sir.'

'Thanks, Bill,' replied Iain.

'This is a great house, Iain. How long have you lived here?' asked Jake.

'Yes, it is pretty special. When Danielle left for med school, I found my former house in Seattle claustrophobic. Probably too many memories of my wife. I always had a thing for modern lines and this is the result.' He looked around. 'Would I do it again? No, the build took two years and probably ten off my life. Very stressful.'

Bill came back in pushing a dining cart, on which rested a leg of roasted venison with a large bowl of vegetables and a jog of red wine jus. They watched as Bill carved and created three plates and the three men talked on, avoiding discussing the reason for their meeting. Jake savored the meal and was glad of the pleasant conversation, finding he enjoyed the two men's company and sharing experiences. In time, they retired back to the lounge area and Iain continued with his story.

'Danielle had been deceased for four days before I received news of her death. To be fair, all the Slovenians had was a dead body and no identification. Eventually, the hotel where she'd been staying reported to the Police that Danielle had not paid for her room and that her belongings were still in her room. That provided the link for the police and, as her passport was in her room, they quickly identified her. They contacted the US embassy and, in turn, I received a phone call from the State Department.

'I contacted my family lawyer immediately and he flew to Slovenia to make arrangements for her remains to be brought back here. I couldn't go. I was devastated, still am.'

Iain paused before continuing. 'Barry, my lawyer, confirmed Danielle's identity and made an application to bring her back to the States. A post-mortem had been conducted and he obtained a copy of that report and he also spoke to the local police to see what their investigation had produced.

'The post-mortem revealed that Danielle had died from an overdose of heroin. I don't need to tell you that my daughter was not the type to experiment with, let alone use, drugs. She detested the drug scene and stayed well away from those in college that were taking drugs.

'Her body had been found near the Piran marina. She was clothed, but her shoes and underwear were missing. The police did not infer any foul play, despite Barry strongly suggesting that Danielle was a doctor and not a drug user.

'Eight days after her death, her remains were brought here and a full autopsy was conducted in Seattle. It was then that I called Pat.'

'How did you two know each other?' asked Jake.

'A close friend of mine, Stephen Muir,' began Iain. 'His teenage son went missing about four years ago. The police lost interest pretty quickly, so Stephen hired Pat, who tracked the kid down and found him in Atlantic City, sleeping rough, but in reasonable health. Stephen had been full of Pat's praise at the time. So, once I made my mind up, I called Stephen, who put me in touch.'

Pat continued the story. 'There were three things in the autopsy performed here which did not match the post-mortem conducted at the hospital in Piran. Perhaps match is not the right word. The autopsy certainly confirmed that there were high levels of opiates in Danielle's blood stream, levels that were high enough to cause death. However, they also found levels of another drug, rohypnol.'

'The date rape drug of choice,' said Jake.

'Yes, that's right,' replied Pat. 'We confirmed later that Danielle was not taking any medication other than birth control and the presence of rohypnol certainly suggested that she had fallen into the hands of some nasty people. Semen was also found inside her vagina and on her clothing.'

'Pat agreed to go and see if he could determine what happened,' said Iain.

'I decided to first fly to Armenia to talk with her colleagues in *Medicines Sans Frontiers*,' said Pat. 'Just flying there is tough enough, took two days from leaving New York. But, I made it and hired a car to get me north into a small region called Shirak. I had contacted their head office in Switzerland and, with Iain's help, we were able to find out where Danielle had been working.

'The head of the mission is a Frenchman, called Pierre Jardine. He spent a generous hour with me and said that they'd only found out about Danielle when he rang his boss in Paris. News is non-existent where this group works.

'Jardine told me that Danielle had been well liked and worked hard, seven days a week, since arriving in the country. A core part of their work is to inoculate people against tuberculosis, but they also have a travelling clinic of sorts. Women doctors are important as Armenian women are reluctant to discuss health issues with men.

'Anyway, he said it had been perhaps four months since Danielle had arrived and there was a short break in their work program. Jardine insisted that Danielle take a break and he clearly remembered how excited they'd been making their plans to travel to Slovenia.'

'They?' said Jake.

'That's exactly what I said. Danielle didn't travel alone to Piran. A colleague, another US-born doctor, Cathy Morgan, went with her. Morgan was about the same age as Danielle and they'd struck up quite a friendship, he told me.'

'How did they travel to Piran?'

'They got a lift into Yerevan by car and then took a flight to Ljubljana, via Kiev. Jardine told me it was Cathy who was keen on visiting Piran. He said she'd been very interested in European history.'

'So, the two women head off for a few days on the Adriatic, a bit of sightseeing. What happened then?'

'Jardine told me that neither of the two women returned to Armenia. He reported this to his superiors in Paris and then learned later that Danielle had been found deceased in Piran. Naturally, I asked him about her and he told me he was very surprised to hear that she'd died from a drug overdose. Danielle would never have taken drugs, he told me. Never. It was he who told me she was not taking any prescription medications.

'I next flew to Ljubljana and drove down to Piran. It's a beautiful place, but I wasn't there to do any sightseeing. The police report included the name of the hotel where Danielle had been staying and it didn't take long for me to find out that, on the day that her body was found, Cathy Morgan had booked out of the hotel.

'Wouldn't the police have known about Danielle's friend and

sought to interview her?' asked Jake.

'Yes, the hotel manager told me that he had told the police that Danielle had booked in with a female friend, albeit in separate rooms, but that fact is certainly absent from the information that was provided in the official police account of the incident.

'I called my team here and got them to work on tracking Miss Morgan down and then I went and had a drink. I had so little to go on and then I went back to the hotel and sought out the manager again. Did he have any idea where the two women had gone on the night before Danielle was found? He told me that they came down from their rooms that Friday night at about nine pm and asked him about night life in Piran. He told them if they were looking for music and dancing, they would need to travel to Koper or Portorož. Portorož is only a couple of miles from Piran, and he was pretty certain that that is where they'd gone that night.

'I was there on a Saturday and, later in the evening, I started to walk around the bars in Portorož. I had a good picture of Danielle on my iPhone and was using that in the hope of jogging someone's memory. By half past ten, I was beat. I must have shown the picture a hundred times. I was also going in circles and found myself back in a bar right on the beach, the Paprika Club.

'There were a lot more people when I went back and some additional staff. I bought a drink and sat at the bar. I started showing the photo, but was having no luck. I was about to go when a young girl asked to see the photo. She told me that she recognized Danielle and had been at the bar on the Friday night before her death. Her name was Tanja, but she didn't want to talk there, so I gave her my cell number and she promised to call the following day. I went back to my hotel.'

Bill entered the room at that point and offered to top up their whiskeys. Iain looked at his guests. 'I think a big pot of coffee would be useful at this point, Bill.'

Pat continued. 'True to her word, Tanja did call the following morning and agreed to meet me for a coffee. She was a regular at the

Paprika club and it was common to meet tourists from Croatia and Italy as well as Slovenians taking their annual holiday. She remembered that night because of the discovery of Danielle's body the following day, which was on the local television and radio. She had arrived there about ten pm with a girlfriend and appeared to have a good time.'

'Why did she notice Danielle and Cathy?' asked Jake.

'Tanja told me that she hadn't really noticed the two, but remembered that one of the women, Danielle, had become very drunk and was escorted from the venue by two men. She recalled noticing that Danielle and Cathy had been sitting in a booth with the two men and, shortly after the three had left the bar, Cathy was found unconscious in the booth. An ambulance was called and paramedics took her off to the local hospital.

'I asked her about the two men and she gave me a look. 'These are two men I do not want to know,' she said. I stressed that our conversation would be confidential and that her identity would not be revealed. She then said that one of the men was called Miro, a regular at the bar, but she did not know the other. She claimed that his name was all she knew and that he was a player. I asked her what she meant and she said he was wealthy and popular with the girls and tourists. Not the kind of man she was looking for, she added.

'At this point I needed some help and looked in the phone book for a private detective. The following day, a Monday, I met Nikki Seztac in my hotel room. I liked the woman immediately and was surprised at her youth. She told me that she had joined the Police in Slovenia, but had not liked the work and had left to help in her Uncle's business as a private detective. I later got to meet Uncle Stefan who told me that much of their work is surveillance, cheating wives and husbands and so on, but he knew the region well and knew the name Miro as soon as I mentioned it. I gave them everything I had and we agreed to meet in seven days. I wanted as much information as I could get on the two men who had left the Paprika Club with Danielle. At that point, I knew that I had done all that I could and needed to find Cathy Morgan.'

Bill came back with the coffee and set the pot down on the table with three cups, sugar and milk. 'Thanks Bill,' said Iain. 'Jake, it's almost midnight. We can continue this in the morning, if you want.'

'This is a story that needs to be told tonight, Iain. I'd like to keep going.'

'Fine by me,' said Pat. 'Don't sleep so well these days anyway.'

'Okay,' said Jake. 'You came back to the States?'

'Yes, another two days travel that I'll never get back. My team had no breaks on finding Miss Morgan. There are a large number of Cathy Morgans here in the US, some of whom were eliminated by age or other reasons, but by the time I arrived back in the States, all the other leads had drawn a blank. Through an immigration contact, we had confirmation that a Cathy Morgan had entered the US from a flight from Rome to New York, three days after Danielle's death. But, from there, we knew nothing.'

5

Slovenia

As Pat Davis was recalling the results of his work, Marko Kovak reclined into the soft leather seat of a big Mercedes S Class saloon as it travelled towards his father's house in Betanja. In the back seat with Marko was a thirty-five year old man, named Stanko Medic. Stanko was the driver of the hijacked truck.

Over the course of the three hour journey, Marko had had plenty of time to think about the current state of his life, particularly as Medic was not much of a conversationalist. Marko had been born in Moscow and never knew his mother. It was only later that he learned that marriage was one of the things his father's vory did not permit among its members. Children were fine, however, and Marko had led a sheltered life in Moscow until he was eleven and they'd moved to Slovenia.

Marko didn't mind leaving Moscow; it was a cold, bleak, gray place. His father purchased a large house in Betanja and had slowly made it into a home, as well as a fortress. For a young Marko, used to the confines of an apartment and the city, the ten acres the property stood on were wonderful and he spent much of his time outside when he wasn't required to be studying. His father employed a number of bodyguards and assistants and they all doted on the young boy as well as helped him prepare for life by teaching him how to defend himself.

At twelve, an Italian woman came to the house every day to

give Marko lessons in both Slovene and Italian. Luckily, Marko was bright and, by the time his father sent him to board at an all-boys school in Milan, he could hold his own in both languages. Till then, Marko never spent much time with boys his own age and, after a slow start and a period where needed to show his peers his prowess in using his fists and his feet, he became a popular, if feared, young man and eventually led his own group of boys, a gang that had no equal within the school.

Despite this, Marko also studied hard and encouraged the boys in his gang to do likewise. He knew that an education was something his father had never had and he did well in languages, history and science and could have gone on to study at university, but his father denied the request. 'You are son of vor,' he'd said. 'You have an allegiance to me and the only work you will be permitted to do is the work of a true criminal.'

To get his point across, he sent Marko to Berlin, where he lived with one of Zoran's closest friends, a member of their vory named Andrei Brankovic. Brankovic and his men provided protection, owned brothels and nightclubs and skimmed profits from much of the illegal gambling throughout the big city. Marko was there to learn. He went out every day with Brankovic's men and participated enthusiastically in all their activities. As part of his 'tuition', Marko lost his virginity to an experienced whore named Mathilda and he developed a taste and an appetite for sex, particularly the rough variety. He also learned that he liked to hurt people and would often take the lead, using a cosh or knuckle duster, when someone needed to learn a lesson.

Brankovic and his men were impressed and, six months later when Marko returned to Slovenia, Brankovic had called his father and told him of Marko's propensity for violence and his skill in enforcing the rules. 'We should make him vor,' he said and then added: 'But you should know that his heart is black.'

When Marko returned home, Zoran talked to his long time deputy, Valery, and asked him to mentor the young man. Over time, Marko learned the way in which his father made his money and money for the vory. The vory's business was very lucrative, but always prone to corruption from the inside and any threat, particularly from within, needed to be dealt with swiftly, severely and transparently when it happened.

The big car stopped and waited for the large electronic gates to open.

'We're here, Stanko,' said Marko. He smiled across at the older man, who clasped his hands tightly, and punched him lightly in the arm. 'Hey, there's nothing to worry about. No shame in being taken at gun point by thieves. If I'd been in your shoes, the outcome would have been the same. Your life is worth more to us than one single shipment.

'Our main focus today is simply to hear what you know. We can't have others disrespecting us in this way. Lessons will be learned, you'll see.'

Once past the gate, they drove up the tree-lined drive and the saloon pulled up outside the side entrance. The driver got out and opened Stanko's door.

'Come, I'll introduce you to my Father.'

Chapter 6

Granite Falls, Washington State

It was past one in the morning, but none of the three men was thinking of bed. 'We knew that Cathy Morgan had joined the MSF organization from Miami and then worked for two years at the Jackson Memorial Hospital,' recalled Pat. 'It was all we had, so I flew down to Miami and made an appointment to see the Chief Nursing Executive, a guy called Terry Pascoe.

'I had a letter from Iain and also an introduction from the MSF, Jardine provided a letter as he was keen to help us. Pascoe was cordial and polite, but refused to provide any information on Cathy Morgan; even when I told him of her importance in a possible murder case. He insisted that her employment records were confidential. He did, however, tell me that she had worked in the hospital for two years in ER.

'So you headed down to ER?' said Jake.

'Of course. I waited down there for about an hour or so. It was coming up to lunch time and I followed a couple of nurses to the staff canteen, waited until they'd bought some lunch and then sat down and introduced myself. I guess I must have a way with people that encourages them to talk to me.'

'That's the cop in you, Pat,' said Iain.

Pat smiled, 'One of the nurses, a Wendy Hudson if I remember correctly, told me that Cathy had been a hardworking young doctor and was well liked by the nursing staff for the way in which she treated them and the patients with respect. I told them why I needed to find her and the difficulties I'd been having. They were sympathetic when I told them of Danielle and her fate and Wendy said that Cathy had married a property developer, but the marriage only lasted six months. The rumor was the man was already married and a divorce was quickly arranged. Wendy was certain that the whole episode led to Cathy looking for how she could do good work elsewhere.

'At this point, I simply asked what her name had been when she first started in ER. Dickson. Her maiden name was Dickson. I called my team and, by the following morning, they confirmed that Cathy was born in Baltimore and a Cathy Dickson was working in ER at John Hopkins.

'I got there that evening, booked into a hotel and called her home address. Her mother answered and I asked her if she could take a message for her daughter, who was working. My message was 'I am a private detective and am searching for Danielle's murderer. Please call.' I got Cathy's mother, Helen, to repeat the message and then waited.

You can imagine how scared this woman was. She'd effectively run for her life after being drugged in a bar and then finding that her best friend and colleague had been found dead in the street.'

'But she called?' asked Jake.

'Yes, the next day at about nine thirty. I told her who I was and that I was working for Danielle's father. She agreed to meet me in the hotel's café. I got over there at the time we'd arranged and Cathy told me that she'd been traumatized by the events in Slovenia. She remembered awaking in the hospital the next day and had been told she'd been found unconscious at the Paprika Club. The doctor told her that they were doing some tests but would not get the results for a few days. She was advised to stay and rest, but discharged herself and went back to her hotel. She didn't know at this point that Danielle was dead, only that she was not in her room.

'Cathy turned on the television and quickly discovered her

friend's fate. I asked her why she didn't go to the police. She said that she just felt fearful. The two men she suspected had been involved in Danielle's death had frightened her and she recounted her warning to Danielle when they'd been in the toilet at the bar. She packed up, paid her bill and took a cab to pick up a rental car. She drove to Rome, paid for a one way ticket to New York and had gone to her mother's house , reverted back to her maiden name. We pretty much know the rest.

'I asked her did she remember the two men. She then asked me what I had found out. I told her about the autopsy results, that Danielle had died from an overdose of heroin and the presence of rohypnol; that her father wanted to see justice done. Cathy said that the rohypnol was consistent with the symptoms she'd experienced. I asked her the tough question and she said that she would be willing to testify in court, but only here in the US. She is unwilling to travel back to Slovenia. I went back to my room, typed up an affidavit on my lap top and sent it to her. She made some changes, got it signed and notarized and here it is.' Pat pulled two pages from a briefcase by his feet.

'This will form part of our evidence supporting our view that Danielle was murdered and the link to our two men. Since seeing Cathy, I have been in contact with Nikki and she has sent over surveillance photographs of the two men we believe are responsible.' Pat reached into the briefcase and placed several A4 size prints on the coffee table. Jake picked up the top one.

'That one's Miroslav Juricic. Twenty-four years of age. His father is Dimitri Juricic; Ukrainian. Made his money in trucks, and now he runs a shipping and logistics business from Portorož, where he lives. Forbes has him at around $5bn. His son likes to be known as Miro, has an apartment, a penthouse, in Portorož, three expensive, late model vehicles in the garage, plays golf, travels and likes his girls. He has a good yacht goes to Trieste in Italy to sail, but also gambles and likes his baccarat. Hard to find out how much money he has. His father set up a trust for him, which provides him with a private income.'

Jake picked up the other photograph. 'So, who is mystery boy here?'

'Marko Kovak. Twenty-three. Friend of Miro's and also his coke dealer. Miro likes his coke, forgot that. He was born in Moscow, mother unknown. Father is Zoran Kovak, a major criminal with known ties to a major criminal network based in Moscow, but with operations throughout Europe. In the time we've been looking, we have found very little background on him, but Nikki told me that her enquiries suggest that that Zoran is responsible for a sizable tonnage of heroin and dope. This comes in through Slovenia's main port at Koper and is delivered to multiple destinations throughout Russia and Europe. Zoran is fifty-four years old and lives on a highly protected ten acres not far from Koper.

'Marko was schooled in Italy at a private school and has been working with his father, as far as we can tell. He is a regular in the bars around the coast, including the Paprika Club, and speaks fluent Slovene, Italian and Russian. He has an apartment in Piran, but he lives for the most part with his father near Betanja, spending his weekends in Piran, particularly when the tourist season is on. Miro is one of several rich young men that he hangs out with.'

'So you see, Jake,' said Iain. 'My daughter was raped and then killed by these two men. This seems very clear. But, you will appreciate that there is a difference between what we know and what we can prove in a court of law.'

Jake looked at the two men. 'Okay, what are you proposing to do now?

'I am travelling back to Slovenia tomorrow night,' said Pat. 'I'll be meeting up with Nikki. With Cathy Dickson's testimony, we are only part way there. What we need is something which more firmly ties our two playboys into Danielle's death. So, we're hoping that we can obtain some DNA.'

'There is an extradition treaty which the former Yugoslavia signed with the US dated 1901,' said Iain. 'And, Hillary Clinton recently re-signed and ratified an agreement which would permit the US to petition the Slovenian Government to extradite these two men. Unfortunately, Pat and I agree that such a course of action would probably be unsuccessful. Zoran Kovak is a very powerful man, connected through a huge system of payments and payoffs to the Judiciary, key politicians, the police and key figures in the port authorities. Zoran owns these people.

'Which is where you come in, Jake.'

Chapter 7

Betanja, Slovenia

Marko and Stanko Medic got out of the car near a side entrance to his father's large house. Stanko was looking nervous and sweat had seeped into his shirt.

'Stanko, what are you worried about? We're just going to have a chat about what happened to you. We must learn from this and ensure it does not happen again. Come.'

Marko slapped Stanko on the back, a gentle prod, and the two headed toward the house. Marko wore a leather jacket which was tailored and included a special pocket on the inside were he kept a cosh filled with hundreds of small lead fishing weights. Marko opened the door leading into the laundry and stood on the threshold, allowing Stanko to go in first. He took no more than two steps and Marko hit him hard behind the ear with the cosh. Marko had learned the best places to render a man unconscious and he specifically aimed for that area as the skull is reasonably thick at that point. If he had used the same force elsewhere, he could have easily killed him.

About thirty minutes elapsed and it was pain that slowly drew Stanko out of his unconscious state. Pain in his head and in his arms and shoulders. As he grew more aware, Stanko opened his eyes which confirmed his fear that he was indeed naked and hanging by his arms and secured to chains above him. He looked around urgently and saw three men in the basement with him. An older man came towards him and he recognized Zoran.

'Stanko, Stanko. What's the world coming to, eh? I've been here for ten years. Never have I lost one fucking shipment. Fucking never, you hear? No-one would dare fuck with me and now this. I suppose you are going to tell me that you don't know the cunts responsible for this?'

It was cold in the basement, but sweat poured down his face, stinging his eyes. 'No, Mr. Kovak, I swear. There were two cars, Mercedes, they forced me off the road and then a gun is pointed at my head. They wore masks. I am sorry…'

'Stanko, your story is possible. Yes, possible. Yet I don't believe it.'

'No, Mr. Kovak. It is true.'

'Only you and three others knew the route and the timing, Stanko. The others I trust. You are new and I don't.'

Zoran turned, said something to his son in Russian and Marko walked over to the trussed man and showed him what he had in his hands.

'You recognize what I have here, Stanko?' he held up his hands, smiling. 'This is a gadget I got out of our kitchen. Our chef uses it to burn sugar on a crème brulee and make the top golden and crunchy. And these, well I am sure you have seen tin snips before.'

'Marko, please, I know nothing about this I swear. Please.'

Valery approached with some rope and Stanko's feet were quickly roped and, using a cleat in the concrete floor, he was trussed so that he couldn't move his legs.

'I am only going to say this once,' said Marko. 'If you tell us what you know, we will let you go. Otherwise, I am going to cut off some of your toes. How many is up to you.'

Marko took a cigarette lighter and lit the gas torch. A blue flame, about three inches long started to glow. 'I saw this in a movie,' said Marko, smiling.

'Please no,' shouted Stanko.

Marko continued. 'I forget which movie now, but the thing is… When a toe is cut, there is a lot of blood. Arteries I think, or is it veins? I no longer remember. Anyway, by using the torch, we can cauterize your wound. Otherwise, you would bleed to death. And you know what?'

Stanko's bladder let go and his urine trickled down his legs. 'What?' he managed.

'It also sterilizes and ensures we leave you germ free. Ha, maybe we should cut your dick first?'

'Marko, please.'

Marko motioned to Valery, who came in behind Stanko and held his legs. Marko firmly grasped Stanko's right foot and quickly severed his little toe, which bounced down onto the concrete twitching. Stanko yelled in agony and Valery let him go, as much in fear that the man would let go of his bowels.

There was a steady stream of blood and Marko brought up the torch and held the tip of the blue flame firmly on the wound. Stanko thrashed and screamed as smoke rose up and he could smell himself burning. Marko stood up.

'Now, Stanko. I am going to cut off the little toe on your other foot. You can stop me anytime.'

'Please, I beg you.'

Marko swiftly dispatched the left foot's little toe and brought the gas torch to bear on the ensuing bleeding. Stanko had never experienced such pain.

Gasping, he managed: 'They threatened my mother.'

'Who is they Stanko?' said Zoran coming forward.

It was all over. Within half an hour, Stanko had told his story, whereupon he was killed quickly by a pistol shot to the head.

Zoran looked at his lieutenant. 'Valery, clean this fuck up. Marko, come with me. Some Croatians are going to die for this.'

Chapter 8

Granite Falls, Washington State

The next morning Jake awoke to the sun filtering through the blinds. He checked his Seamaster, 09:07. He climbed out of bed and recalled that it had been after two before the three men retired to their beds. Jake had not given an answer to Iain and wanted to think on the proposition he'd been made. This morning, he felt certain of his response and a plan formed as he showered, shaved and put some fresh clothes on.

There was a knock on his door and Bill put his head around it. 'Good to see you are up, Mr. Walker. Breakfast will be ready when you are.'

'Thanks, Bill. I'll be right down.'

Jake went over to a small bureau by the window. He sat down and started to write some lists on a note pad

Five minutes later and Jake skipped the elevator and went down the stairs and in to the kitchen. Pat and Iain sat at a decent size breakfast bar, drinking coffee and picking at the remains of a cooked breakfast.

'Good morning, Jake,' said Iain. 'Sorry, we didn't wait for you.'

'Would you like some breakfast, Mr. Walker?' asked Bill in front of a large stainless steel range.

'Just coffee for the moment, thanks Bill,' replied Jake. He took a vacant stool at the breakfast bar and looked at Iain. 'You know that there are lots of things that could go wrong on an operation such as this?'

'Yes, we know, Jake. We hope we can minimize the risks by our choice in you and in good planning.'

'I have some conditions. If you agree to meet them, I will try to bring your daughter's murderers back to the US to face trial. Firstly, I am going to need five weeks to prepare. I can't do this alone and want to be able to pick my own team. I have three men in mind. Like me, they won't be physically or mentally ready to go over to Slovenia and snatch these two men. So, I need one week to get the team together and four to get them fit, to train and to plan.

'We're also going to need a safe-house in Slovenia. This needs to be out of the way, but close to both Portorož and where Marko lives with his father. It also needs to have at least two roads for access and escape. Three would be better. Naturally, it should be furnished and ready in five weeks' time, including fresh food. No booze, however. Lease something for six months and pay in advance. Use a corporation and explain you need a corporate retreat.'

Jake consulted his lists and noted Pat taking notes in his own small notebook.

'Now, even with a private jet, we can't take weapons with us as we need to pass through Customs, wherever we land. Here is a list of what we are going to need.' Jake tore off a page and pass the note over to Pat. 'Some of it will be unavailable, get the next best alternatives. I have no special contacts in that part of the world, so this is going to be a difficult, but critical task. Nikki may have some people who can assist. That part of the world should be awash with arms, so hopefully it won't be too hard.

'There is some equipment I can buy here and take over with us, clothing, communications, night vision stuff and so on. But, weapons and ammunition will need to be sourced locally. I will need two SUVs, either BMW or Audi, my preference is for the former. Both should be easy to purchase, new if possible. Black is the color and they should be V8s. With a five week lead-time, this should be one of the tasks to complete first. Once you have the vehicles, get them into storage and use them, in turn, to store the weapons. We're going to fly in, probably from the US, using your plane, Iain. I assume this is okay?'

Iain nodded.

'You have two pilots in your employ?'

'Yes, Paul Lawson and James Reilly. Both contractors, but good men.'

'How do you rate them and your level of trust?'

'James works for a number of business people and celebrities here in the US. Very discrete, former Air Force and well regarded in the industry. Paul is the junior, but they work together. James operates under a company structure and has been flying me for four years.'

'Okay. Go and see him personally. Book his time and that of his co-pilot for the next three months. Tell him enough, but downplay the risks. Make it sound like a taxi service, an offer he can't refuse. You will need to hire a parking spot for your Cessna and ensure it is gassed and ready to go at a moment's notice. James can make the arrangements once we are sure of our timing.'

'There's a small airport at Portorož,' said Pat.

Jake looked at him. 'I'm surprised, but that's good. Book a couple of rooms at a good hotel nearby; pay for a month. If you can't secure the services of your pilots, you are going to have to find alternatives. Let me know, I still have some contacts that might work out, even if they're not rated for the Cessna.

'Okay, money. Iain, you offered me an immense sum. Up front, I don't want it and don't need it. But, there's an element of personal risk and my team will want compensation for that risk. They're all ex buddies, men I knew in my previous life and some of them didn't exactly fall on their feet when they got out. I am also going to have expenses in the initial phase and when we get on the ground in Slovenia.

Right now, I need five-hundred thousand in cash and a further one-and-half million in this bank account.' Jake handed Iain another note with the details. 'When we get to Slovenia, I want a further three million, one million for each of my team – I'll supply details later. I will also require one-million in cash in a safety deposit box at a major bank, or what passes for one in Slovenia. Let me know the details.'

'The money is no problem, Jake,' said Iain.

'If we bring these boys back, I want a final three-million for my team, and two mil. for Pat here, whatever the outcome.'

Iain didn't blink. 'Okay, but what about you?'

'If we succeed, I'll talk to you when we get back. If we run into trouble and my team become wounded or die, they still get the final million dollars.'

'That sounds fair,' said Iain.

Jake looked at Pat. 'Pat, get physical evidence however you can. Hair is easiest, but fingernails, blood from a syringe. Hire some girls, whatever. If we can't get some DNA, everything falls apart. It will also fall apart if the DNA doesn't match samples taken from your daughter. Have you thought about that, Iain?'

Iain looked at Jake. 'No, I haven't. But, if it doesn't match, this whole operation will be canceled. You also need to know, Jake, that the samples on Danielle only delivered the one DNA profile. Even though we are certain Juricic and Kovak were both involved in Danielle's death, the evidence only points to one person. So, I would focus on Kovak first. He is the one with criminal and drug connections. Get his DNA first. If it doesn't match, we go for Juricic. If that doesn't match, there'll be no point going. If that's the outcome, your men will still get paid half if that's okay.'

'Fine.' Jake drank some of the coffee. 'Alright, Kovak is our target.' He turned to Pat. 'When we hit the ground, Pat, I will want a full briefing from you and Nikki. I want to know what this man does each day and each week, any routines you observe. Is he armed? Does he have protection? Is he under surveillance? Who is a potential ally for us? Who is likely to be an enemy? Who's in Zoran's pay? Complete details of where he lives...

'Marko is going to be very difficult to profile. Get some of your team here involved if you must. I want to know as much as I can about Marko's father and who he's involved with. What are his ties to the US? Everything. Whatever you do, be discrete. I don't want anyone forewarned.

'I also want you to track down these three men,' Jake handed Pat another note. 'Message me the details as soon as you have located them.'

'Iain, I want to head up to Montana, tomorrow if possible, and will need that half mil. in cash. And, a four wheel drive.'

'Done,' said Iain. 'You okay with this, Pat?'

'Mine's the easy part.'

Jake called to Bill, who was discretely putting some dishes into a dishwasher. 'Bill, any chance I can have what these two have just enjoyed?'

Chapter 9

Twenty miles west of Philipsburg, Montana

The wheels of the Suburban click-clacked across the gravel towards the large timber house. Twenty miles of dirt and Jake had been glad of the four wheel drive capability of the large SUV. Jake drove to see Joe Grant, one of the Instructors that had been on Jake's Special Forces Selection back in the 90s.

Jake took in the details of the house at the head of the drive. It was built of timber and stood proud on the slopes of a gentle valley which led up towards several hills which would soon be white with snow. A large cleared area surrounded the house and a smaller cabin stood off to one side. Thick pine covered the slopes as far as Jake could see.

Jake pulled in an area set aside for parking at the end of the drive, next to a near new Nissan pick-up. As he got out of the SUV, the man he'd come to see came out on to the veranda. A German shepherd also emerged from the house and came down the steps.

'Dog, hold,' said the man to his dog. The dog stood still his eyes never leaving Jake.

Jake called out. 'Joe, it's me Jake Walker. I'm sorry, I should have called.'

'S'okay,' said the man and the dog retreated back up the steps and lay down near his feet.

Jake walked toward the house and stopped at the bottom of the steps. 'How've you been Joe?'

'Come up Jake, Dog won't mind you.'

Jake walked up the steps and stopped at the top. He held out his hand, which the older man shook. Joe still had the buzz cut, albeit gray, piercing, hazel eyes and he was clean shaven and tanned.

'Dog, got a name,' said Jake as he bent down and gave the animal a scratch behind his ears.

'Nope. Just Dog. What the hell are you doing up here of all places? I heard you got out.'

'It's a long story, Joe.'

'Well, I've got plenty of time. Come on in, just made some coffee.'

Jake followed Joe into his house. Dog stayed on the veranda. It was a solid house, with all walls, internal and external, made of the same raw pine logs. Jake admired the craftsmanship. 'This is a beautiful house, Joe.'

'Glad you like it.' Joe went into his kitchen, around a bench and retrieved two mugs from a shelf. 'Black okay?'

'Black's great,' said Jake, pulling up a stool and planting himself on one side of the bench.

Joe filled the mugs from a battered steel jug on the range. 'So, what brings you all the way up to Montana? Heard you were living in LA.'

'I'm preparing a team for a mission, Joe, and I need to get some men and myself ready. Knew you were up here and couldn't think of a more qualified person.'

'How'd you find me?'

'I'm working for a guy up in Washington State. He has a private detective. I'd heard you were up here; that you were taking in corporate types for team building and so on. Gave him your name and he had an address before I even put the phone down. How're things going for you?'

'Been good, Jake. I never married and like my own company. I took retirement three years ago, put my savings into this place. My own slice of heaven. I don't advertise widely, take in groups every month or so, whenever I feel like it, no shortage of takers. Each group has different requirements – a bit of abseiling, sleeping outdoors, trail walking, and fitness. Helps pay the bills and I kind'a enjoy it, watching city folks push themselves and finding their limits. What sort of mission you planning?'

'Can't tell you just yet, Joe, but I will if you take us on. It's overseas and involves risk to me and the team I've picked. It'll be me and three others, all former buddies, and a couple of them will be a challenge to get them ready. Figure I'll be back in around six days' time, have allocated four weeks to train and prepare.'

'I'd love to help Jake, but I've got a group coming in two weeks' time.'

Jake reached into his jacket and pulled out an envelope. 'Guy in Washington State is paying well for what he wants us to do. There's fifty in there and another hundred when we leave.'

Joe looked at Jake. 'This all above board?'

Jake held his gaze. 'Yes, Joe. I wouldn't involve you or myself in anything illegal. We're simply seeking to help a man who needs and deserves some justice.'

Joe thought about the money. He needed a new dam and wanted to get some goats, try his hand at cheese making. And one of those new solar systems... 'If it were someone else, I'd be telling 'em to fuck off.' He paused. 'Alright, I'll do it.'

'Great. Give me your bank account details and I'll wire in another twenty-thou' for things we're going to need.' Jake handed him a list.

Chapter 10

Austin, Texas

After leaving Joe Grant's place, Jake boarded a plane at Bowman Field and was in Texas that evening. He took dinner in his hotel room and slept soundly.

After breakfast, Jake got in his hire car and headed for where he knew Andy Francis was working as a stunt man. It was Jake's first time on a movie set, albeit behind a barrier so the public could watch what was going on. It was a cop movie, a sequel to one Jake hadn't seen, but had heard about, and all the action for the morning was taking place on the roof of a small six-story office building at the edge of the city.

Over a period of an hour, the spectators could hear but not see the action, which involved filming a gun fight on the roof. After a while, the sounds of gunfire ceased and they saw preparations being made for someone to fall off the edge of the roof. A couple of men were assisting the stunt man and Jake could tell from their actions, they were rehearsing how the stunt would go. A huge airbag sat on the pavement adjacent to the building, perhaps ten yards square and five or so high, which was constantly fed a stream of air from a couple of large compressors.

Cameras were staged in several locations across the front of the building, including two remote units on cranes. Jake watched as someone came over to the man on the roof, who faced inwards, and brought down a clapper board. Action, thought Jake. Two shots rang out and then the man on the roof toppled back, stepping off the ledge. He fell backwards with his legs and arms outstretched directly into the middle of the cushion. That took guts and a lot of trust, thought Jake.

The crowd cheered loudly and the man stood up and clambered off the airbag onto the ground. A large stain of movie blood sat across his chest. A number of film people came over to shake his hand and several patted him on his back. Jake recognized Andy and watched as he walked away toward a staging area on one side of the building. He followed.

Andy disappeared into an RV and Jake took a seat on a nearby bench and waited. Fifteen minutes went by and Andy emerged; he'd changed into jeans and a t-shirt. He locked eyes on Jake and then went to walk away.

'Hey Andy,' called out Jake.

Andy stopped and turned. 'Fuck me, is that you Jake?'

Jake stood up as Andy came over and they embraced and then stood looking at each other, seeing how kind or otherwise the passing of the years had been. Andy was about six-two, one-eighty and wore his fair hair long to the shoulder. It was an unusual look, but it suited him.

'Some stunt there, buddy,' said Jake, feeling Andy's biceps. 'You're looking great, even the hair.'

'Been growing it for this role. Only a few scenes, but I'm getting my face out there, you know? You're looking good too. What the fuck are you doing in Austin, fucking Texas?'

'Looking for you.'

Andy checked his watch. 'Well you found me. Hey it's not even lunch time, but how 'bout we get a drink? My workday is over.'

'Sure, lead the way.'

It wasn't long before the pair found a good hotel a block away, went into the bar and ordered a couple of bourbons.

'Cheers Andy,' said Jake, tapping his glass against Andy's. 'How long you been in the movie business?'

'Coupl'a years. Friend of mine told me a production company was looking for someone who could handle explosives. Right up my street and beats contracting over in the Middle East. But, as you saw this morning, I've also been doing stunts on camera.' Andy paused and took a sip of his drink. 'Haven't seen you in… I dunno, must have been the 'Stan in '02.'

'Yep, that clusterfuck of a mission in the east, the one that was over for us before it even begun.'

There was a pause of about thirty seconds. 'You were good that night, Luke,' said Andy, referring to Jake's call sign.

'Haven't been called that in years. Anyway,' Jake looked at Andy in the eye. 'I'm setting up a team for a mission overseas. You were my first pick.'

'What sort of mission?'

'Can't tell you, yet. We're still gathering some facts together. If you say yes, the pay is good; I've been hired by someone with very deep pockets.'

'I dunno, Jake. Doing well here. It's a good life working in the movies.'

'Where's home these days?'

'Atlanta. But, I'm only home half of the year.'

Jake pulled an envelope out of his jacket pocket. 'There's fifty inside, just for saying yes. There's four weeks of training, one million each when we go and a further one million for success, which is also paid if you don't make it back.'

'Fuck, Jake. It's a little hard to make a decision based on that.'

'The man who has hired me wants us to locate some men and bring them back to the US. They won't be willing to come with us, so we're going to need to persuade them. That's all I can tell you.'

Andy drank the rest of his bourbon and took the envelope, looking Jake in the eye.

'Your job will still be here when you get back. Hell, you can start your own outfit with the money you are going to make.'

'Where and when?'

'Butte, Montana; Airport diner at midday on the 12th. You'll learn more when you get there. Okay?'

'I'll be there.'

'One more thing.'

'Yes?'

'Your measurements…'

Chapter 11

Portorož, Slovenia

It was after eleven pm and two young women wove their way steadily back to their hotel, having a bit of giggle, arm in arm. They'd been to several of the beach bars and were on holiday from Norway. Both were backpacking and had been away from home for six weeks, having that overseas trip which their generation often saw as being necessary before going on to university and a life of work.

The blonde woman, Birgitt Nilsen, said, 'What did you think of the barman at that last place? He was cute and liked you I am certain.'

Her friend, Arnfrid Jonsen, the taller of the two with long, black hair, replied, 'I agree. Why did we have that last drink?' She laughed and punched Birgitt lightly on the arm.

'Hey, no-one forced you.'

'Anyway,' said Arnfrid, it was you he was chatting up. I think we should go back there tomorrow.' She giggled and swayed against her friend. 'I may even let him take me home.'

'Are you trying to set a record?' said Arnfrid.

'You're only young once, and we'll be home in two weeks. The boys at home are so lame.'

Presently, they reached their hotel. At forty Euros a night, it was no palace, but safer and more comfortable than the backpacking places.

As they entered the reception, Arnfrid stumbled and realized she was more inebriated than she would have liked. Birgitt helped her to their room and paused at the door.

'Hey, you want some pizza? There is a place open, just along the street.'

Arnfrid went into the room. 'You go. I need to lie down.'

♦

Outside, in his Mercedes SUV, Marko watched as the blonde woman came out of the hotel and walked past him. He'd been at the same bar as the girls and was annoyed that he hadn't had the chance to talk to them. He found it hard to go out clubbing alone and, when he'd asked Miro to meet him, Miro fobbed him off with the excuse that he had company. Then, that bitch Rhonda had called him a whore, in Russian no less. He'd nearly hit her.

He started the engine and drove around the block parking next to the café. He got out of the car and leaned against the front fender. He saw the woman notice him as she approached the café.

'Hi,' he said, flashing her his best smile.

Birgitt remembered the man from the bar. He was dressed in jeans and a stylish, open neck, white shirt. The car and the watch on his wrist clearly suggested he had money.

Perhaps the pizza could wait...

Chapter 12

Kentucky

The day after his meeting with Andy, one of the people on Pat's team, Paula Gerretson, called and gave him the address of the second man for his team. He took an afternoon flight to Louisville, where it was after eight pm and he hired a car and booked himself into a hotel. He'd eaten on the plane and went straight to bed.

Jake was up early the next morning and he bought a coffee and cheeseburger at Burger King before driving up the interstate to his destination, Sparta, where he hoped to find Tony Evans, a man he'd served with in Afghanistan. Jake plugged the address he'd been given into the Sat Nav. and sat back for the forty minute drive.

In due course, a voice told him 'you have reached your destination' and he pulled over opposite a sixties style house clad in vinyl. Old cars and parts of cars littered the front yard and up the drive toward a large free standing garage at the rear of the block.

Jake went up to the door and knocked. More than one dog barked in response and he could hear them scratching at the door. He was about to leave when the door cracked open and two small dogs beat themselves up trying to get through the screen door. A woman's face appeared and Jake saw that she'd been sleeping and clutched a gown around her.

'Mindy, Cindy, git,' she growled at the dogs, who fell silent, but attentive, their tails wagging furiously.

'Hi ma'am, sorry to bother you. My name's Jake; a friend of Tony's. Is he in?'

The woman peered through sleepy eyes. 'A friend, huh?' She looked at Jake closely and saw the new car across the road. 'You'll find him at the track, that's where he usually is.'

Jake turned gave his thanks and went back to his car. 'The track' had to mean the speedway on the other side of the interstate. Jake plugged the destination into the Sat Nav. and he pulled into the parking lot ten minutes later. As he got out of the car, he could hear the sounds of a powerful car. The gates were open and Jake walked in and made his way to the main grandstand, taking a seat opposite the pit area. He saw a couple of crews working and a beat up Chevy was doing laps of the circuit.

After Jake watched the car lap the track five times, it swung into the pit lane and came to a stop in the pit area. One man helped the driver out while another jacked up the front and went underneath. Jake stood and found his way to a tunnel which went under the steep bank of the track and into the pit area. As he approached the crew, he could see the driver and another man were having a bit of an argument.

As Jake went forward, he recognized the driver, Tony Evans, one of the guys from Jake's operational detachment alpha, or ODA, in Afghanistan. The argument appeared to be about the pace of the car and Tony's skill at getting around the track. Jake let them go for a few minutes and then Tony noticed Jake for the first time. He looked surprised.

'Hi Tony.'

'Fuck me,' said Tony.

Jake went forward and they embraced. The other man wandered off muttering to himself. Jake checked out his former buddy and noticed he had a few pounds on him, but the gray-green eyes were clear and his smile was genuine.

'Why don't we grab a seat somewhere and I'll tell you why I'm here.'

They left the car and walked over to a dugout, where there was some shade.

'So,' began Jake, 'always knew you were into cars, but this I didn't expect.'

'When I got out in '07, I came back here because my sister was here.'

'The woman at your house? We've met, although I didn't get her name.'

'Her name's Judy. Weren't many jobs for an ex-soldier. Still aren't, but the Army paid for me to go back to school and I qualified as a mechanic. I work in an auto-shop in town and pick up work when the racing's on. There's three of us throwing money away on the car over there, but we enjoy it. You got out in '04, right?'

'Yes. Had a bad night in Baghdad, lost a couple of mates and more. Afterward, I found I had also lost my enthusiasm for the job.'

'I know what you mean. I couldn't see myself doing twenty-five. Army just isn't the same these days and the fucking politicians don't have the guts to put the resources in to do the job properly.'

'I know. Now it's all private contractors. No-one cares when they get killed or injured.' He reached over and put his hand on Tony's shoulder. 'How'd you like to earn some good money for a couple of month's work?'

Tony looked at him. 'What are you into Jake? I heard you were in security.'

'I was,' said Jake. 'Had a bit of an 'incident' down in Panama a couple of months ago. Made me realize I wasn't enjoying it anymore.' He paused and looked away, taking in the sights. 'A man wants me to go overseas and bring back two men. Two bad guys. Our employer has got deep pockets and I'm setting up a team to go and do it.' He looked back at Tony. 'I'd be grateful if you would come along.'

'How grateful?'

Jake pulled an envelope out of his jacket pocket and tossed it to Tony.

'Let's just say, it could be big enough to get you a faster car – and a better crew. There's fifty K in there. It's yours. Meet me in Montana in four days' time for a month of training. Then, if you get on the plane, you get one million, plus a further million if we're successful, which you will also get regardless if you get injured or we die in the attempt.'

Tony thought for a few seconds. 'How long will we be away?'

'No more than a coupl'a months. Remember Andy?'

'Spider? Sure.'

'He's coming. I've got one more in mind. Four of us in total.'

Tony looked at Jake closely and put the envelope into a pocket in his racing suit.

'Good. Meet me at the airport diner in Butte, Montana, midday on the 12th. Okay? Oh, yes. I need your measurements to make sure your kit fits when we get there.'

Chapter 13

Portorož, Slovenia

Birgitt approached Marko and replied in English: 'Hello. You were at the bar tonight.'

'Yes, sorry we never met. Johan, the barman, had your attention.'

Birgitt swept the hair out of her eyes and smiled at him. 'I am Birgitt. Are you here for something to eat?'

'Marko.' He held out his hand and she shook it gently. 'I live just up there, about five minutes away. Why don't you come back to my place and I can make you a sandwich or something?'

He was so attractive and his suggestion to go up to 'his place' gave Birgitt a bit of a thrill, a challenge. *Why not?*

'Okay.'

♦

The promised five minutes elapsed and they stood in the elevator heading up to the sixth, the top, floor of Marko's apartment block. Marko held her hand and Birgitt didn't object. Marko felt himself get hard.

'This is a beautiful building,' she said as the doors opened.

'Your English is good. Where is your home?'

'Arnfrid and I are from Oslo.'

Marko knew his capital cities. 'Ah, Norwegian. I would love to go there.' They stopped at his door. 'We're here.'

He opened the door and allowed Birgitt to enter, admiring her figure under her dress and wondered what color underwear she wore.

Birgitt noticed the apartment was very masculine with almost no ornaments, pictures or personal items, certainly no photos. A kitchen, in fashionable white was on the left, again immaculate, with a large lounge-dining area to her front. Large windows looked out to a balcony with a view of the coast. A big, flat screen television dominated one of the walls with equally large surround sound speakers before a black leather sofa. A weight machine in the corner confirmed her view that he looked after himself.

Marko went into the kitchen and got two wine glasses. 'What do you think?'

'It is very nice. I like the view.'

Marko poured two glasses of red wine. 'Here, come outside.' He opened the glass doors and went out onto the balcony and stood against the glass railing.

Birgitt joined him and he handed her a glass. 'What about the food?'

'I'll make something soon. *Na zdravje.*' He clinked his glass against hers. 'That means to your health,' he added.

Birgitt looked at him. 'In Norway, we say *Skål.*'

Marko took a sip of the wine and stroked her arm. 'You are very beautiful Birgitt.'

He pulled her toward him and kissed her gently on the cheek. He also made sure she could feel his erection as their bodies came together.

'I need to go to the bathroom,' said Birgitt. *Perhaps I should have stuck with the pizza*, she thought.

'Sure, just through the bedroom there, he pointed to the left.'

Birgitt put her glass down on a table and went through toward the bedroom.

She closed the door to the en-suite bathroom and checked her face in the mirror. *This is not a good idea Birgitt. Tell him you are tired and get out of here.*

She flushed the toilet, washed her hands and opened the door. Marko was sitting on the bed. 'You are better?'

'I'm actually feeling a little tired. Do you mind if I go? Give me your number and we'll get together again. We are here for a few more days.'

Marko stood up and went and put his arm around her. 'Come on my girl, you know you want it.'

Birgitt went to get out of his embrace, but found he was very strong. 'Please Marko, I would like to go.'

Marko picked her up and threw her onto the bed. She sat up and Marko hit her with his fist, splitting her left eye. Birgitt fell back and screamed. Marko jumped on top of her, slapped her twice and clamped her mouth shut. He manhandled her to the top of the bed and opened the top drawer of his side table. From inside, he pulled out a handkerchief and stuffed this into Birgitt's mouth. She was still struggling, but no match for Marko, who reached again into the drawer and brought out a tie, which was looped and incorporated a slip knot. This he slipped over her head and around her neck.

He was hugely aroused and the voice inside that told him this was wrong was amply drowned out by a chorus of yes, yes, do her!

Marko flipped her on her front and, not worrying about her zipper, ripped her dress apart, starting at the top. She was wearing black, matching underwear. He ignored the bra and ripped off her bottoms exposing her. With one hand firmly holding her down, he took off his jeans and boxers.

Birgitt's head was in a spin. She tried to take the gag from her mouth only for Marko to grab her arm, which he then twisted behind her back and up. She was gagging and then he was inside her. He was large and the pain was almost too much for her. She felt him going faster and faster and then he was pulling on the tie around her throat. She tried to get her fingers around it, but he was pulling very hard, her head now well off the bed. She couldn't breathe and she started to slip toward blackness.

At that point, Marko ejaculated and, such was the force of his orgasm, he lost control of his legs, which buckled beneath him.

It was a full minute before he rose to his feet. The girl wasn't moving, so Marko went into the bathroom to urinate and clean himself. When he returned, the girl was still lying there.

What have you done Marko? This is a new low for you.

Fuck off! The bitch wanted it. They all do.

Marko shut the little voice out and thought hard about how he was going to get rid of the body.

Chapter 14

Silver City, New Mexico

From Kentucky, Jake flew to Houston. It seemed a central location to wait for information about the final pick for his team, Eddie (Frogman) Martinez. Eddie had been a Weapons Sergeant in the Special Forces and Jake had served with him in Iraq. Eddie had also been with him on the night their Blackhawk helicopter was shot down by insurgents over Baghdad in late '03.

Jake took his discharge shortly after that event and he'd heard that Eddie had stayed on for the full tour before going back to the States where he was given an instructor role. Jake kept tabs on several former buddies and heard that things went bad for Eddie when he got back in '04, that he'd turned to drink and, when the excesses could no longer be covered up and started to affect his job, a medical discharge resulted.

Jake stood at the cab rank waiting his turn when Paula called him on his cell. She told him that Eddie'd been cashing his disability checks in Silver City and was a long term resident at a mobile home park. Jake took the details and walked back into the terminal to get a plane to Albuquerque.

Once there, it had been too late to go further that night. So, following a night in one of the hotels around the airport, Jake returned and found a charter pilot willing to take him to Whisky Creek airport where he hired a rental car. He noted with satisfaction that the Impala had Sat Nav. and plugged in the trailer park's address. It was only five miles from the airport and he was driving through the entrance to the park ten minutes later. Jake checked the time, 11:13.

He stopped at the reception and went in to find where Eddie had his trailer. The owner of the park was helpful and gave him directions. As Jake emerged from the reception area, he remembered seeing a general store a block or so away. So, he got back into the car and went into the store buying some steak, a salad that just required some dressing, some milk, juice and cola. Five minutes later, he re-entered the park and pulled up outside Eddie's trailer.

With the groceries in one arm, he knocked on the flimsy door of the trailer. 'Eddie, hi it's Jake, Jake Walker.'

There was silence for perhaps fifteen seconds and then a response: 'Okay, come in.'

Jake opened the door and went up into the trailer. There was a strong smell of alcohol and body odor inside. Jake put his purchases on a table. Eddie sat on the edge of his bed at one end of the trailer. He was drinking cheap scotch and most of the pint bottle was gone.

'Hi Eddie. How've you been?' Jake went over to the bed and sat down next to his friend. He put his hand on his left knee and squeezed.

'Jus' another day, Jake. What the hell brings you to the ol' Silver City?'

'Been lookin' for you, Eddie.' Jake looked through the trailer, not as messy as he'd expected. He turned and looked at his friend. Unshaven, hair longer than he knew Eddie would like it. He wore a singlet and shorts. It was warm inside and Jake got up and cracked open a couple of windows. He sat on the bench seat near the open window.

'What happened Eddie?'

Eddie looked up and then out of the window. 'Always bin a drinker, Jake. You know that. It's jus' that I used to have a reason to stay sober each day. Now,' he spread his arms, 'this the only reason I got.

'When you left the war, I stayed on and finished the tour. Lost another four buddies in that time. You knew some of them too. When I came home, they gave me a job as an instructor, but I wasn't sleepin' too good without this,' he held up the bottle. 'Before I knew it, I was drinking in the mornings too.

'They tried to help me. I went to see all sorts of Doctors who reckon I got pos' traumatic stress. Next minute I'm pensioned out, with some coupons to see some more doctors. Found my way here after trying to live properly in 'Frisco. Bin here about two years. Always liked the sun.'

Jake got up and looked around the small kitchen. The gas was connected and he was soon grilling a couple of steaks. 'I'm going to make you something to eat. Why don't you go and have a shower and then we'll talk, okay?'

Eddie grabbed a towel, found a clean t-shirt and headed off to the shower block.

Jake made up a salad and, by the time Eddie reappeared, two meals sat on the dining table and two chipped glasses of orange juice. Jake noted Eddie looked much better. He smelt better. Jake started to eat and reflected on a lack of breakfast.

'I'm setting up a team and I want you on it.'

Eddie looked up, he was really only picking through the food.

'You were the best weps specialist I ever worked with, Eddie. Where we are going, I need someone who can shoot and not miss.'

'Aren't you in security these days?'

'Was. Last assignment made me think of other things to do.'

'What's the mission?'

'I can't tell you today. Tomorrow, I'm heading up to Montana, where the team will assemble and we'll do some training before the op starts.'

Jake pulled an envelope out of his jacket pocket. He reached inside and counted off fifty one-hundred dollar bills. He pushed it across. 'The man who has hired me is wealthy and will pay us well for what we do. There's five K, just for talking to me today. In the morning, there's a nine-thirty charter flight back to Albuquerque. If you meet me at the airport, I'll give you the other forty-five in this envelope. If you complete the training and commence the op, you get one-million, with a further million if we are successful.'

Eddie picked at his teeth with a fingernail. 'Two mil? Can't even imagine what you'd need me to do to earn that sort of dough.'

'Nothing illegal, pal. We're on the right side of things. I'll tell you some more if you turn up tomorrow. It's a dry op, Eddie. No booze. It's a chance to turn your life around.'

Jake stood up. 'I hope to see you tomorrow.' He held his right hand out and Eddie shook it.

Chapter 15

Portorož, Slovenia

Pat Davis and Nikki Seztac sat in a BMW three series that Pat had hired at Ljubljana airport. They were parked across the road from Marko Kovak's apartment block, albeit on the opposite side of the building overlooking the entrance to the underground garaging.

When he picked up the BMW coupe, Pat had liked the feel of the car so much, he decided to head straight to the BMW dealership to see about buying the two SUVs Jake wanted. This turned out to be harder than he had thought, particularly as he wanted the X6M, Motorsport, top of the range, both in black. Initially, the BMW Dealer in Ljubljana told Pat it would take eight weeks to get the two cars shipped. So, Pat gave the man five-thousand US dollars, with a promise of a further five, whereupon the man was on the phone to BMW in Munich and the cars were delivered three days later. Pat organized a lock-up garage in Ljubljana, which was where they were parked. Both were black and had privacy glass all round. Importantly, they were four wheel drive, had Sat Nav. and, with a twin-turbo four liter V8 and sequential eight speed gearbox, very quick.

After arriving in Slovenia, Pat had given Nikki the task of finding a suitable property and locating someone who could sell them some weapons and Nikki quickly found them a suitable safe-house. Just south of the main highway between Ljubljana and Koper was the small town of Pivka. Nearby, Nikki had found a large house, with a triple garage under the roof line, set on several acres and well off the street. There were two driveways as the block fronted two roads, making it ideal for their purposes. As instructed, Nikki paid the owner six months' rent in advance using a company name supplied by Iain.

'Any luck with weapons, Nikki?' asked Pat.

'Yes, has been hard for me, but a friend has a contact and we are meeting him tomorrow. This guy is an agent, a how you say it, come between.'

'That's go between. You know him?'

'No, but my friend has used him and believes he can get what we want. Discretely and with no questions.'

'What about visas for Jake and his team?'

'Their US passports will get them through without a visa. Same if they need to cross into any of the other European countries.'

'That's good. What about Kovak senior?'

'A very shadowy and careful man, that one. He has a Russian passport, but also one from Slovenia. He has been made citizen here, which enables him to travel throughout Europe. Can't find anything about his past, where he was born, nothing. All I can find is that he came here from Moscow and has links to a major crime syndicate in Russia.'

'You mean the Russian mafia.'

'Could be, but more likely he belong to a vory, a criminal brotherhood. If so, he would have prison record somewhere. I am making very discrete enquiries. This man has links everywhere and my own questions will raise attention, so I am being very careful. The police, politicians, the authorities at the docks in Koper, many, many people are in his pay. He's never been caught doing anything illegal, but my contacts suggest he is very large importer of drugs, mainly heroin and cannabis. His job is to ensure safe passage of merchandise to his network further up, in Europe and Russia.'

'And the son, Marko?'

'Again Russian born and he has the same status and passports as his Father. He lives with his Father, but comes here, mainly in the warmer months, to party at the various bars and nightclubs. His apartment is on the top floor. His Father and him are seen together regularly and my contacts believe that Marko is being groomed to succeed him at some point in the future.'

They were silent for a few minutes and Pat noticed the garage doors rolling upward. He checked his watch, just after nine pm. 'This could be our boy.'

They watched and, sure enough, Marko's Mercedes SUV drove up the drive and out onto the street. The driver had a quick look and then headed off toward the town center. 'Let's go, said Pat.'

The two got out of their BMW and headed quickly across the road and down the ramp to the garage. Pat caught the bottom of the door just in time and it obligingly rolled back upward. They entered the garage and avoided the lift, which they knew required an owner's electronic tag for operation. Instead they headed toward the fire escape and Nikki handed Pat a set of latex gloves, which they both put on.

The entered the fire door and headed up the stairwell, but at the top, the fire door was locked and Pat opened a small carry case and pulled out a lock pick gun. He checked the size of the lock, selected the right pick, which he inserted into the gun and placed the pick into the lock. A couple of presses of the trigger aligned the lock beads and the door unlocked.

'How you get through customs?' asked Nikki.

'Told them I was a horse dentist and that I used this to clean teeth.'

Nikki smiled at him, before opening the door and giving the corridor a quick check. All was quiet, so they went along until they reached the door to Marko's apartment. Pat thanked the builder for buying his locks in bulk. It was the same type as the fire door and there was no dead lock. *This boy feels safe.*

In seconds they were inside. Muted light came from the bedroom and they headed over there. The room was immaculate, bed made up, no clothes or other things lying around. *I hope he's not that clean*, thought Pat.

In the bathroom, Pat turned on the light. Again, nothing out of place, towels all lined up. The counter was clear, so Pat tackled the drawers and Nikki checked the cabinets. 'Here, look at this,' said Pat, holding up a hairbrush. 'Nothing, not one hair. This is impossible. No-one has a hair brush this clean.'

'Look here,' said Nikki, pulling a small wooden box toward him. He opened it and there was an injecting kit inside and two small bags of white powder.

'Seems to confirm things,' said Pat. 'But we can't take it as evidence, or even photograph it. We're here illegally, remember?'

Nikki put the box back. 'I have an idea,' she said and headed over to the shower enclosure. She got down on her knees and unscrewed the drain cover. Peering inside, she said: 'Go into the bedroom and see if there is a coat hanger, one of the wire types.'

Pat was back a minute later. 'We're in luck. A lot of designer suits and street wear. This is the only one.' He handed the hanger to Nikki, who unwound it and made up a crude hook.

After a couple of tries, Nikki retrieved a small wet clump of hair, which she held up so that Pat could see. 'Now you know why you hired me.'

Pat pulled a zip lock bag from his pocket and held it open so that the Nikki could place the sample inside. Five minutes later they were back in the BMW.

Chapter 16

Silver City, New Mexico

It was nine-thirty am on the day after meeting Eddie Martinez at the trailer park. It was the 10th, two days before Jake would rendezvous with the team in Montana. Eddie had still not arrived and Jake was contemplating his next move and whether they could do the job with just three of them.

At nine-forty, Jake had just decided to go when he spotted a cab coming down the road toward the airport. On the chance it might be Eddie, Jake decided to wait and, in due course, Eddie emerged from the cab, wearing jeans, boots, a clean t-shirt and carrying a hold-all. He paid off the cab and walked over to Jake.

'How're you feeling, Eddie?'

Eddie raised his sunglasses to show two bloodshot eyes. 'Sorry I am late, Jake, it's hard to get a cab to the trailer park. Didn't have a good night, but I didn't have a drink after you left. '

'That's good,' said Jake noticing that Eddie was perspiring. 'It's going to be tough, but you are going to thank me.' He pointed to the open baggage hold in the twin engine plane. 'Put your gear aboard and we'll get going.'

Presently, they were at ten-thousand feet heading toward Albuquerque. The ride was fine, a few bumps, but Eddie was looking a bit green.

'One thing I need right now are your measurements, foot size and so on. I need to make sure your kit fits when we get to Montana.'

Eddie gave him the information.

'I'll give you the rest of the money when we reach Montana,' said Jake. 'There are four of us in all. I don't think you know Andy Francis or Tony Evans, the other two. I fought with them in Afghanistan.'

'I've heard of Tony,' replied Eddie, 'but not Andy. What's the plan when we get there?'

'You remember selection?'

'Who doesn't?'

'Well, we're not exactly in fighting condition and, for what we're planning, I figure we'll need every advantage. We also need time to set up and plan So, we're going to be doing some fitness, weapons and other training over the next four weeks. And, the link to selection is Joe Grant.'

'Fuck no!'

'Yes, the same sadist that pulled our sorry asses around Fort Bragg all those years ago. These days, he's retired, but he has a remote property where he takes in suits and takes them through fitness and team-building. Earns well out of it.'

Eddie had been clutching a sick bag and, even though he had eaten nothing since yesterday, still found something to spit into it

Jake patted him on the back. 'The next plane's bigger, Eddie. You'll be fine.'

Chapter 17

Butte Airport, Montana

It was just before midday on the 12th and Andy and Tony were on time, sitting in the airport diner, both sipping sodas. The diner was filling up for lunch service, but they'd been sitting at the bar for over an hour, both having flown in that morning. It'd been over eight years since they were last together and they didn't initially recognize each other. Of the two, Andy looked less recognizable because of his long fair hair, but from the quick glances at the man, he became more and more certain he could see Tony Evans (whose call sign had been Sensei (the Master)).

Andy walked over to the man, now certain. 'Tony Evans. How the hell are you?' He thrust out his right hand.

Tony looked up at a large man with long hair. He struggled and then got it from the eyes. He shook Andy's hand warmly. 'Hi, Andy. I guess you're waiting for Jake too?'

Andy sat down next to him. 'Yep.'

'You're looking fit, but what's with the hair?'

'You don't like it? Helps me blend in, besides I'm doing movies now, only small parts and they needed my hair long.'

'Movies huh?'

As the two men chatted and caught up on their respective lives,

Jake and Eddie were exiting their plane. They had flown to Salt Lake City and stayed one night in one of the hotels near the airport. Eddie had the shakes, had tossed and turned all night and Jake wished he'd had the foresight to obtain some Valium, something that was on Joe's shopping list. They picked up their respective bags from the carousel and headed over to the diner inside the terminal. Jake spotted Andy and Tony straight away and walked over.

'Here he is,' said Andy.

They all shook hands and Jake introduced them to Eddie. 'Eddie and I fought together in Iraq. I probably wouldn't be here today if it weren't for this man.' He turned to Eddie who'd refused food and drink on the plane. 'You ought to eat something, or at least get a coffee down you. I'm going to get our hire car. You guys stay here and I'll be back.'

After sorting out the rental and paying for four weeks, Jake went back to the team. 'Okay, let's go.' He tossed Tony the remote. 'You're driving.'

There were a large number of cars in the rental park. Jake stopped at a red BMW X6M. 'Here we are.'

'Nice,' said Andy.

Jake went up to the passenger door and touched the handle, whereupon the door unlocked. 'Press the tailgate button, Eddie,' said Jake. Eddie pressed the button and the tailgate swung upward automatically.

'Fuck me,' said Eddie.

The four men stowed their bags and got into the BMW. Jake was in front with Tony. 'Where's the key?' said Tony.

'Doesn't have one. You have the remote, so the car assumes you are the owner. Simply press the start button, there,' said Jake point to a big red button on the console.

'What will they think of next?' said Andy from the back seat.

Jake turned to Andy. 'The rental company only has two of these in their entire fleet. Cost me four grand just so that it could be here waiting for us, and a grand a day for the next four weeks. This is identical to the vehicles we'll be using on the operation. We'll have two of them, so you and Tony will be training on this over the next few weeks.' He turned back to Tony. 'Sounds quiet, doesn't it?'

'What's under the bonnet?'

'Twin turbo, four-liter V8. Zero to sixty in less than five seconds. See the M button near your right hand?'

'This one?'

'When you press that, all the car's systems go into sport mode. From the handling to the responsiveness of the throttle. There's an instruction manual in the glove box which you can look through.'

Jake fiddled with the complex menu on the screen until he was able to activate the Satellite Navigation system. He punched in 'philips' until he was able to select 'Philipsburg Montana' which he then pressed. 'Okay, let's go. It's about sixty K or so to Philipsburg and then a further twenty K of gravel to Joe's place.'

'Joe?' asked Tony.

'Joe Grant,' replied Eddie.

'Not the instructor from selection?' asked Andy.

'Same one,' said Jake. 'He's agreed to get us into shape.'

Tony started to drive out of the parking lot, following the routes marked out on the screen. 'Shit, this thing's even got a heads up display.'

Chapter 18

Ljubljana, Slovenia

Zoran had received a meeting request from Pavel Novak the previous day and travelled to the capital. At precisely twelve-thirty, he pushed open the door of the *Zlato Runo* restaurant and went inside. Close behind him was his lieutenant, Valery Petrov. The restaurant was popular and only a few tables were empty.

A waiter approached. 'Sir, a table for two?'

Zoran knew where Novak would be seating. 'No thank you, I am meeting the person over at that table,' he pointed to the far corner.

'Of course.'

Valery went to the bar and Zoran sat down opposite Novak, who was the Director of the Uniform Police, a very senior policeman. Novak displayed a youthful face and, at thirty-nine, had enjoyed a stellar rise through the ranks since he joined the force at the age of eighteen. Novak was Zoran's chief source of protection and money paid to him went upward as well as down to lower level officers. The arrangement enabled Zoran to operate without interference.

Novak was eating and Zoran noted a plate of *Hachapuri* (Georgian cheese bread) and a plate of *Chashushuli* (beef and vegetable stew) sat nearby. He was also drinking a glass of the house red.

'Hello Pavel. You are looking well,' said Zoran, placing the newspaper he'd been carrying on the table.

Novak paused to finish a mouthful. 'Thanks for coming Zoran.'

'Not at all. What can I do for you?'

'I heard about the hi-jacking of your truck.'

'Yes, very unfortunate, but is sometimes a cost of business, no?'

Novak finished eating and took a big mouthful of wine from his glass. He tapped his nose and leaned forward. 'Word I hear is that there are bunch of young Croatians flashing a lot of cash around Zagreb at the moment. Seems coincidental, perhaps not. Maybe you should take a trip, see where they got their money?'

'Thanks, Pavel. I already know who is responsible. I just haven't yet figured a means to ensure it doesn't happen again. If there's any trouble, it will happen over the border.'

'Good.' Novak paused and finished the remains of his wine. 'There is another matter. A bit more delicate.' He gathered his thoughts. 'Your son, Marko…'

'Yes?'

'Most weekends he is down at Portorož. Do you know what he gets up to?'

'He is a young and handsome man. He likes to hang around people of his own age. A lot of pretty tourists visit the coast and I am sure he gets to fuck quite a few. I set him up with an apartment so that he could spend his weekends there.'

'I know. What you don't know is that a couple of tourists, pretty, young woman, have been found dead.'

'And?'

'In both cases Marko was seen in their company, one several months ago, one last weekend, a Norwegian student.'

'That doesn't prove anything.'

'I'm pretty sure that Marko is involved, or even responsible, for their deaths. The American found dead earlier in the year near the marina. She was a doctor and has a wealthy father in the US. There is an American, a private detective, who is sniffing around you and your son, asking questions.'

Zoran hid his surprise.'I know Marko, Pavel. I am certain he would not be involved.'

'I don't think you know him well at all.'

Zoran remembered the words of Andrei in Berlin (*you should know that his heart is black*) 'I will talk to him.'

'Your money can only buy so much from me, Zoran. If it happens again, I will arrest him myself.'

'What do you know about the American?'

'He has travelled here several times. He is definitely investigating what happened to the American doctor and, now that he is looking closely at you and your son, I am pretty sure he suspects your son. Proving it is another matter, as you would know, but I would be extra careful if I were you. The American's name is Patrick Davis and he is staying at the Kempinski in Portorož with a woman he has hired, Nikki Seztac.'

Zoran rose to go. 'Thank you for this information, Pavel. I will take care of things.'

'Don't make a mess, Zoran. There are some things that even I cannot clean up.'

Zoran left his newspaper on the table.

Chapter 19

Montana

'I've never driven anything as good as this,' said Tony, caressing the leather on the steering wheel.

'Tony, at the end of this you'll be able to afford the two-hundred Gs they cost,' said Jake. 'Whatever you do, try not to crash it, the insurance doesn't cover it off road.'

The big red BMW pulled into the parking area adjacent to Joe's home and the four men got out of the car. 'How are you, Eddie?' said Jake as he looked around.

'Been better, Jake. It's been a long day.'

Joe Grant opened his door and came down the steps, his dog bringing up the rear. He was wearing black work wear and black, army issue boots, which held a high shine from hours of spit polishing.

Jake introduced the team as they got their gear from the trunk of the BMW.

'Right,' bellowed Joe, before Jake could finish. 'Forget about your gear and fall into a line over there.' He pointed to a line scratched into the gravel.

Tony whispered to Jake: 'Is he kidding?'

'No I am not fucking kidding, now move it!'

The old habits came back to them and, within about 15 seconds or so, the four men stood approximately one arm's length apart in a rough line facing Joe.

'Ten-hut!' The four men came to attention and Joe walked back and forth in front of them. 'I am being paid to get you guys into some sort of condition and, from the look of you, it's going to be a real challenge as you no longer have the youth you had when we last met. You've travelled a long way today, so you can have the afternoon off to acclimatize to the brisk autumn we enjoy here in Montana and to check and prepare your gear.

'We start tomorrow. Reveille is at oh-five-thirty hours. You will have five minutes from reveille to be out here, just as I am dressed, with the exception of a t-shirt instead of this,' he patted his black shirt. 'After PT, you can shower and breakfast is at oh-seven-thirty here in my dining room. That's all you need to know for the present. Dinner tonight is at eighteen hundred. I expect you to be wearing what I am from here on. You won't need your civilian gear and can stow it at the top of the wardrobe in your rooms. I will call you soldier, or use your old call signs. You will address me as sir. Is that understood?'

There was a muted 'Sir, yes Sir.'

'IS THAT UNDERSTOOD?'

'SIR, YES SIR!' came a louder response.

'Okay. Dismissed.'

The four men picked up their bags and headed off to their cabin and Joe went back into his house. Once inside, they found there were six separate bedrooms which opened onto a lounge area with large sofas a couple of flat screen televisions, plus a dining and kitchen area. There was a large fridge, a washing machine and dryer and two large bathrooms at one end. The quality of the fit-out and furnishings was better than Jake had expected and then he remembered who Joe usually catered for.

On four of the bedroom doors were the call signs they used back in their ODAs – Luke, Spider, Frogman and Sensei. Jake went into his room and put his bag on the ground. He opened the wardrobe and saw that Joe had done the shopping as requested. There was underwear, socks, t-shirts, two pairs of Army issue boots, a pair of Adidas runners and, hanging up, six black work-utility shirts and matching pants.

He opened the third door and found there was a Glock 19 9mm pistol and an Olympic Arms semi-automatic carbine chambered for the 5.56mm NATO round. There was also camping equipment and a back pack, no doubt for spending some nights outside.

Tony entered Jake's room. 'You seen the gear?'

'Yes, just checking it now,' replied Jake, picking up the Glock and checking the mechanism. 'These are all new, we'll need to clean off the protecting grease.'

'Eddie doesn't look too good.'

'No, he's been spending his days on the bottle. It's going to take him a week to detox and get all that shit out of his system. While you're here, tell the guys to shower, shave and get dressed. The boots are new as well, so we'll need to start wearing them. Then, we should get our weapons stripped and cleaned. Okay?'

'Sure.'

Talking about Eddie jogged Jake's memory and he headed up to Joe's house hoping that Joe had been able to get some Valium, a pretty addictive drug, but it would help Eddie with his withdrawal.

♦

Jake woke and checked his Seamaster: 05:10. *Twenty minutes to get ready*. Last night, the conversation had been light. Jake thought it had been a combination of tiredness and a mindfulness of what they were preparing for that had settled around them. The meal had been very good, braised steak that had been going all day and plenty of fresh, homemade bread, but Jake was unsurprised to see the men retire early to their rooms to sleep. Eddie had needed no encouragement after Jake palmed him twenty milligrams of Valium after his meal, drugs that Joe had bought mail order from Canada. Jake had a plan to wean him off the drug over a two week period, but it would help him sleep and experience less tension.

At five-thirty precisely, Joe entered the team's cabin. He didn't play the bugle, so he banged two pot lids together, which had the desired effect.

'Everyone outside in five minutes,' he boomed in his best parade ground voice.

Only Jake and Tony made it. Andy came next, followed by Eddie, a full one minute late.

'Ten Hut!' The four came to attention. 'Not a good start. You are a team. When the team fails, everyone fails. Everyone down in the push-up position.' Jake and Tony started toward the ground. 'As you were!' The four men resumed attention. 'The word is Go. Remember this. Now, the push-up position. Readdddy, Go!

Joe held them in that position for a minute, until their arms ached. 'Right. Fifty push-ups in your own time. Go!'

Even Jake and Andy were struggling, but Eddie and Tony only made about twenty before their arms started to give. 'Keep going,' Joe roared. Eddie was resting on his knees. 'Alright, everyone on their feet.' He paused. 'Fucking pussies. I've seen fitter pensioners than you lot. And to think each one of you passed Selection.' He paused. 'We are going up that trail to your right. At precisely two-and-a-half miles is a large boulder, about seven yards wide, with a smaller boulder on top. It is about one thousand feet higher than we are here. We will do the same run every morning. By the end of your stay here, you will be doing the round trip in thirty minutes. Any questions?'

There were none. Joe adjusted his chronograph. 'Go.'

Jake and the three others headed up the trail, which looked like it had been built by loggers. He concentrated on his breathing and putting one step in front of the other. After a few hundred yards, the figure of Joe Grant went past him and headed off. Jake attempted to match his pace for a hundred yards or so, before he realized he just wasn't fit enough.

Andy came up beside him. 'I guess the good part is the second half is downhill.'

Jake managed a smile and the two kept a reasonable pace. After about two miles, the trail became quite steep and Jake found he couldn't maintain a run and started to do a fast march instead. Andy also found the going hard and Jake caught up to him. Eventually, they could see the boulder, just as Joe had described it, with Joe standing to one side.

As they touched the boulder and turned to go back, Joe told them their time. 'Twenty-three minutes. You need to bring that down to at least seventeen to complete the run in thirty. I will see you two down the bottom. Wait there until we all get back.'

Jake and Andy headed back down. Although it was downhill, the trail was uneven, with plenty of stones, large and small, and holes. They both went cautiously. After a couple of minutes, they saw Tony, who was laboring with the slope. 'Keep going, Tony, almost there,' said Jake.

A further minute and they saw Eddie, who was also finding it tough but was not ready to quit. 'Come on Eddie, not far to the top, then it's all downhill,' said Jake.

It would be a further twenty-five minutes before Joe, Eddie and Tony came down the trail. Eddie looked half dead and sat on the ground, retching.

After they were showered and dressed in clean kit, they enjoyed a cooked breakfast, except for Eddie, who only managed some toast and coffee. There followed a weapons refresher where Jake told them that, even though they didn't know what type of weapons they would have on the op, it was important that they learned to strip their weapons and reassemble them.

In the live practice that followed, only Jake consistently got good groupings from both the pistol and the carbine. They completed the day with another session of PT, strength training this time, some abseiling, more live practice and finished at five o'clock. After dinner and, by the time they had cleaned their kit, Jake wasn't the only one to find he was climbing into bed before nine pm.

Chapter 20

Seattle

It was mid morning and Iain Fisher was reading on his laptop when he noticed a black Ford sedan negotiate its way up his driveway. Iain was not expecting anyone and he went to the window and saw two men emerge from the car, both in white shirts and conservative ties. They had hung up their suit jackets in the rear of the sedan and paused to put them on. *Feds for sure.*

He went back to his table and tried to focus on a board paper regarding a planned merger. He'd been trying to concentrate more of his time on fewer things. The proposal before him had some flaws and he was trying to create a succinct and compelling argument against the proposal. Now that he had visitors, he would need to put it down.

Bill called through on the intercom and Iain pressed the talk button, 'Yes Bill?'

'Two gentlemen to see you, Sir,' said Bill, reading from two business cards in his hand. 'Special Agent George Simmons and Special Agent in Charge Hank Grady. They're from the FBI, Sir.'

'Thanks Bill, show them up.'

He recalled now the phone call he'd received from a Special Agent Simmons just after they'd buried Danielle. The day after in fact. He'd offered his condolences and told Iain to call him if there was anything about his daughter's death that he wanted to discuss.

Bill appeared at the entrance to Iain's study. 'Here you go gentlemen, Mr. Fisher.' He looked at Iain. 'I'll leave you to it, Sir. Call me if you want anything.'

'Thanks Bill, I will. Hi there, Iain Fisher, do come in and sit down, he pointed toward a leather lounge.

Simmons was about six-four and about twenty-five or so, regulation haircut, fit by the look of him. Grady was in his forties, about five-nine, but carried himself well and not a gray hair to be seen. The older man approached and held his hand out. 'Hi, Mr. Fisher, Hank Grady and the young man behind me is Special Agent George Simmons, who I believe spoke to you on the phone some time ago.'

Iain took the man's hand and nodded to the younger man, 'George,' they sat down, Iain in one of the armchairs. 'Can I get you anything?'

'No, we're good, thanks Mr. Fisher,' said Grady.

'Well, what can I do for you?'

'It's about your daughter, Danielle, and the circumstances of her death.'

'I see.'

'We have reason to believe,' began Grady, 'that you don't believe the official version of the events of her death.'

'What official version would that be?' said Iain cautiously.

'That she died of a drug overdose,'

'And why might you think that?'

Grady looked at Iain closely and thought hard about how much he could say. He knew that Iain had paid for a private autopsy, the presence of Rohypnol in the girl's bloodstream and so on. He also knew about him hiring Pat Davis and the trips the man had been making to Slovenia. He wanted to help, but he also wanted to ensure that Iain Fisher was not off on some wild crusade, a vigilante who could destroy their own efforts in the region.

'I know that you have evidence of foul play, Mr. Fisher.' Hank began cautiously. 'I even know who you suspect, a certain Marko Kovak, twenty-three year old son of Zoran Kovak, who goes to church every Sunday and files his tax returns with the occupation of 'business man'. We know who Zoran Kovak and his son really are, as do you, I suspect. But what we know and what we can prove are two different matters. And that applies to you also. We've come here today just to have a chat, to make sure that you know what the boundaries are here.'

Iain stood and went over to his window. 'Did you know that I have a signed and properly notarized affidavit from the woman who accompanied Danielle on her holiday and was present when the Kovak boy and another man, Miroslav Juricic, took her out of a nightclub to rape her and murder her?'

Grady didn't know that and looked at the younger Simmons, could see that he knew nothing either.

'That's excellent, Mr. Fisher, if true. But I suspect it is still insufficient for us to make any formal enquiries. I understand you have employed a private detective, Mr. Patrick Davis, to look into things on your behalf.'

'That's right. It was Pat who located the other woman and we might have other evidence too.' Iain paused, unsure how to put it. 'Would your position change if we had DNA evidence which linked Marko to my daughter's murder?'

Grady paused, putting his words together, again on the back foot. 'DNA evidence? Funny thing DNA evidence. The expert you put up on the witness stand will state categorically, ninety-nine-point-nine-nine per cent that the DNA samples match; that there's only one chance in thirty-million that the samples didn't come from the same person. But, Mr. Fisher. It matters not one bit if you didn't follow procedure in obtaining the DNA samples, obtaining the perpetrator's permission and so forth. You're a smart man. You know how good defense attorneys can be at getting good evidence thrown out of court?'

'Yes, I know this,' conceded Iain. 'I won't be doing anything unless I have further, substantial evidence, witness testimony, for example. I assure you that Pat Davis is simply clearing up a few matters for me.'

'Thanks for that, Mr. Fisher. 'You know that the US has no extradition treaty in place with Slovenia?'

'Yes, I did. Suggesting that if we get sufficient evidence, the boy would need to be tried in Slovenia.'

'That's right, Mr. Fisher. Unless, we had the evidence and he decided to visit America... You know what I mean?'

'Yes, I do.'

'Good. Don't take things on yourself.' He placed his business card on the coffee table between them. 'Call me or George here if you need any assistance.'

Outside in the car, Grady turned to his younger protégé. 'Simmons, I want you to keep a close eye on this, okay?'

'Sir?'

'We've wanted Kovak for a long time, George. His existence is an embarrassment to the Slovenians and their President has sought our help. We know his son murdered Fisher's daughter.'

'But, the evidence is circumstantial, Sir.'

'So far. Fisher's now suggesting that they've linked the boy's DNA, but it's almost certain that the evidence would be inadmissible. Let's just say if Fisher's private dick obtains more evidence, perhaps eye witness testimony from others, perhaps from this other man, Juricic, we could do what we can to assist? If we get this boy's ass, we may get our chance with his Father, and he's a much bigger fish. Keep a rolling brief on this, okay?'

Chapter 21

Betanja, Slovenia

Marko was playing on his *PlayStation* in his bedroom. The game was the very latest *Medal of Honor* game in which Marko played the role of a US Navy Seal operative with the code name of 'Rabbit'. He was good at playing this game, having spent hundreds of hours mastering the art of moving around the digital battlefield and quickly shooting the enemy soldiers. He heard a knock on his door.

Marko paused his game. 'Come in.'

It was Valery. 'Your father's in his study and wants to see you.'

Marko went downstairs and stood before the door. He didn't knock, just opened the door and went in, closing it behind him. Zoran stood by the large window beside two empty chairs, one of which he pointed to and Marko crossed the room and sat down, crossing his legs.

Zoran didn't speak. So, Marko broke the silence. 'You are worried about something, Papa?'

'Yes, you could say that,' Zoran replied, taking the other chair across from his son.

'What is up?'

'You is up, Marko. It is you that I am worried about,' replied Zoran, looking at his son.

'But why?'

'I have just learned about an American woman. She was found down at the Marina in Piran, dead of a drug overdose several months ago. She was a doctor working for a charity in Armenia, here for a few days to holiday with a friend.'

'I read about this in the paper.'

'Last weekend, another young woman, found strangled. She was raped and beaten. My sources tell me she was a Norwegian. My sources also tell me that you were seen in the company of both women.'

'Who can tell? I am seen in the company of many beautiful women, many of them tourists.'

'You were in Portorož on the weekend?'

'Yes, so what?'

'What happened?'

'Nothing, I swear. A few drinks, I was in bed, alone, by midnight.'

No, Marko. I don't believe you.'

'I swear, papa. I have done nothing.'

'It is too much of a coincidence. If you weren't my son, you would have been arrested by now.'

'I…' began Marko.

'NO! Hear me out. I have had to pay extra money to the police to ensure things are kept quiet. I was told that my money would not protect you a third time.

Marko was sullen, but knew when to keep his mouth shut.

'Now, there is another matter I must deal with. An American private detective. A good one, I am told, who is working for the father of the dead doctor. He is looking into my affairs and into yours.'

Zoran stood up. 'From hereon, there will be no partying in

Portorož. If you don't like it, I will sell the apartment and the cars. You hear me?'

Marko turned red, but it wasn't embarrassment, it was anger. 'You can't sell my property, I have fucking well earned it.'

Zoran grabbed his son's shirt front and pulled him upwards. 'You have no idea about anything. Least of all respect.' He threw him back into the chair and sat down. Marko was still angry, but also scared.

'I have two sisters and two brothers, all younger than me. Yet, I don't know where they are or even if they are still alive.' Marko looked at his father. 'There was little laughter in our little house when I was growing up. All I remember was the cold and how hungry we always were. You know nothing about hardship, about how respect is earned.

'I know you have had little say in your upbringing, and no mother. But I have done my best in the absence of my own family for the past forty years. Being a member of our *vory* has brought its reward to me and to you, my son. But, the rewards come with lifetime obligations and responsibilities. Lifetime, remember, and that goes for you too. It's like the words in that song from long ago 'you can check out, but you can never leave'. It's time that you realized who you are and to start taking responsibility for yourself.

'Now, go and get ready. We are going to do some detecting work of our own.'

Chapter 22

Montana

Jake sat on the ground and looked into the fire. The others were already there, enjoying the warmth as the coolness of the clear night started to make its presence felt. A dinner of cold rations had been consumed and all the men could feel the tiredness in their bodies after walking into this beautiful high mountain lake. Fifteen miles? It felt twice as far given how far they had climbed.

The day also marked that two of their four training weeks had gone by and he was pleased at the team's progress. Tony and Andy had been getting to grips with the BMW, learning how to tap the SUVs immense power and torque. Tony had more experience and natural ability, which was not surprising given his part-time hobby, but pretty soon, Andy was able to power slide around corners and do handbrake turns with ease.

Likewise, the daily five mile run was no longer a burden, although Andy and Eddie had had some problems with blisters. Even Eddie was able to keep running all the way to the top, but had yet to crack the thirty minute time. His appetite had returned and he was no longer taking large amounts of Valium, although Jake still allowed him two-point-five milligrams, half a tablet, each evening to help him sleep.

"How's everyone feeling?" asked Jake

The men discussed the day and Joe talked about what time they would need to get up to catch some fish.

After five minutes or so, Joe excused himself and Jake thought it time to discuss planning. 'I had a call from Iain Fisher yesterday,' Jake began. 'Told him of our progress, that I think we will be physically and mentally ready in two weeks.'

'What's the plan?' said Eddie.

'Well, at its simplest, our plan was to snatch Kovak and fly him back to the States, whereupon he'd be arrested on the suspicion of murder of a US citizen. Fisher now tells me that, for this to work, we need a Federal arrest warrant. And that's the issue, his lawyers tell him we don't have enough evidence to get one.'

'What do you mean?' said Andy. 'They have that woman's evidence, don't they. The one that got away.'

'It's not that simple. Fisher told me his investigator had found some hair samples in Kovak's flat and that it matched the DNA they'd found in his daughter's body. You know, the DNA within the semen they found inside her. Anyway, in order for Fisher to convince a Federal Prosecutor to go before a judge to obtain an arrest warrant, this DNA needs to be legally obtained. There needs to be an audit trail back to the person giving the sample and, in most cases, the person's permission. Any judge will want to see evidence that the sample has been lawfully taken by appropriate people, who can attest that it comes from Kovak and then point to the improbability that the samples came from different people. We don't have this, and the evidence from the Morgan woman is not enough. The DNA simply provides more proof, even if we can't use it against him.'

'So, we go over there and put a bullet in his head,' said Andy. 'That's the way most of the rich people get justice or revenge.'

Tony looked at his buddy. 'It's probably how we'd all handle it, Spider. But Fisher is the client and he said at the outset that he wanted justice in an American court. So, there is no point bringing him back if we can't put him in jail.'

Andy extended his arm to make a pistol, pointing at the fire. 'I hear ya, Sens. The Kovak boy is just a hood, a criminal. I wouldn't think twice as I double-tapped the Russian trash.'

'What about a confession?' said Eddie. 'We snatch him and then get his signature to a confession. Or we go over there and ask him politely for some blood?'

'I know you're all trying to be helpful,' said Jake. 'Anyway, the upshot of our conversation is that you should now have been paid a mil each, including me. I decided I needed money after all and Fisher has heaps of it.' Jake saw the subtle eye movements and so on as his team digested this. All of them needed a cash injection and to be free from worries for a few more years. It felt good, despite the news from Slovenia. 'We are to keep going, we'll keep working on a plan to snatch him from a vehicle, or in a hotel or similar room. Meanwhile, Fisher and his detective are going to keep looking, to see if there are other witnesses prepared to come forward.

'Sensei and Spider. Two BMWs have been purchased and are in a shipping container at the safe house, a property that's been leased not far from the Kovak's place. I am told they are the same as the one we've been training on. The property should have everything we will need, including the weapons to do what is needed to be done.'

'What about the other guy? Weren't there two of them involved?' said Tony.

'Fisher says the other guy's a playboy and that he's no longer interested in him.'

'Okay.'

'Fisher's pilots are on the payroll and ready to go at twenty-four hours' notice. Everything appears to be in place,' concluded Jake.

'We don't have enough intel on Kovak and his father,' said Eddie.

'Yes, Frog. It worries me too. Hopefully we will have more to go on when we get our feet inside Slovenia.'

Chapter 23

Portorož, Slovenia

Over the following week, Pat and Nikki made further enquiries, sought further witnesses, but no one wanted to talk. It was a Wednesday and Nikki awoke just after eight am and went into the bathroom to shower. They'd been staying in the Kempinski, an older hotel on the Portorož waterfront for a week and she was getting increasingly worried about the course of their investigation. She'd worked with her Uncle Stefan in his private detective business for five years, ever since she left the police force disillusioned and unhappy about the lack of opportunity for woman and the petty corruption within the force. She owned an apartment in Ljubljana, something made possible through an inheritance from her Father, and was looking forward to going home and reconnecting with her few friends. Yet she was also feeling worried as a close neighbor had reported someone asking questions about her whereabouts and Stefan had also raised concerns, reporting that the police were following him. It was becoming apparent that their investigation into Zoran and Marko Kovak was getting someone's attention and it was the kind of attention they didn't need. The money she was earning was considerable, a half a million dollars, a fortune, and her share was fifty per cent, but what was her life worth, she wondered?

She stepped out of the shower, toweled herself dry, went into the bedroom and looked at herself in the mirror. At thirty-two, she was still toned and slim and her jet-black, shoulder length hair with a long fringe worn down across her face gave her a determined look and caused many to look twice, men and women. A natural athlete at school, she'd been a good long distance runner and had even contemplated running professionally before joining the police force, a job she believed in passionately as a young girl, but no more. She still loved to run and managed to exercise several times a week and this showed in strong limbs and very little fat on her body.

She checked the time on the alarm clock and focused on the day ahead. Through a close friend, she'd organized the purchase of weapons for Jake's team and had a meeting later in the day at the safe house where she was going to take delivery of an assortment of guns and explosives. She looked in her wardrobe and selected her black jeans and a white blouse. A short leather jacket which she wore when riding her Honda motor bike completed the look she was after. She put some gel into her hands and ran her fingers through her hair until her hair sat the way she liked it and then applied some red lip stick. She was ready for the day.

She picked up her wallet, passport and key ring and put these into the various pockets of her jacket. She checked her phone for emails, nothing important, and picked up her bike helmet before knocking on the adjoining door in the apartment. She heard Pat acknowledge so she entered and saw Pat on a sofa watching the news on CNN. 'Good morning Mr. Patrick,' she said and, seeing through the open door to the balcony that the fine, Autumn weather they'd been having was likely to continue, remarked, 'nice day for it.'

'Morning, Nikki; it sure is. Sleep well?'

'A full ten hours. Can you imagine? Feeling good.' She headed over to the bureau and, checking the electric kettle contained water, switched it on. 'You want a cup of tea?'

'Yeah, sure, thanks,' replied Pat as he watched the 'talking head' describe the increasingly inexplicable response from the National Rifle Association to yet another shooting incident in Arkansas, a probable murder suicide in which a man had shot his three children and wife before turning the gun on himself. He shook his head. He loved his news and thought back to the time when CNN reported real stories and gave opinions that resonated with people. Now, they were no different from any of the other commercial news stations. Mainstream, all censored and designed to suit whatever the media owners wanted to say, taking out the real stories and giving them sound bites of bullshit. But, at least CNN told him how the Celtics were going and he could forget, for a moment, the seemingly endless removal of the constitutional rights of ordinary Americans…*Never used to be this way. Probably have more rights as a Slovenian...*

Before long, Nikki brought two mugs of tea over to the coffee table and sat next to Pat on the sofa. 'Thanks,' said Pat and he hit the remote turning off the television. 'I got a call in from Iain Fisher, earlier.'

'Yes, a week to go before your team arrives.'

'That part of the planning is going well. Sadly, we don't think we have enough evidence to convict our boy.'

'Surely, we now have DNA. Is how you say, inconvertible?'

Pat smiled at the malapropism. 'I think you mean incontrovertible. But you're right, the DNA evidence matches and we know our boy is responsible. We just can't use it, can't get a warrant for the boy's arrest, even with the evidence of the other woman who was with Danielle that night.'

'So, where does that leave us?'

'We need to get other evidence which supports the woman's testimony. Then, if our plans go right and we get him over to the States and charged, prosecutors can legally obtain some of the boy's DNA and we'll get our conviction, perhaps the death penalty.'

'So what are you thinking?' asked Nikki.

'We're not sure we can proceed at this point. Entrapment could be one avenue, but it's a really long shot. A last resort really. Iain's asked us to look into the other guy, Miro Juricic, see what we can dig up.'

'I see. I've had some success with the weapons and will be going out shortly to meet with a man who can deliver weapons to the safe-house. The two BMWs are in the shipping container at the property. I thought it best to leave them there, probably more secure than the garage.'

'Okay, that's good. What did you manage to get?'

'This guy has friends high up in the Russian Army, men who have stockpiled tons of ordinance, warehouses full of everything from tanks to submarines he told me. I gave him Jake's list.' Nikki passed over a page from a small notebook. 'Four machine pistols, handguns and rifles with scopes and one sniper rifle, with a night vision scope. Smoke, flash and fragmentation grenades. Rocket launcher and missiles. He also said he could provide the Russian equivalent of the American claymore. And, the rest of the stuff, ammunition and so on listed there. All was possible he told me.'

'Well done, Nikki. How much?'

'That's Russia for you. Everyone can be bought these days and any criminal or citizen for that matter can buy this stuff if they have enough of the right money. He wanted half-a-million US. I gave him fifty thousand in cash and we agreed on two hundred thousand. It's a good deal for what we are getting.'

'I agree. You get a receipt?'

Nikki smiled. 'I'm meeting him at eleven this morning. He is a personal friend of one of my closest associates, so I am not expecting trouble. I can do this alone.'

Pat again thanked God that he'd found one person in Slovenia with integrity and skill and he'd entrusted her with five-hundred-thousand in cash to enable her to do her thing, hiring the house and so on, leaving Pat free to do what he did best, sleuthing. It'd helped that Iain had deposited one-hundred-thousand into Nikki's bank account at the start with a promise of another four if the mission succeeded.

'Good,' he replied. 'You'll have to as I'm booked on a flight at midday, heading back to the States to have a meeting with Iain and Jake. Things are quiet over at the Fortress,' Pat referred to their name for Zoran's home in Betanja. 'He hasn't left the place in five days now, neither has his son.'

Nikki looked at him, 'How you know this?'

'Well, you know how there is one road to get there?'

'Yes.'

'Well, I considered staking him out but got one of my team to send me some of these via courier instead.' He pulled a small black device from his pants pocket, about the size of a remote control for a garage door and handed it to Nikki, who looked at it carefully.

'So that was delivery the other day. What is it?'

'Very cheap, but effective technology, only fifty bucks on eBay. It's a GPS tracking device. Parents put them in their kids' backpacks so they can track where they go. Women hide them inside their husband's car or briefcase. Here, pass me your iPhone.'

Nikki picked up her iPhone from the table and passed to Pat who pulled a small note out of his wallet.

He swiped it to open the menu and went into the App Store, searching for the App which monitored this particular brand of GPS device. 'Here,' he said, showing Nikki the screen, 'this is the App you want, free as you can see.' He pressed 'install' and the phone asked for Nikki's AppleId. Pat held it for her to place in her password. Less than thirty seconds elapsed and he opened the software.

'These numbers here,' he pointed to the three numbers on the note on the coffee table. 'The top one is for the device I placed onto Zoran's Mercedes Saloon while he met with your Chief of Police the other day in Ljubljana. Just under the rear bumper bar against the fuel tank.'

He tapped in the number of the device. 'The password is

'Zoran' for all three devices,' which he entered on the screen. 'See, his car hasn't moved since he got back from the meeting that day.'

Nikki held the phone and saw a map of the area and a blue peg-shape which she saw was up near the road adjacent to Zoran's house. She squeezed the screen with her fingers, zooming out and confirmed the location relative to theirs. Not far, perhaps thirty minutes, drive, twenty on the bike.

'It was you who told me Zoran didn't drive and always travels in the Merc. saloon with the armor-plated glass and souped-up engine, so he must still be at home. I put one on Marko's SUV the following day. Second number is Marko's device. Third number is this one.' He retrieved the small device from where Nikki'd put it on the table and slipped it back into his trouser pocket.

'Anyway,' he stood up. 'I have to go to the convenience store and get a few things for the plane trip.' He picked up his wallet from the table and headed for the door. 'You need anything?'

'No, is okay, Pat. See you soon. Be careful,' she added. 'They know we are looking into their affairs.'

'Thanks, I will,' said Pat and went out and closed the door softly behind him.

Nikki drank some of her tea and looked down at the list of numbers. The second on the list was Marko's SUV. She pressed the menu button and the software asked for the 'Device Number'. She picked up Pat's note from the table, entered the serial number from the note and the password 'Zoran', and then pressed 'Locate'. She put the note in her jacket pocket and waited for the screen to refresh.

She heard a screech of brakes outside in the street and looked at the screen on her iPhone. *Just outside the hotel. It couldn't be...*

She slipped the phone into her jeans, jumped to her feet and rushed over to the glass doors fronting the balcony which were open. From the balcony, she looked down and saw two men flanking Pat, pistols drawn, as they bundled him into the rear door of an SUV.

Marko's SUV. She heard a knock at the door and looked over the edge as the SUV sped away down the street.

Three floors up; she estimated twelve meters to the pavement below. It was a long way down, too far to jump. She climbed up and over the balcony and looked over. She started to climb down and, hearing two gun shots, she lowered her body into the space below her. As she lowered her head past the floor of the balcony, her legs dangling below her, she saw the front door of the apartment fly open and two men rushed in. She hung from her hands, holding onto the slab of the balcony and swung her body inwards, landing awkwardly, but okay nonetheless, on the balcony below. *Thank God I wore flat shoes today.* She tried the door, locked; went back to the balcony rail and rushed the glass door, striking it with her right shoulder and all the force that her fifty-five kilogram frame could muster. It shattered into thousands of tiny shards and she was into the empty room, same as the one above. She rushed to the door, flung it open and headed for the stairwell to her right, glass pieces falling in her wake.

She headed down the first flight and, as she reached the landing, a shot whistled past her head and she felt a sharp sting as some of the concrete ricocheted into her face. Another shot rang out, but she didn't look back, racing down the stairs, jumping the last four as she reached each landing. She reached the foyer to see a number of staff and guests looking on in fright and she decided to take the rear door, which led to the garden area, figuring Marko's men probably had the front covered.

She didn't stop running until she was four blocks away. She ducked into a coffee shop and asked for some water thinking about her next move and how they could rescue Patrick. She realized she'd have to leave her Honda back at the hotel for now and decided to get a rental car so she could pick up some cash from the bank and make her meeting at the safe house. She pulled out her phone and checked that she had Iain Fisher's number. *The sooner she called, the sooner the team could be there on the ground...*

Chapter 24

September 5, 02:13, Granite Falls, Washington State.

Iain completed the final response to a due diligence questionnaire. As a non-executive Director of a company that developed intelligent systems for the integration of solar power into homes and commercial properties, the company had drawn the attention of a much bigger player in the market and had offered the shareholders a very good price. Personally, he didn't want the major shareholders to sell up. They had a good team and the product was world class, but money talked and the offer was way above current market valuation. He couldn't see any way other than to vote for the shareholders to accept the offer.

His cell phone rang and he saw that it was a blocked number. Tempted to let it go to voice mail, he relented and accepted the call. 'Hello.'

'Iain; it's Nikki.'

Iain heard a woman out of breath and realized he was talking with the woman Patrick had hired in Slovenia. 'Nikki, what's up?'

'The Russians captured Mr. Patrick. Less than an hour ago, right in front of the hotel.'

'No. Are you sure?'

'Of course. They came for me too, but I jumped off the balcony and ran for my life. They were shooting…'

'Okay, calm down. Where are you now?'

'I am still in Portorož.'

'Any idea where they've taken him?'

Nikki knew exactly where they'd gone. All three GPS transmitters where within one hundred yards of each other, at Zoran's house, the Fortress, in Betanya. 'I am pretty certain they took him to Zoran's place, about half an hour from here.'

Iain thought quickly. 'We'll fly out there tonight. I'll get onto Jake right now.'

'Thanks Mr. Fisher. I'll call my Uncle as I am going to need his help with the cars and other preparations we have made. Even though Mr. Patrick is a strong man, a good man, I need to be prepared that he will tell his captors of our plans. So am taking precautions. I cannot return to the hotel or go home for the present.'

Iain knew that Nikki lived alone, one less thing to worry about. 'Give me your number so I can reach you and stay out of sight. Someone'll call you as soon as we know what the plan is.'

Chapter 25

Betanja, Slovenia

Pat didn't stand a chance. He saw the SUV driving rapidly toward him as he came out of the hotel and it distracted him allowing two large men to grab him, one either side, pressing their pistols against his torso. 'Get in the car,' said one as the SUV screeched to a stop in front of them. He briefly thought of resistance, but a thick, meaty hand grabbed his neck and pushed his head down so that he could get into the SUV. *Stupid, Pat. You idiot!*

Another man already sat next to the far door and he quickly found himself sandwiched between two men with very wide shoulders, both holding Glock pistols and expressions that said don't try it. His other assailant climbed into the front passenger seat. A younger man drove and Pat could tell from his profile and the eyes in the mirror, that Marko Kovak was driving.

Pat could have kicked himself for being so naive, so incautious as to believe that their enquiries, however discrete, would not have gone unnoticed by these people. People that had infiltrated so much of the country, with paid officials in the police, military and judiciary. No, they were never going to just stand by without making contact. So, perhaps that's what this was all about; to warn him off.

What worried him now, more than anything, as they headed towards the outskirts of Portorož, was that they weren't disguising their intentions or their destination by blindfolding him. They wanted him to know; they were brazen and didn't care. *Shit, if a police car had been on the scene at the hotel, it probably wouldn't have made any difference.* He glanced out the window as they passed the dockland area of Koper and headed toward the main road which headed North East to Ljubljana.

Marko regarded him through his mirror from the driver seat. 'You like our country, Mr. Davis?'

Pat decided he wasn't going to entertain the little thug of a man and kept quiet.

'I think you do. You have been here several times now. We have a beautiful coastal region. But you know this already.

'You don't want to speak? Is okay, we can talk later. I am going to show you where I live. I think you will like it.'

A cell phone rang and Marko accepted a call from a phone in the console. He put the handset to his ear and listened. 'Okay, see you there.' He hung up the call. 'Your associate, Ms. Seztac…'

'Yeah, what about her?' said Pat.

'It seems she can leap from hotel balconies. It matters little, we know where she lives. I am glad you are now talking.'

Pat felt thankful that Nikki had escaped. *If she had escaped…* It was him they wanted, not the local help. He now hoped that Nikki could get word back to Iain and have enough good sense to stay low and out of sight.

Within ten minutes, they were out of Portorož and on the main highway to Ljubljana. Pat closed his eyes and focused on this breathing. He knew where they were headed and, twenty minutes later, Pat felt the car take a right turn and headed up the road that led towards the Fortress. Pat had not seen the place and took in the details as the SUV came to an intersection, well hidden from the tree-lined road, where he turned left and headed into the pine forest. Pat saw a sign 'ZASEBNEGA' (keep out or private, he surmised) and they followed a well maintained gravel road for perhaps two miles, most of it uphill. Zoran's home came into view at the end of the road and they slid through a high, motorized gate and rolled up a gravel drive toward a large, sandstone house. Marko skipped the front entrance and drove to the left stopping outside another entrance. He stopped the SUV and turned off the engine. The two thugs either side of him got out and, with their pistols pointed in his direction, Pat exited out the right hand door.

Marko came up to him. He was about six foot and well built. *From the gym*, thought Pat. 'It is a large house, Mr. Davis. No? Come, let's go inside.' He headed through the doorway and Pat followed, finding himself in a corridor which opened into a larger corridor and, to his right, a large foyer, resplendent with marble floors and wood paneling. Marko turned as they filed through and Pat stopped, well aware of three guns pointed at his back.

'The house was first constructed by aristocrats in the eighteenth century. Probably rebuilt three or four times since. When my father and I came here in the 90s, it was a ruin, but one with very solid foundations. This whole site sits on solid rock and is well fortified on all sides. The Nazis occupied it in the last world war. But as the Russians advanced, and they faced retreat, they blew most of it up.

'Did you know I am Russian?'

'Yes, I did know that.'

'Good, I am glad you are talking to me. We have a basement here and I was contemplating taking you down there, but would much prefer that we have a nice, civilized talk instead.'

He spoke to the men in Russian and turned toward the foyer and headed up the staircase as they led Pat away.

Chapter 26

Montana

Jake lay on his bed, unable to sleep. His wakefulness was unusual as the hard days of physical exercise meant they were all hitting the sack at about nine, not waking until Joe came into the block and called them to reveille. Tonight, his dream had been unpleasant, but he couldn't remember the details, which evaporated within seconds of his waking. The previous day had been busy and the afternoon's unarmed combat left his ribs sore from a round-house kick he'd sustained from the one-on-one with Andy. He was only bruised he knew, but he winced slightly as he ran his fingers along his chest.

Despite the soreness, he felt the best he had since, well since Special Forces Selection. They all did. Joe knew his stuff. They ran just about everywhere and he now reflected on how clever the man was as all of them, Eddie included, had put on ten pounds, all of it muscle and their torsos and arms were solid and ready. It wasn't gym muscle either; they'd built it sweating, from carrying pine logs, climbing up ropes, the constant push ups. And, the five miler each morning.

Jake's time was down to twenty-three minutes, twelve up and eleven down; Andy and Tony were not far behind and even Eddie was now doing it under thirty and had cracked twenty-eight minutes that very morning. There'd been no beer or alcohol of any sort and Joe had pumped calories and protein into them knowing that they needed fuel and energy, but also protein to build and develop their muscles. It had been good, tasty, healthy food as well. They would miss it when they left.

That afternoon, they'd been doing unarmed combat, a mishmash of boxing, Judo and Kung-Fu. Again, Joe's experience came good and he proved a match for them all, having expertise in each of the disciplines and a physique which belied the fifty plus years of the man. Jake knew he was enjoying himself as well. Despite his growling and the constant 'Readdddy, Gos' he barked at them on the chin bars, doing press ups and on the ropes, Jake saw the glint in his eyes and his pleasure at delivering what he'd promised, men who were ready to fight.

His cell phone, a new iPhone, vibrated on his bedside table and he saw it was Iain, which he instantly realized was not good; his dream had been a warning. He pressed 'Answer' and said, 'Iain, what are you doing awake at this hour?'

'How's the training going?'

'We're good, better than I thought we'd be. What's up?'

'I just had a call from Nikki. I need you to gather the team and fly over there as soon as you can.'

'Why, what's happened?'

'Nikki told me that Pat was bundled at gun point into our boy's Mercedes SUV early this morning, Slovenia time, just outside their hotel in Portorož.'

'Shit, no.'

'I know.'

'This means that Zoran is onto us, or at least knows that Pat has been making enquiries about him and his boy.'

'Yes, Nikki told me she only just escaped with her life as two armed men entered the hotel room and tried to kill her.'

'How did she get away?'

'Over the hotel balcony to the floor below. She said they'd been outside the room and came in shooting.'

'Okay. Are our pilots ready?'

'Yes, I've been making calls. They're logging a flight plan to Portorož as we speak. The rest of the arrangements are ready. Nikki has the house, weapons and the BMWs. We just don't have a plan now.'

'Other than to rescue Pat?'

'Yes, I was hoping you'd see the immediate objective I had in mind. He's part of the team, Jake. Can't sacrifice him to get our boy.'

'I understand.' Jake checked his Seamaster, 03:13. 'What's the flying time to Slovenia?'

'I don't really know, Jake. James was going to work it out and let me know. They are on their way to Butte Airport as we speak to ready the plane. I suggest you gather your kit and your team and get over there too.'

'Okay. I'll call you from the airport,' said Jake heading into the common area outside his bed room.

He knocked on Eddie's room, entered and saw his friend asleep. His eyes opened and, seeing Jake's face and the hard resolve he saw there, he swung his legs onto the floor. 'Luke, what's up? We goin'?'

'Yes, we are. Right away. Get the men and our gear ready to move in ten minutes. I'm just going to see Joe.'

Eddie was already moving.

Chapter 27

Betanja, Slovenia

As he entered his Father's study, he noted that Valery was there at the big desk with his Father, the two of them looking at something on the laptop.

'Marko, good. You have the detective, Davis?'

'Yes Papa, he is down in the library. I wanted to talk to you first.'

'What about the other one, the woman Seztac?'

'We missed her, but we know where she lives and she won't get far. She'll be dead within the week.'

'What do you plan to do with Davis?'

'Question him, find out what he knows, what he is planning?'

'He knows nothing. They have no proof, no evidence against you or me.' Zoran looked at Valery, who nodded. 'You waste your time, Marko. I told you this. He is either planning to kill you or go home. You will see.

'Anyway, we have business to attend to and you are coming with us.'

'Where?'

'A place called Brežice, near the Croat border. Come over

here.'

Marko went over to his Father's desk and they made room for him around the laptop.

'Recognize this truck?' said Zoran, pointed to the screen.

Marko looked and said, 'Yes, it's one of ours. Runs up every week to Luxembourg.'

'This picture was taken this morning by friends of mine in the Police. It is currently in a warehouse in Brežice, which is also a temporary home to eight Croats, who work for this fucker here.' He brought up another photo on the screen. 'His name is Carlos Radic, born in Monrovia, from good parents, which is a shame. He now controls almost one third of the drug trade in Croatia, is moving into Bosnia and now, it would appear, into my territory, with the nerve to take my shipment, my truck and to kill my driver.'

Zoran walked to the window and looked out. 'Our intelligence tells me Radic is in Brežice, with about ten men, and we are going to fly over there today and kill every last one of the fuckers.'

They heard a knock at the door and it opened. Zoran arose and saw who entered. 'Boris, my brother, come, come.'

A big, stocky man entered the room. He was well dressed in a dark gray suit, white shirt, no tie. His head was shaved and there were multiple tattoos on his neck and hands. A second man entered, similarly attired, also with a shaved head and tattoos.

'Zoran, it's been a long time.'

Zoran approached his guest and they embraced, kissing each other on the cheeks. 'Thank you for coming. You know Valery and this is my son, Marko.'

Boris nodded toward them. 'We've just come from the airport at Divača. This is Gregor. We flew from Moscow to Zagreb, where I dropped off four of my men. We then flew here.'

'What's your plan?' ventured Marko.

Boris looked at Zoran, who nodded. 'We're going to fly to Brežice shortly, where we will meet the rest of our team, finalize a plan and rest up. By four am tomorrow morning, we'll be outside the warehouse and then we'll go get our truck and shipment back; kill a few dogs too. About right, Zoran?'

'Yes, with you and your men, plus three of us and the element of surprise, it should be easy.'

'What about our guest, the Detective?' said Marko.

'Tie him up. Leave one of the men here, Petr, and the two that failed to get Seztac. They can stay here to look after things until we get back tomorrow morning.

Marko stood up and exited the study to attend to his father's orders.

'Boris, you come in my car with me and Valery. Marko can take Marin, Tosya and Gregor here in his SUV. Follow me and we will head to the airstrip.'

Chapter 28

Butte Airport, Montana

Tony drove like he was competing in a time trial for the world rally championship. The team had confidence in him, had experienced his ability to power slide around corners and knew of the BMW's awesome power, the kick in the back, when Tony floored the accelerator. Even so, the ride was a mixture of pure fear and exhilaration as Tony powered the four ton SUV at speeds which were illegal throughout the Union. What made it all the more frightening was the darkness and Jake thanked again the research that he'd done on the BMW as it xenon lights lit up the trail ahead easily and even moved to light up the road when they went around bends. *Why couldn't America make cars like this one?*

Jake had nearly asked Joe to come with them, to drive the SUV back so that it could be cleaned, as the vehicle was filthy and it was clear it'd been driven in rough country. As he hung onto the hand strap above his head, he was now glad he'd said fuck the insurance bond and Joe, he was sure, would not have needed the excitement of their hour long trip to the interstate, and a further mad dash, perhaps fifteen minutes, to the airport.

Around five minutes from the airport, Jake glanced over to see they were traveling in excess of one-hundred miles per hour. He called their pilot, James Reilly, using a cell number Iain had provided.

'Hello.'

'James, this is Jake Walker. Pleased to talk to you finally. We are five minutes from the airport. What do you want us to do?'

'Okay, the airport is small, unmanned at this hour. But, we have properly contacted Border Security, we've logged an international flight plan and our intentions are known. You have a cover as documentary film-makers.'

'Yep.'

'Okay, there are a few other planes parked in the general aviation lot, but ours is the only Cessna Citation, the only jet. You've been aboard it before I believe. Drive straight up to the plane and we'll get loaded and on our way.'

'Great, see you shortly.' Jake ended the call and saw they were already on Harrison Avenue. He tapped Tony's hand which gripped the gear selector 'Slow down now, mate, you've done well.' Tony eased off the gas and dropped a couple of gears. Jake pointed toward the aircraft sitting on the apron. 'See the planes to the right there, the larger one, the jet? That's us. Just park next to it.' Jake turned round. Eddie and Andy were also holding tight to the hand holds above their heads. 'You too good?'

'No problems,' said Andy.

'Good to go, boss,' said Eddie.

Ten minutes later they were all aboard, except for Tony, who had gone to park the BMW. Someone would contact the rental company later so that someone could pick it up and, no doubt, send Iain a bill for a clean-up and to fix the likely damage to the suspension and underside.

James emerged from the cockpit, while his co-pilot, Paul, completed the final paperwork. 'Jake?'

'Yes, hi James,' replied Jake, walking forward and shaking the younger man's hand. He turned introduced Eddie and Andy.

James nodded. 'Hi guys.'

'We're going early. Did Iain tell you the reason?'

'Yes, we know. The detective, Patrick, he's been kidnapped, right?'

'Almost,' said Jake. 'Pat's been sniffing around, but I don't think there'll be a ransom demand. They'll take him somewhere as they'll want to know what he knows and why he's been so interested in them.'

'Who's they?'

'A long story, James. I'll talk to you and Paul later, once we are on our way. Promise.'

'No problems. We're cleared for take-off, but can't take off until six am, just the rules around here. Once we're up, our flight path will take us to Harrisburg, a small airport in Pennsylvania, where we'll top up the tanks before the flight to Spain, again a small airport at a place on the west coast called Vigo. It will take us eleven hours to get there and we'll stop for around an hour to refuel. Then straight onto Portorož, a further two hours flying time.'

Jake looked at his Seamaster, 05:30. 'What time you figure we'll get in?'

'All goes to plan, we'll be on the deck in Portorož at four am local time.'

Tony came up the steps and into the cabin. 'Here's Tony. Tony, this is James, our pilot.'

'Hi Tony. Good, we can get moving.'

Jake held up his iPhone. 'You okay if I use this?'

'Sure, no problems Jake. That stuff the commercial airlines sprout about electronic devices affecting navigation systems... All bullshit. But, pretty soon, we're going to be fifteen ks up, fifty-thousand feet, so you might have trouble getting a signal.'

'Okay, I'll make my calls now.'

Chapter 29

Slovenia

The taxi driver, a naturally grumpy Serb, Nikki'd decided, complained constantly about the state of the roads during the half hour drive from Portorož, even more so as he negotiated the rough track which led to their safe house, about five kilometers to the east of the small town of Betanja. Nikki gave the man an extra twenty Euros to shut him up and stood outside the shipping container, which sat to the side of their safe house. Ten kilometers to their north was Zoran's property. It sat three kilometers off a main road, at the top of a hill, with a sheer ravine on two sides, very private.

As she waited for her Uncle Stefan to find a set of pliers from inside the house, she reflected on how lucky they'd been to find this place. The seven acre property was owned by an Italian couple, who lived in Catanzaro in Calabria, Italy. They would normally have been here enjoying the relative cool climate, but their son, who lived in France, had taken ill and they'd forgone their summer retreat to look after him. Prostate cancer, the estate agent had told her. Fully furnished, the house had everything they'd needed, but with Pat now taken by Zoran, she was extremely wary that its location would soon be known. She pulled out her iPhone and checked, for the fifth time in the last hour, that the three GPS transmitters, one each on the vehicles and the other, hopefully still in Patrick's pocket, were in the same location. They were.

Uncle Stefan was almost sixty and Nikki was sure that his abstinence from alcohol and a vegan diet had helped to keep the man healthy and fit. She looked around, peering through the woodland upon which the property sat. She had a feeling they were being watched, but could see nothing. She tried to relax and almost jumped as her Uncle returned..

'Here go, Nik,' said Stefan as he walked over with the pliers he'd found in the garage. Nikki had already unlocked the padlock securing the container, but Pat had insisted on using a special wire seal he'd purchased at a hardware store enabling them to tell if the container had been tampered with. The seal was intact; a few snips and it fell to the ground. They pulled open the doors revealing the two BMW X6Ms inside.

Nikki had both remotes and stepped inside the container to the first vehicle and climbed inside. Two minutes later and both SUVs sat on the driveway of the property, black, bright and shiny in the sunlight which filtered through the trees.

Nikki tossed the second remote to Stefan, who remarked, 'Very nice. What's our plan?'

Nikki'd been thinking constantly about a plan for the last two hours. The two BMWs were the best they could buy for speed on the highway and their capacity off road, but Jake had forgotten about blending in and the two luxury SUVs stood out like the proverbial in this part of the world. Her apartment had off street parking, but they couldn't be seen anywhere near Ljubljana. The more she thought about it, Zoran's network of informers, including the Policija, were just too abundant to risk them being out in public at this time. She looked in the back of the vehicle and confirmed that the cache of weapons was securely covered by the screen which rolled over the trunk area to hide its contents from outside observers. Now that Slovenia was part of Europe, the border crossings into Italy were unmanned and she couldn't think of a better plan.

'Let's head over the border to Trieste, eh? I think we can find a good hotel where these two can sit safely in an underground car park while we get some rest.'

'Sounds good, I'll follow you.'

Chapter 30

Betanja, Slovenia

Marko went to his bedroom and opened one of the cupboards in the wall where he kept his toolkit, a selection of weapons he had accumulated over the years. He scanned the several pistols, selecting his newest 9mm *Strizh* (Strike One or Swift Bird) automatic pistol, a treasured gift from Valery on his most recent birthday. He picked up three loaded magazines and, as they would be tackling the Croatians in the dark, a laser targeting device which clipped onto the side of the barrel. He turned this on and saw that it was fully charged. He thought about taking the Beretta MX4 sub-machine gun, also a new toy, but realized he'd only had a few minutes of practice with the gun. *No, the Strizh would suffice.* He picked up a set of handcuffs, a length of stout chain, a padlock and closed the cupboard.

He quickly changed into black pants, a t-shirt and shrugged into a dark blue crew neck pullover. He checked himself in a mirror and took a stance with the pistol, adopting what he thought was the classic stance when shooting the pistol, legs apart, both hands on the weapon, sighting along the barrel towards his target. He pulled off a couple of imaginary shots and slid the pistol into a shoulder holster he would put on later. He contemplated a jacket and thought better of it.

He took one last look around his room, *tidy enoug*h, and went out to the corridor which bisected the third floor, descended the staircase to the ground floor and entered the library. His Father read few books, but that didn't stop him wanting a properly stocked library, wood-paneled on two walls, with views to a terrace and garden beyond. It contained the complete works of Chaucer and Dickens, as well as many reference books and auto biographies. *Wasted on me as well.*

Marko closed the door and nodded to Petr who stood by the window covering Pat, who sat on a deeply padded, leather sofa, one of two in the room. Pat had his hands in his lap and couldn't disguise the fear and what Marko decided might have been pity as Marko took his pistol over to a cabinet and set it down.

'Patrick, you don't mind if I call you by your first name?'

Pat looked up, but said nothing.

'Didn't your Mother teach you to be polite when meeting strangers for the first time? How do the English say it? Knowing one's manners. But then you are an American...'

He picked up the pistol, inserted a magazine and pulled back the slide to cock and load the weapon. He walked over to Petr and gave him the cuffs and chain, before putting the pistol into a shoulder holster he'd put on over his sweater.

Petr walked over to the empty sofa and moved it so that it sat against one of the large, wall to ceiling bookcases. He put the chain on the sofa and motioned with his right hand for Pat to come to him.

Pat didn't move and Marko walked away from the window, holding the pistol in his right hand, pointed right at Pat's head.

'Mr Davis. I want to find out what you've been up to. You've been asking lots of questions about me and my Father.' He wagged the pistol from side to side. 'You will talk to me and tell me what I want to know.

'Fortunately for you, I have to go out with my Father and we won't return until tomorrow. Then we can have some fun, yes?

'You will talk to me, Patrick. I am very good at getting answers. I think you know this already.

'I am going to give you two options. A night on the couch over there, or a night in our cellar?'

Fifteen seconds elapsed. 'Silence means the cellar, Patrick. Petr?'

Petr moved toward him and stopped when Pat said, 'Alright Marko, the couch, okay?'

'Now we're getting somewhere. Stand up, turn around and put your hands behind your back.'

Patrick stood up and did as instructed. Marko nodded at Petr, who moved in and slammed a punch into Pat's kidney area. Pat flew forward, pain flooding his back and he cried out. Petr pulled him roughly to his feet and cuffed him.

Marko dumbed down his anger and aggression and said, calmly, and slowly, 'I can make our time together very painful for you, Patrick. I don't like to hurt people. That is the honest truth. Now, sit the fuck over there or I'll let my man fuck you up the fucking ass, you hear me?'

Pat could feel the bruise in his back coming up and knew he'd be pissing red next time. He looked at Marko, trying to keep his contempt at bay and walked over to the sofa and sat down. Petr looped the chain through the nearby radiator and through Patrick's handcuffs.

'Padlock?' Petr asked.

Marko reached into his pants pocket and withdrew a solid brass padlock which he handed over. Once Pat was secure, he motioned to Petr to join him outside and, once in the corridor, spoke to him in Russian. 'He is yours to look after until we return.' He gave him the key to the padlock. 'I don't want him touched. A little water, but no food, okay?' Petr nodded. 'I am going with the others to kill some Croats. Vlad and Sasha will drive us to the airport and then return here to share the guard duties. You are in charge until we return tomorrow.'

'Yes boss.'

Chapter 31

Butte, Montana

As the Cessna taxied to the runway, Jake retrieved Nikki's contact details and called her. Three rings and she answered. 'Yes,'

'Nikki, it's Jake. How're things?'

'Not so bad, Mr. Jake. I am with my Uncle Stefan in the vehicles, am using Bluetooth, what a car, no?'

'Where are you?'

Jake felt and heard the Cessna's engines power up and then they were gathering speed.

'These cars are too visible here at the moment, so we have just crossed the border into Italy and are heading to Trieste for the night. The cars and the weapons are safe. We'll pick you up tomorrow at the airport.'

'That's good thinking Nikki. Any idea where Pat is?'

'Yes, I am pretty sure they have taken him to Zoran's place, we call it the Fortress.'

'How sure are you?'

'Pat had a GPS transmitter with him when they picked him up. I am also tracking one attached to the cars of Zoran and Marko. Yes, I am sure he is there. Alive? I don't know. He had just shown me how to track them using my iPhone before he was snatched in front of the hotel.'

'What about your family?'

'There is only me and Stefan, Jake. No children, brothers, parents. Otherwise, I would be very worried.'

Jake felt the wheels leave the runway and the sheer power of the plane as its twin Rolls Royce engines pushed them higher and higher into the dawn sky.

'Okay, that's good. We've just taken off.' He looked at his Seamaster: 06:05. 'We'll touch down in Portorož in thirteen hours, okay? What time is it there?'

Nikki looked at the display in front of her. 'It is just after two in the afternoon.'

'Alright, in the morning, drive to Portorož and find somewhere quiet to wait, somewhere no more than five minutes' drive to the airport. Be in position by three am. We'll have to clear Customs, so add perhaps half an hour. I will call you on this number when it's time to pick us up, you got that?'

'Sure, we'll be there.'

'Don't forget what you are carrying, Nikki. Our mission will be compromised if you are picked up. You've enough weapons there to start your own terrorist group.'

'Don't worry, Mr. Jake. These cars drive themselves.'

'That's what worries me. Bye Nikki.'

He checked his cell signal and saw it was down to two bars. *One more call.* He recalled Iain's number and pressed 'call'. It was answered immediately. 'Jake?'

'Hi Iain, not much time. We've just taken off, refueling at Harrisburg and tomorrow in Spain. We'll land at Portorož around three am Slovenian time. They are eight hours behind us.'

'Got that. What are your plans?'

'Don't know Iain, until we see what equipment we have and scope out this Fortress of Zoran's and what we are up against... I just don't know.'

He waited and then looked at the phone. He'd lost the signal. *Ah well not much more to tell him anyway.*

Chapter 32

Ljubljana, Slovenia

Zoran and Boris sat in opposite corners in the back of the Mercedes. Valery drove carefully.

'Thank you for coming Boris,'

Boris reached over and placed a big left hand on his friend's knee, giving it a squeeze. 'What are we for, Zoran, our *vory*, if not to pull together when we are threatened? This Croat cunt, Radic, I will kill him myself, you know that.'

'Yes, I know my brother. I must be getting old for this to have happened. They are testing us, these younger men, seeing what we are going to do. We'll show them.'

'These things happen, Zoran. We'll always have people who want what we have and it is a cost of doing business. Sometimes we need to show them the extent of our strength. Is why I came. Andrei would've come as well if it was needed, you know that.'

At the mention of Andrei Brankovic, the head of their *vory*, Zoran thought back to their last meeting when he'd told him that his son had a black heart.

'Anyway,' said Boris, clapping his hands, 'I need some excitement; it's been a long time since I felt like this. You too, I'm sure. The plan is to fly to Cerklje, the military airport just south of Brežice, get our planning done, set the alarm clock, get some rest and they'll be in God's hands by breakfast, you'll see.'

'Military airport?'

'Cerklje was a former cold war airport when the country was Yugoslavia. On the base, you can still see the remains of a large surface to air missile site. The Army has a small barracks there and the Air Force uses it, but not much. Is no problem for me.' He grinned showing a mouthful of gold-capped teeth. 'I am a celebrity flier in these parts don't you know?'

The two men watched the scenery for a few minutes.

'What is the business back at your house? With your son, Marko?'

'He is young, Boris. You were young once.'

'I don't understand.'

'We've had a private detective, an American, asking about Marko, and about me. Marko wanted to find out what questions he needs answers for, what he knows and picked him up this morning. We will deal with him tomorrow when we return.'

'An American, a detective? You must know why, my brother.'

Zoran sighed. 'Yes, I know why, my friend.' He paused, thinking about how to say it.

'Tell me, Zoran. I have no sons, but I know how they can misbehave.'

'Marko,' he began. 'Marko has become tired of fucking the tourists, his tastes go to something bad. You know what I mean?'

'No, Zoran. Tell me.'

'Marko is an attractive man, with money. I bought him this apartment in Piran. Yet, he has been drugging girls and then fucking them.'

'No?'

'Yes, Boris, I couldn't believe it myself. A woman died. No, two! It cost me a lot with the Policija to make it go away. One of the women was an American, a doctor.'

'So, the American is working for the parents of the doctor?'

'Yes, I believe so. His father that Marko has done this and now he is sniffing into my affairs.'

'Zoran, these things happen. How many people have you killed, eh? Put it into perspective. It sounds like Marko needs to be busier; perhaps we can initiate him into *vory*. It is time, no?'

Zoran looked ahead and saw they approached the airport.

'Yes, I will deal with this American myself,' said Zoran. 'Show his employer that we are not people to be fucked with.' He looked through the windscreen and saw a large, vintage plane come into view, definitely Russian. 'What the fuck is that, Boris?'

'That is our transport. It's the only thing in my garage that can take off on such a puny runway as this one. This is a civilian airport, although I believe it was used by the military in the world wars. Built by the Italians, but as you can see, it is for small aircraft only. That is an Antonov, Zoran. Built in 1972, she is over forty years old now. I found her on a scrap heap. She cost me one-hundred US dollars.' Zoran looks at him. 'No kidding, she'd been sitting in this scrap yard for ten years. I've had her fully rebuilt. Cost me millions. She's not my best, not my preferred, but built to last, one of the safest planes you can fly.' The Mercedes pulled to a stop next to the giant turboprop. 'Come, I will show you.'

They got out of the Mercedes and Boris said, 'Listen, forget about your troubles back home, eh? Let's focus on killing these cunts. Next week, I will return personally and we will plan how we are going to deal with the rest of Radic's gang. We'll teach them not to fuck with Russian men!'

Chapter 33

Portorož, Slovenia

Dimitri Juricic sat behind the simple, worker's desk in his office and looked out to the Adriatic Sea, a view he never tired of. At sixty-nine, he'd been born poor, dirt poor, in the Ukraine and had worked almost his entire life to amass the fortune he'd now accumulated. His working life commenced at age nine, when his older brother by two years, Viktor, took him by the hand and down to the labor boss in one of the coal mines near Chernvonohrad in the West of the Ukraine. Back then in the 1950s, the Ukraine was part of the Soviet Union and, for many young boys born into the Ukrainian working class, you worked or you didn't eat from a very early age. This was particularly the case when fathers died, as had his own Father and many others in the coal mines of post-war Soviet Russia. So Dimitri went into the pits and crawled into the narrow coal seams to retrieve the coal by hand, working twelve hours a day for six days each week until he was fifteen.

Shortly after that birthday (he remembered there was never a cake, but usually some meat or fish), he decided to leave his Mother and older brother and jumped on the train to Kiev. He remembered carrying no bag that day, just the one set of clothes that hadn't been down the mine and the shame he'd felt with no possessions other than a diary, a gift from his brother, and a pitifully, small amount of money he'd been able to save. He swore that his own family would never grow up hungry and poor and he'd worked himself up from being a driver of trucks to the owner of a multi-billion dollar transport and logistics company that operated throughout Europe and the Middle East. Some luck, he told himself, but mostly through hard work and determination. And, he'd never forgotten his Mother and brother and had bought them homes and given them money as soon as he was able.

He was thinking about Miroslav this afternoon, his only son who he dearly loved despite everything. His beloved wife, Marie, died from a sudden stroke some nine years earlier and Miro, he knew, had somehow been damaged by her sudden departure, when aged fifteen at the time. Despite everything he tried, the best schools, private tuition, the threats and the money, he now accepted that his son was who he was and Dimitri just tried to be the best Father he could, forgetting about his own ambitions for the boy, now a man.

Miro had shown no interest in any sort of work, especially a role in his business and, when he'd turned twenty-one, Dimitri had given him a private trust, a lifetime annuity, a generous one. He loved Miro, but was painfully aware that he lacked any business acumen, or a desire to work within the business. So his company would be sold, eventually, and he remained hopeful that Miro would take an interest, a vocation, anything other than the aimless pursuit of leisure.

Dimitri owned several pleasure craft in some of his favorite places in the world and one of those was in the capital of the Bahamas, Nassau. Miro may have led a life of leisure, but he shared his passion for boats and sailing in particular. He kept his own small yacht at the marina in Piran and regularly sailed up the coast to Trieste in Italy, to participate in regattas and races. Dimitri's brightest hope for Miro was that he might pursue a professional career in racing, so he encouraged him. The yacht he owned in Nassau was large, contained four state rooms and he'd not used it since his wife died. It needed a refit, whether he kept it or sold it. So, he'd sent Miro to organize the works that were necessary and hoped the trip might consolidate his interest in boats and sailing. Who knew?

Still, Miro had been happy to go, pleased for the opportunity to escape the Adriatic's August heat and see a part of the world he hadn't been before. Miro left seven days ago and promised to keep in touch. But, just the one phone call four days ago and now he couldn't be contacted; kept getting the message that his phone was out of service.

He would try to reach him at his hotel.

Chapter 34

Las Vegas, Nevada

Miro was not thinking about his father or his yacht as he pushed another ten-thousand chip into the circle marked 'P' for Player and awaited his cards from the Baccarat dealer. He was up around $200,000 in this session, but had dropped almost half a million dollars since he'd arrived in Vegas the previous day accompanied by a new girl, Sabina, who stood at his shoulder.

Sure, he liked his boats and had been diligent enough in Nassau to hire someone to oversight the refit of his father's yacht, but that was the end of it. To Miro, the yacht was ostentatious and hideous, with fixtures that went back to the sixties. Not a thing of beauty in his opinion, so he did the bare minimum and then went out to find the party scene, to get some coke if he could and to get laid.

Once he'd achieved these short term goals, his addiction to gambling and a little voice in his head suggested he head over to Vegas, where he'd never been. A trip to the US Consulate to get a visa and then the one flight was all it'd taken to be sitting here at the Bellagio, a five-hundred dollar a night suite upstairs and this beauty at his elbow.

The beauty at Miro's elbow, Sabina Thomas, was bored. Miro had promised her a fun time, but all he'd done since they arrived at the hotel the previous day was gamble.

Twenty years old, Sabina lived in Nassau in the Bahamas, where she'd met Miro in a night club a week earlier. Like Miro, she came from wealthy parents, her father a banker, and she had her own apartment in Palmdale, where she eked out a hopeful modeling career and dreamed of becoming an actor. Like any attractive girl with money, she had no end of male suitors and her life was a never-ending series of lunches, boat trips and parties. Miro was an attractive man, a great lover she'd soon discovered, and he also had his own money.

So, travelling on her British passport and not needing a visa, they'd boarded the daily American Airlines service, flying first class as befitted their money and status. The suite at the Bellagio had been great as well, but this was too much. Five hours last night and six today. Sabina didn't mind gambling, but she was starting to wish she'd stayed at home. One last try.

'I'll see you in our room,' she whispered in his ear. 'Please don't be too much longer, Miro. I want you.'

Miro turned as she walked away and watched her sassy away in a tight, short, white dress she'd bought just for him. And, he wasn't the only one looking either. He wasn't blind and knew Sabina was bored and that he should stop gambling and pay her some attention. It'd be cheaper too.

He'd hired a red Porsche at the airport and the phone number of a 'reliable' coke dealer sat in his pocket, a name that had cost him a c-note from a fellow coke aficionado (he recognized the signs), a security guy he'd seen earlier in the day coming down the corridor near his room. He pushed his stack of chips across to the dealer and was sitting in his car five minutes later punching the man's number into his cell phone.

The sex with Sabina would be so much better with a little snow...

Chapter 35

September 5, 10:15, Las Vegas, Nevada

Frank Avery got out of his Acura, a work vehicle, and walked over to the Mercedes Sprinter van, parked in a side street of an older neighborhood, five blocks from the strip. The van was nondescript, only its three aerials and black tinted windows suggested the vehicle was law enforcement and belonged to the US Drug Enforcement Agency, the DEA. He stood at the rear and waited for the occupants inside to unlock the doors.

Inside the van, Senior Agent Richard Kowalski listened to his headphones watching his monitor and, as Avery approached the rear of the van, a new window popped up on his screen and he saw Avery approach from the camera mounted on the inside of the van's rear door. He took off his head phones and tapped the shoulder of his partner, Agent Denise Tahoe, who was closest to the door.

'Denise, you wanna' let Frank in.'

'Sure,' replied Tahoe, who popped the locks with the van's remote and watched as her boss opened the door and climbed inside the specially equipped vehicle.

There were four consoles with fixed seats in the rear of the van and Avery sat in one of the vacant seats and regarded his team. 'Denise, Rich'. How're things goin' today?'

His two agents looked his way, glad of the distraction.

Surveillance work was a tough job sometimes, hours of nothing with the occasional thrill as their work culminated in a bust, another dealer arrested.

Two blocks away, the suspect of their surveillance sat in the kitchen of a house that he owned, surrounded by four of his gang and the usual posse of women, who sat watching television in the lounge room. James Vincent Taylor came to the DEA's attention after several anonymous tip-offs from neighbors and other people who would like to see him knocked off his very high perch. At twenty-two, James owned several homes and condos throughout Las Vegas, drove a new BMW M3 and he didn't appear to work for a living.

The DEA knew that he dealt in cocaine; they were just having trouble proving it. They didn't know where he got his supply or where he kept it while it was being cut and dealt to his customers, hundreds of people throughout the city. They had the house under surveillance, a high-resolution camera beamed vision 24-7 to the DEA van from a house across the street and they had a dedicated, legal wiretap in place on his land line. A call came through as Kowalski talked to Avery about their afternoon; he flipped the switch to the speaker phone.

'Hi, is this Jim?'

'No Jim here. Who wants him?'

A pause. 'Name's Miro, friend of Carlos.'

'Don' know a Carlos, man.'

'You know, works at the Bellagio. S'where I'm staying, you know.'

'You buyin' bro?'

'Er, yeah…'

'Drivin'?'

'Yes, a rental.'

'You got Sat Nav.?'

'Yes.'

'What type of car?'

'It's a Porsche. A 911, red,'

'Go to the Super 8 Motel, off East Rochelle, you got that?'

'Super 8, East Rochelle. Yes.'

'Drive into the car park, stay in your car and wait, okay?'

'Thanks, see you there,' but the man had already hung up.

'A typical call,' said Agent Tahoe. 'Although this guy's new, not a regular, almost certainly flown in to play the tables, snort some coke…'

'We won't hear the call go to the courier,' said Kowalski.

'No?' said Avery. 'How do you think it goes down?'

'It will be a text to the courier, from a non-traceable twenty buck phone using some sort of code,' said Kowalski. 'One courier will pick up the mark's money and a different person will come and deliver the product.'

'At least this time we know the rendezvous,' said Tahoe. 'Ninety-nine times out of a hundred, all we get is 'usual place' and the person's first name. They match the name to a list and the meeting place is known, but not to us.'

'Clever system,' remarked Avery. 'Any point in staking out this motel?'

'No way, boss,' said Tahoe. 'These guys can smell a cop a mile away. Hell, they probably know we're watching them. No, we stick at it and our Jimmy will slip up. He's amassing assets way beyond his earnings and we will get to confiscate those assets soon, I guarantee it.'

'Okay, at least call the red Porsche into the cops. It'll give them probable cause if they stop a male in a rental 911.'

Kowalski turned to his terminal and entered the caller's details into the system used by the Las Vegas Metropolitan Police Department.

He pressed 'enter' and a rough description of Miro's red 911 Porsche came up on dozens of screens in the police vehicles doing the rounds of America's largest gambling city.

♦

Miro drove into the motel's car park as directed. There were only two other cars in the lot and he pulled up in the middle. The trip had only taken five minutes and he looked up at the hot sun and listened to the engine ticking as it cooled. Funny how he'd thought it was much later. He picked up his cell phone and saw it was not even eleven o'clock. He picked up his room key and punched in the hotel's telephone number into his cell.

'This is the Bellagio Hotel. My name is Kimberley, how can I help?'

'Yeah, hi, this is Mr. Juricic. Could you put me through to room 1007.'

'Putting you through now sir.'

Miro heard the phone ringing in their suite. After about seven rings, he was about to hang up when Sabina answered. 'Hello.'

She sounded sleepy. 'Hi Sabi'.'

'Hi baby.'

'I won't be long, just gone out for a minute.'

'Where are you?'

'Just getting something nice for us both.'

'You going to gamble again, Miro?'

'Nah. I'm getting bored with it too. Time for us to have a good time in this town. You got some champagne in the fridge?'

Sabina got off the bed and checked. 'Yes, we have champagne.'

'Well I'll bring something to go with it. Why don't you get in that big bath and I'll be there before you know it.'

He ended the call and waited. Five minutes went by and he noticed a white coupe pull up and then enter the car park, parking next to Miro's Porsche so as to face the opposite direction. He saw a white male with short cropped hair, gold jewelry, mirror shades.

'You Miro?'

'Yes.'

'This your wheels?'

'Yes, er, no, a rental.'

'What do you want bro'?'

Miro thought. 'Er, I want to buy some coke.' He didn't want to appear cheap. 'Can you do twenty grams?'

'Twenty grams of snow, huh? How much you got there in cash bro?'

Miro had never bought cocaine. He'd acquired the taste through the wealthy party scene he was part of back in Slovenia and Italy. Later, he'd met Marko and only had to ask and he gave him a huge big bag of the shit. He'd cashed in his chips at the Bellagio and had two-hundred-and-forty-thousand dollars in hundred dollar bills in the jacket on the passenger seat. He did the math and offered $150 per gram. 'Three grand, okay?'

The man opposite was smart and quick. He'd been doing this for a while and recognized a chump when he saw one. The going rate, particularly in the current depressed economy, was $80 a gram. He countered, 'Fuck you man, you gonna' need four-thousand dollars for twenty grams.'

'Sorry,' said Miro. 'Sure, no problem'. He knew he was being ripped off, but didn't care too much and reached for his jacket, pulling out one of the ten-thousand dollar bundles he'd taken from the cashier. He counted off forty bills and passed them across to the man in the coupe.

The man flashed him white teeth and wished he'd asked for five.

'Now stay here and someone'll be along shortly.' The man drove off slowly.

Miro looked around the bleak motel lot, a far cry from the ostentatiousness of the strip a few blocks over. He'd planned for Sabi and him to stay for a week, but now realized that he should have taken her elsewhere. He'd chosen Vegas precisely because he could gamble. His addiction had started with some friends in Monte Carlo three summers ago, where he won a few thousand dollars on roulette. Now, he regularly travelled to casinos throughout Europe, without the knowledge of his father, to play baccarat, his favorite game. His income was fixed and this put a ceiling on his losses, but he knew his losses had now amounted to several million Euros. Maybe they could ditch this place and head to Los Angeles, someplace with no casino?

He didn't want to go back to Slovenia either. Marko had poisoned the place for him. He used to enjoy bedding the young tourists and backpackers, the thrill of the chase and the feeling as they said yes. But the three occasions Marko had drugged and raped those girls had given him nightmares. Especially, when Marko had overcooked the drugs he'd injected into the girl that last time. The other two girls had recovered, a bit shaken sure, but to have killed someone?

To make matters worse, he'd found that he couldn't do it, couldn't get it up with a drugged and unconscious girl. It had appalled him and several counseling sessions were required, without getting to the facts of course, before his equipment started to work properly. But Miro knew about Marko and, more and more, he'd wanted nothing to do with the evil man. He'd been a fun companion at first, very charming, and Miro hardly needed to do anything to find himself in the arms of a young German or Irish girl. But, the death of that woman had been the end and, ever since, he'd rebuffed Marko each time that he sought his company. Still, Miro knew who his father was and, given what he knew about Marko, he was thinking about skipping Slovenia altogether, buying a place in Italy, perhaps back in Nassau. Then again, those damned casinos.

A blue Suzuki, a small hatch, entered the car lot and pulled up alongside. The window came down and a small brown paper bag was tossed over the gap by a Negro woman. She didn't say anything and didn't wait for Miro's thanks. He looked in the bag and saw four small bags of the white powder. He pulled one out and looked around. The lot was deserted and he hadn't seen another human being other than the two couriers. He unsealed one of the bags and put the small finger of his right hand inside, gathering a small amount of the powder under the finger nail. He brought this to his nose and sniffed it down, feeling the familiar buzz, like he'd just jacked into a better power source. His eyes seemed to focus more clearly and it was like he had super hearing and super vision.

He pressed start on the dash and the engine came to life. *Time to go see Sabi and have some fun.*

Chapter 36

49,000 feet over Atlantic Ocean

As Miro exited the car park of Motel 8, Jake got out of his seat and walked forward and pulled open the door to the cockpit. James and Paul stopped their conversation and looked back.

Jake looked forward at the magnificence of the sight before him. The sun was just rising and he could clearly see the curvature of the earth. 'You guys are lucky to get to do this job, you know.'

James and Paul regarded each other. 'Yes, Jake, we know,' said Paul.

'Sorry, pal, there's no jump seat in these things,' said James. 'Paul, I'll take the first shift. Why don't you get some breakfast and some zeds in the back with the boys?'

Jake moved back and allowed Paul to climb out of the co-pilot's seat. 'Thanks Paul. I'll be coming back shortly to brief the men.'

He climbed into the vacant seat and James handed him a pair of Ray-Ban Aviators. 'Thanks.'

'Can't do this job without a good pair. Sun'll be up higher quite soon. When we travel east like this, the day gets condensed. Twelve hours of sunlight might only mean five when we're travelling east at close to the speed of sound. You'll see, it'll be dark in about five hours or so.'

'We go that fast huh?'

'Just shy of the magic number. I could get us there in a dive, but the aircraft isn't really designed for that. Right now, I don't have to do a thing,' James pointed to the dash, 'all on auto-pilot. But, Regulations require two pilots for this type of aircraft even though they can, theoretically, take off and land themselves. Anyways, how'd you end up here today, Jake?'

Jake took some time to explain to James, his own personal background, that of his men, and didn't hold back about their ultimate objective, Marko.

'Yes, I knew this was a bit of black op. Iain's generous retainer for doing nothing told us that. Now I know some more of the background, I admire him, and you, Jake. You have something rare in this day and age. Integrity.'

'Thanks for the complement. To be honest, I'd be happy to kill this little shit of a man, given what he's done, but I respect Iain and his restrained anger. If we were to simply kill him, Iain would not feel justice was done. But for now, we're just going over there to retrieve Pat Davis. If they've tortured and killed him, however… Until I talk more with Nikki and scope out Zoran Kovak's home, a place we've dubbed the Fortress, I just don't know what we're up against. Pat was supposed to brief us on arrival. Now we need to go and save his ass.'

'Appreciate the briefing. When we get to Portorož, we'll refuel and go and get some sleep, leave the soldiering to you guys. But, we're only ten minutes' drive from the airport. So if you want us ready to roll, call my cell.'

Jake took out his cell phone and added James' number as a contact. He handed back the Ray-Bans and extricated himself from the seat. 'Thanks James.'

Jake headed back into the cabin and poured himself a coffee from the pot warming in the galley. The boys sprawled at the back and Paul reclined in one of the forward club chairs, his eyes closed.

He went past and took up the remaining seat at the rear of the cabin.

'This is what I call class,' said Andy, his arms behind his head, mirror shades on his head. 'Gonna get one too, once my movie career takes off.'

'You believe this mother?' said Eddie, smiling broadly. 'Be lucky to own a ultra-light, you know?' laughing now.

Jake and Tony joined in the laughter and Andy saw the funny side and laughed too, knowing he was with friends. 'Seriously, boys,' broke in Jake pointing his hand at Andy, 'I saw this man fall backwards, that's with his face heading into the sun, from six stories. Thirty meters about right, Andy?'

Andy nodded, happy with the jesting.

Jake's face turned serious again. 'You all know why we're here. We don't have enough to snatch our boy, Marko. Therefore, we're travelling to Slovenia as Patrick Davis has been taken at gun point and is being held at the large home of Marko's father, Zoran Kovak. That's not his real name and he has kept his past very quiet. I know nothing more about the man and his criminal activities than I've already told you.'

The others kept quiet. They knew pretty much what Jake knew as they'd had plenty of time to absorb the background that Jake had amassed through his conversations with Iain and Pat. 'We have another fuel stop to make in Spain and then a short flight to Portorož in Slovenia. We should land there around nineteen-hundred Montana time, oh-three-hundred in Slovenia. So, I suggest you wind your watches back by eight hours.

'What about the cars and weapons?'

'I called Nikki just as we were taking off. She's a resourceful woman. They came for her too and, by her description of what happened, had no plans to take her alive. She escaped, called her Uncle and they went and picked up the vehicles and weapons. Took them over the border to Italy, where they'll be much less visible. They'll drive to

Portorož in the morning and wait somewhere until we've cleared customs and then pick us up.'

'Then what?' asked Eddie.

'I guess we find somewhere to hole up and then head up there to scope the place out. Nikki has promised me a plan of the area. Not much more we can do until then.'

'What weapons will we have?' asked Tony.

'Sorry boys, forgot to ask. I think Nikki was able to get most things on the list. They just won't have made in the USA stamped on them.'

Chapter 37

Las Vegas, Nevada

Officers Paula Johnson and Ozzie (Oswald) Garcia sat in their Metropolitan Police sedan, outside *Ballys*, an older casino, on East Flamingo Road. They'd just assisted the casino to eject a patron who'd become angry when he'd lost all his money. It was a common call for them. This time the guy was abusive, but not violent and he hadn't been drinking, which was rare. He'd gone quietly as soon as they'd turned up. Ozzie was glad, their shift ended in two hours and he could do without the paperwork.

Ozzie checked the screen for updates. 'Anything happening?' asked Paula.

'Not much, Oz, couple of accidents on the south side. What say we do a lap of the strip and see what comes up?'

'Okay, sounds good. Maybe we can stop for a coffee?'

Paula Johnson started the engine and checked her mirrors. A vehicle was approaching, so she waited and they watched as a red, late model Porsche came up the street behind them. It wasn't speeding. In fact, it drew their attention as the man was driving slowly, perhaps only doing ten miles per hour or so. As it went by, the man looked over and smiled at them. Paula pulled out in the street. 'You see that?'

'Sure did. There's a red Porsche 911 on the watch list too.'

'Yeah, why's that?' They approached the strip, about twenty yards behind the Porsche.

'DEA logged it an hour or so ago. What say we pull him?'

'Okay, just wait till we're round the corner.'

The lights turned green and the Porsche turned left onto the strip. Paula pressed her switches, giving the sirens a short blast and the strobes went off. They saw the man see them in the mirror and he signaled right and pulled over to the side of the road. Keeping the lights flashing, Paula pulled in behind the car. She got out, while Ozzie checked the DEA entry on the system in the cruiser. Couldn't be certain this was their man. Man had identified himself as Miro, simply Miro. Car certainly matched. He got out of the car just as Paula was checking the man's license details. He walked forward and said, 'What you got, Paula?'

'Slovenian driver's license, current. Miroslav Juricic,' she looked up. 'Where's Slovenia?'

Ozzie walked up the driver's door and pushed his shades onto his head, looking at the young man before him. Miroslav, Miro... They had probable cause. He put his hand on the handgun at his hip and said in his nicest possible cop voice. 'Excuse me, Sir. Could you please get out of the vehicle?'

Chapter 38

Seattle

George Simmons sat in his cubicle eating a sandwich. He had just listened to a phone message from a Detective Richards in Las Vegas, telling him that a Miroslav Juricic was in their custody. He checked back through hundreds of unopened emails and found what he was looking for, a system-generated email which would have alerted him that Juricic had entered the country; if he'd looked at it.

George sat back in his chair and closed his eyes. He had fourteen cases currently on the go, including two kidnapping cases and a bank robbery. He received over a hundred new emails a day and the pressure had been getting to him. After they'd met with Iain Fisher, he'd met the physician who'd performed the second autopsy on Danielle Fisher and also travelled to Baltimore to interview Cathy Dickson and go over her affidavit. She was a convincing witness, but both he and George knew that, without further evidence, the investigation would go nowhere. George had put some notes into the various federal systems and two of them had now borne results.

As Juricic had entered the country, his name was automatically checked against numerous databases, including several maintained by the FBI. George had flagged the man in a way that would allow him entry, but so that he would be alerted by email, a system-generated message, that he was now on US Territory.

The second result was how the various police forces around the country worked. It was normal for the Police to check a suspect's details against the FBI's National Crime database, which records persons of interest. Marko Kovak and his father Zoran were listed in the system, but Juricic's name was also in there, as George had put him in. The system worked. The Vegas Police had pulled him up for some reason, he'd ended up in a cell and they'd plugged his name into the system which gave them George's contact details and a request to please contact.

He picked up the phone and dialed Richards in Vegas.

'Richards,' came a man's reply.

'Detective Richards, my name is George Simmons. I work in the FBI's Seattle office. I'm returning your call about Mr. Juricic.'

'Oh right, thanks George for getting back to us.'

'You got this boy in custody, that right?'

'We do, George, yes. Only been in the country a couple of days, flew in from Nassau in the Bahamas, stayin' at the Bellagio.'

'What happened?'

'Seems our boy had the misfortune to call a coke dealer whose line is being monitored by the DEA. We think he just wanted some coke to use, take back to his hotel, where he's staying with a young woman, a British National, Sebina Thomas, who accompanied him from Nassau. Only known him a short time, we think.

'Anyway, he calls this number, where he got it we don't know, but DEA are listening in on the conversation and log the man's car and first name. Then, as he's tooling up the strip, just had a taste you know, a couple of our officers spot him goin' a bit slower than he should. They check through the log in their cruiser, and this gives 'em probable cause to stop and search.'

'And?'

'Twenty grams of coke and almost a quarter of a mil. in cash.'

'Shit, what's he planning?'

'Well, we figure his story stacks up. Money's from where he cashed his chips at the casino. Guy has a seven figure bank balance. And, twenty grams sounded better to him than five…

'Don't matter though. We have enough to put him in jail, given the amount he was carrying. Standard procedure here is put all names into our system, which then goes and makes multiple enquiries here and overseas. Your name comes up, hence my call.'

'Well, it seems the system works Detective.'

'Call me Bob.'

'You charged him, Bob?'

'Yep, possession of a trafficable quantity of a Class A prohibited drug with intent to deal.'

'He lawyered up yet?'

'Nope, but he called his girl. Currently, sitting in a holding cell. What does the FBI want with him?'

'We believe he may have information which would help with a murder enquiry.'

'I see.'

'Cheers Bob, Going to see if I can fly down there today. You got a cell?'

George finished writing down Bob Richards' number and called his boss, Hank Grady, who answered first ring. 'George?'

'Boss, I need to go to Vegas.'

'Like on holiday?'

George told him about the conversation with Bob Richards.

'Go for it. Let me know exactly what goes on. Juricic will want to know what sort of deal we can give him. If, as we suspect, he did not have intercourse with the girl and had no part in her murder, I think we might be able to do something for him in exchange for his testimony against Kovak.'

'I dunno boss, seems such a long shot.'

Hank didn't mention that, from another talk he'd had with Iain Fisher, there was a reasonable chance that Marko Kovak would be visiting the United States. 'I know, I know. Listen, I'll get onto the Federal Prosecutor's Office. I know a guy there. I'll have a confidential, hypothetical chat with him. See what we might be able to put on the table.'

''Kay, boss. I'll call you later.'

Chapter 39

Las Vegas, Nevada

Miro sat in a holding cell in Area Command, on South Las Vegas Boulevard. He reckoned he'd been there for around six hours or so. It was hard to tell when there was no natural light. At least they'd put him into a cell alone. It had a comfy steel bench slash bed, a toilet pan and a basin. The walls were bare concrete, painted gray some time ago, judging by the graffiti which covered them. Miro couldn't think how his predecessors had managed to have pens and sharp things to write with, but the wall was covered in the musings of the people who'd been there before him.

They'd allowed him a phone call earlier, but when he dialed his Father's home number, correctly working out that it was late in the evening in Slovenia, the phone system told him that the call could not be placed. So he called Sabi. She went into a fit of hysterics and rage, but agreed to call his Father and took down the name of the arresting officers. Then I'm going back home, she'd added. This place sucks and so do you.

Miro agreed with her on that. The buzz from the coke had worn off long ago. Those two cops thought they'd caught Pablo Escobar when they saw how much cash he'd been carrying. All polite, Sir this and that, but once they'd spied the powder and the money, it was 'face down on the ground, fella' or something like that. A knee in the back, cuffs on tight and, before he'd caught his breath, a further three cruisers were on the scene. They hadn't laughed when he'd said, 'Shit guys, it's just a bit of coke.' That's when he realized just how much trouble he'd created for himself.

The slot in his door cracked open. A woman's face, a cop, peered through the gap. 'Prisoner, you have a visitor. Your lawyer, I believe. Please put your hands in the slot below.'

Miro got off the bench and shuffled over wearing sneakers without laces. He put his hands through the slot and was cuffed. He pulled them back and the door was unlocked.

'Follow me,' she said, standing with another cop, a male who looked at him like he was dirt. They led him along to an interview room and sat him down opposite a youngish man, wearing spectacles, shaven head. *Probably bald*, thought Miro, somewhat unkindly.

The man looked toward the cops. 'Stephen Pallas. Are the handcuffs necessary? I understand Mr. Juricic has not been charged with a violent crime of any sort.'

'Take them off, Mary,' said the male cop, which she did and the two of them were left alone.

'What time is it?' asked Miro.

Pallas looked at his watch. 'It's almost six pm, Mr. Juricic. Is that a correct pronunciation?'

'Yes, that's correct.'

'Your father called me, that's why I'm here.' Miro nodded and Pallas looked at the papers in front of him. 'Says here you were arrested just before eleven this morning?'

'That's about right.'

'What were you doing to give the police cause to pull you over?'

'Nothing. I was driving properly, using my indicators. I was almost back at the hotel…'

'The arresting officer's report states that the Drug Enforcement Agency had logged a watch and detain for a red Porsche and your name. How would they have your name?'

Miro thought, but couldn't link his phone call. 'No, I don't know how they knew my name. I have never been arrested, never had trouble with police or authorities.'

'Okay, Miro. Is that what you like to be called?'

'Yes, Miroslav is too long, too hard to say, particularly for Westerners.'

'Well, it seems clear from what I've read, that you were not pulled up for a traffic violation. You have a Slovenian license, which allows you to hire and drive a rental car here in the States.' He paused, thinking. 'Here in Nevada, Miro, the Police usually require what we call a probable cause that your vehicle contains evidence of a crime or contraband - drugs. Where did you get the white powder?'

Miro proceeded to tell him about how he got the number and had bought the drugs at the motel, before heading back to his hotel.

'Why'd you buy twenty grams?'

'I don't know really. I just didn't want to sound, you know, cheap.'

'The going rate too, Miro, it's about eighty a gram, max a hundred and the more you buy the cheaper it gets. So, you were robbed too. Anyway, sounds like they had probable cause from the phone call you made, but I think we can argue possession only. You can substantiate the money. There'll be video at the cages at the *Bellagio* we can obtain.'

'That's good isn't it?' said Miro hopefully.

'Yes, it is. But, I don't think it will be enough to keep you from jail time.'

'You're joking. Please tell me, Mr. Pallas, that you are inexperienced and that I will be able to get out of this and go back to my life. That I can say I'm sorry, pay a fine. Spend some time in rehab if that's necessary. Money's no object here.'

'I wish that were the case, Mr. Juricic. Sadly, in this age of the 'war on drugs', this country of mine comes down very harshly on users and dealers of drugs, particularly cocaine and heroin. Under four grams and I could get you bail tonight, get you quickly arraigned before a judge, plead guilty pay a fine. No lawyer in Vegas can do that when you've been caught with twenty grams in your possession. I'm really, really sorry. The fact that you are not a US citizen will only make them more determined to obtain a conviction and the attendant publicity.'

They heard a knock on the door and a cop they hadn't seen before opened it. He addressed Pallas. 'Excuse me Sir, could I see you for a second?'

Outside, the new cop said, 'There is an officer from the FBI here, Sir. Requesting an interview with your client.'

◆

After his lawyer left, Miro sat in the room for about an hour. It could have been more, or less. He was tired and hungry and realized he hadn't even had a drink of water in all the time he'd been there. There was a one-way mirror to his right and the rest of the room was bare, except for the bolt down furniture. His stool became uncomfortable, so he sat on the floor, his back to the wall, closed his eyes and tried to contain the panic that was building in his chest.

The door opened and he saw his lawyer enter followed by another man, young, clean cut, short hair and dressed in a good suit, well built. *This is my FBI man.*

They entered and Pallas closed the door behind them.

'Hi Mr. Juricic. I am Special Agent George Simmons of the Federal Bureau of Investigation.' He came closer and held out his badge and security card. Miro stayed on the floor.

'Listen, I've spoken with the Sherriff here. I understand you've taken no sustenance since your arrest?'

'He means you've had nothing to eat or drink, Miro,' said Pallas.

'I know what he means. I'm not uneducated, Mr. Pallas.' Miro got to his feet. 'And the Sherriff is correct.'

George continued. 'Well, Mr. Juricic. I can take you to the canteen; get you a coffee, a soft drink, a sandwich. You are still under custody, without being charged at present,' he looked at Pallas, who nodded, 'and will need to promise to behave… Or we could stay here and talk.'

'What will we talk about?'

'How we can help each other. How you can avoid going to jail.'

A female cop led the way from the interview room to the canteen, which was reasonably empty, a few lone figures grabbing a coffee and some food, checking messages on their cell phones, or watching the muted television on the wall. George led them over to a side table and asked the cop to leave them alone. 'You want coffee, a sandwich?'

'A water and a coffee, and a sandwich with ham, or something like that.'

George handed Pallas some money and said, 'Would you? I promise not to start until you return.'

'You want a coffee too?' said Pallas.

'Sure, just black would be great.'

George studied the man opposite who stared off into the distance avoiding eye contact. He looked beaten and he'd only been in custody a few hours. George was tired as well, a dash to the airport, two hours in Delta coach, sitting next to a woman who would have touched two-twenty on the scales, easy; *Should'a made her buy two fucking seats!* Then the hassle of finding a cab, a further twenty minutes with his boss on the phone, a further thirty waiting for the Sherriff to see him, and then using all his personal charm and skill to persuade him that he should relax his rules; so that Miro, his lawyer and himself could have a confidential chat.

Sheriff Horatio, G, Johnston had needed a good reason. George said to him: 'Sheriff, we have good evidence our boy down there might, just might, have evidence to convict a nasty little Russian man of murdering one of this country's citizens. A doctor who was doing charity work for *Medicine Sans Frontiers.* You and I know that Mr. Juricic is not a drug dealer. But the law is the law and the fact that he is likely to go to a Nevada jail gives me a lot of leverage to see if he would be willing to give me that evidence. I'm asking you nicely to let me take him to the canteen, with his lawyer present, so that I can have a chat with him. I hope that is good enough reason for you.'

It was, but was also going to be long night.

Pallas returned with a tray and they gave Miro some time as he re-hydrated and ate his sandwich.

Miro felt himself recover and took his time. He wiped his mouth and hands carefully and said: 'Okay, Mr. FBI man. How can you and I help each other?'

'Has Mr. Pallas here gone over your case?'

'He has.'

To Pallas: 'He was Miranda'd properly?'

'He was.'

'And what's your likely take on what'll happen to him now?'

Miro looked at his lawyer, who looked at George. 'He'll be taken to Clark County Detention Centre later tonight, perhaps tomorrow morning. At his arraignment, which could take a week before it happens, he can apply for bail, but the prosecution will object and the Judge will deny it. Prosecutors will point to his potential flight risk, his wealth, and the large quantity of drugs in his possession. He will reside in Detention for anywhere from two months to six before being tried. We can't argue the drugs were not his. We can't argue his 4th

Amendment Rights were violated, which in any event doesn't apply to motor vehicles if the police believe reasonably that the vehicle contains evidence or contraband, which they did. The DEA have him on tape talking to a known criminal.'

George looked at Miro. 'Prosecutors, shit, Judges for that matter, love cases like yours Miro. You're not a US citizen, you are wealthy and you will be shown to have blatantly disregarded the State of Nevada's tough laws on drugs. I'm guessing you will go to the Nevada State Prison and it will be for a minimum of two years.'

George let that sink in and drank his coffee. 'Miro, I am here to offer you a deal.

'I'm not here to trick you, trap you or coerce you. I'm not recording this and even if I were, I couldn't use what you say in a court of law, nor could I call Mr. Pallas here to corroborate what you said. That is why we are out of the interview room, so that what I say and what you say remains confidential. Okay?'

Miro still had no link to anything. But, he clearly understood that he was going to jail. Perhaps, he could make a 'financial contribution', just like he would if caught in Slovenia…

'Okay. Do you know a man called Marko Kovak?'

A shiver passed down Miro's spine and everything fell into place, like those moments in movies where you know exactly who the killer is, the clues all lining up. He could feel the blood drain from his face. 'Yes, I know Marko,' he finally managed.

'Do you know what Marko does for a living?'

'Not really, he's a bit like me, I guess. He works for his father sometimes.'

'Do you know what his father, Zoran Kovak, does for a living?'

'He's in transport, trucks, imports, that sort of thing.'

'Miro?

'This won't work if you don't tell me the truth. I'm going to trust you with things I know. I need you to trust me that I am not here to get you. Now, what does Kovak senior do?'

Miro looked George in the eye. 'He imports drugs, a big man in the Russian mafia, I suspect.'

'Correct. His group of Russians is one of the largest sources of marijuana, heroin and cocaine in Europe. Stuff comes in from Colombia, Afghanistan and Pakistan, mainly, often taken through Africa and then freighted by sea to Koper, where Mr. Kovak trucks it overland to his associates in Russia, Europe and Asia.

'His son, Marko. You spend time with him? Going to nightclubs, that sort of thing?'

'Yes, when he is in town. Not lately though. I've been avoiding him.'

'Why's that?'

'I don't enjoy his company as much as I used to. He and I don't see eye to eye.'

'I see. Do you remember a night in May this year? Friday the eighteenth I think it was. Where were you that night?'

Miro knew the questions were going to get increasingly difficult to answer. He knew that lying would only get more difficult. 'We were at the Paprika Club. It's on the beach at Portorož.'

'Who's 'we'?' said George, looking for a lie.

'Marko and I.'

'Go on.'

'Marko told me one afternoon he was bored with fucking the *'popotniks'* the backpackers. He said they smelled, gave bad head and had no sophistication.

'I didn't agree. Sure, they were easy to pick up, but I enjoyed the chase and when I took them home, sometimes two at once, I looked after them, loved them for a short time. I'm not bragging; it is how it is for me and I know my money attracts them too.'

George knew when to keep quiet.

'One time we were out and he just picked on a girl, someone who was by herself and dropped a tablet in her drink.' Miro looked away. 'Of course, the girl became confused, appeared very drunk, so we helped her out of the bar and into Marko's car.'

'What happened next?'

'Marko fucked her, back at his apartment. It has an internal lift from the basement car park.'

'And, you?'

'Couldn't get it up. Marko teased me about it. Said we had to try one more… He did it again, and it had the same reaction from me.'

'What happened to the girls, those first two times?'

'After he'd finished, he'd put their clothes back on and just drop them somewhere quiet in the city. In an alley, or down near the waterfront.'

'And you helped him?'

'Yes, but the girls were okay; it was only a strong sedative that he gave them.'

'Tell us about the third time on May 18th, Miro, at the Paprika Club.'

'There were a couple of Americans. They weren't backpackers and we learned they were doctors. We talked to them, chatted them up. Catherine, she liked me… But, Marko had to ruin it.'

'How so?'

'The other woman, a pretty girl too, Danielle. Marko over-did things. They weren't ready to take us to bed. We would need all our charm and skill to get their panties off.' He smiled and tapped his head. 'I know the signs. Marko went too hard, too early. He could see it too, but I didn't see him drug them. Too quick even for me.

'One minute we were having a good time, the next we are helping this poor girl down the street and into his car. We argued in the car. I told him it had to stop. I was weak. I'd seen him deal with people and there were stories about him, that he'd killed people.'

'What happened back at the apartment?'

'I took some cocaine, took my clothes off, but the thought of making love to an unconscious woman, an unwilling partner. It was not for me.'

'Why did he give her heroin?'

'She woke up while he was doing her. She couldn't move; he'd given her a powerful drug. He told me later that she'd sneered at him. I said that he'd killed her. He said he hadn't meant to, he'd just wanted to give her a bad headache, confuse the situation in her mind.'

'Did you believe him?'

'No. He's a nasty person. Evil in many ways.'

'Thanks for telling me that Miro. Danielle's father has been gathering evidence, sufficient evidence to prosecute Marko Kovak, here in the United States. Presently, the evidence he has, the evidence that the FBI now has, is only circumstantial. You know, insufficient. I'm sure we could match Marko's DNA to the semen found inside Danielle's vagina during her autopsy. And, I'm starting to be certain that we won't find a match to your DNA. But, that still leaves you as an accomplice to the girl's murder.'

Miro kept quiet. He'd a good idea where this was going and didn't like it one little bit.

'Right. If I walk out of here now, you will go to the Detention Centre on remand for two to six months. And, I think you are starting to realize that even you, with all your wealth and influence, can do nothing to prevent you going to jail for at least two years. Unless…'

'Do you have any idea who Marko's father really is, Agent Simmons?

George had tapped all the sources of information on Zoran Kovak, but the file was very thin. Choosing to operate in a fringe country like Slovenia meant the major law enforcement agencies had added very little to the file beyond a few small details. They didn't even know where he'd been born, or when. 'We don't know a lot, Miro, but we do know that Zoran Kovak joined a criminal brotherhood, a *vory*, when he was doing gulag jail time in Russia for the attempted murder of a policeman. As a senior person in this brotherhood, Zoran runs a major part of their drug operation.'

'What do you think Marko's father will do when he learns of your plans, and my involvement?'

'He will try to find you and kill you, Miro. He will also try to find and kill your Father.'

'It won't just be him, George. It'll be his whole fucking *vory*. Marko is essentially one of theirs. Which means if I help you, I won't have any sort of future. And you want my evidence in exchange for what?'

'We have spoken with the State prosecutor, Miro, Benjamin Nash. Is that his name, Stephen?' Pallas nodded. 'The State of Nevada would drop its charge of drug possession, in return for your testimony, your evidence.'

'And then what?'

'We'd give you and your Father a new identity, and citizenship, here or in Europe. You have money.'

'My life would be ruined.'

'It's already ruined, Miro. And don't forget you were an accomplice to Ms. Fisher's murder.'

'You said you wouldn't use this against me.'

'Miro, we already know what happened. You've told me nothing tonight that I didn't already know. Are you prepared to gamble now that we can't gather sufficient evidence to implicate you in Danielle

Fisher's death?'

The young man opposite looked absolutely dejected, like he'd been condemned. 'I know that this is a shit-sandwich, Miro. You made it when you broke our laws and went against your own instincts, your own moral compass and helped Marko to murder an innocent woman.'

'I didn't help him.'

'That is not how a jury would see it, Miro.'

The young man in front of him was thinking, his head no doubt weighing up all the bad options before him. George stood up. 'I'm going to the bathroom. When I come back. I want your answer. If you agree, we can have your Father somewhere safe in the next twenty-four hours. You too, for that matter.'

George walked through the canteen, looking for a rest room and glanced at the clock. It was almost nine pm. He'd done his best...

Chapter 40

Over Italy

They'd made good time from the small airport at Vigo on the west coast of Spain. Everyone slept on the leg from the US and they were keen to get on the ground and put their training into action. Jake looked up as James came back into the cabin. He grabbed a bottle of water out of the fridge and dropped into the seat opposite Jake, who was in a forward seat facing the rear.

'Hey, James.'

'In about ten minutes we'll begin our descent into Portorož. They normally don't take flights after hours. You can thank Pat for setting this up so that I was able to call them yesterday and ensure that tower control and customs would be present, effectively coming in six hours before they usually do.'

'How'd you manage that?'

'We have them convinced that Bear Grylls is flying into Slovenia in three days' time. That and a promise of a cash donation when we land. To charity of course.' James patted the bulge in his shirt pocket, 'I have it covered, part of doing business in many parts of the world.'

'I'm not sure what this guy will know or ask, but you and the team are here to do some location shoots, so that when the star arrives, you already have some footage and a good plan of where he'll be going.

Tell the customs guy, we are dropping the Bear off on top of Mount Triglav. He'll be impressed. He will stamp our passports, will want to check through our bags, but not too much I hope. Then you can call Nikki and the guy should let your cars come straight onto the apron and pick you up.'

'Okay, James, sounds good. I have no idea when, or indeed if, we will be back. Whatever happens, I'll call you every twelve hours at six o'clock, with the first call this evening. If I don't call, head back to the US immediately.'

James nodded and held out his hand. 'Good luck, buddy.'

Jake shook it. 'Luck's for those that aren't prepared.'

Twenty minutes later and all four men were pulling out their gear from the Cessna's luggage compartment, assisted by Paul. James remained inside the plane, completing the post flight checks and his log book. Jake had already called Nikki once, to check she was in position and would call again when they were ready to go.

An official car approached from the perimeter and pulled up to the plane's rear. A young man got out, dressed in uniform with insignia on the side, a peaked cap and he had a pistol in a holster on his hip. *Dobro Jutro*', said Jake (good morning was one of about six phrases he'd practiced.)

'Good morning, Sir. How are you?'

'We're fine,' said Jake. 'I'm Jake Walker, personal assistant to Mr. Grylls.'

The Customs man came nearer and held out his hand. 'Welcome to my country, Mr. Walker.' Jake shook the man's hand. 'My name is Tomaz. Could you get your passports together and place your luggage over there.' He pointed to a lit area of the apron.

'Sure, Tomaz, no problems.'

'And could you direct me to the pilot Mr. Walker.'

'Our pilot is up in the cockpit, Tomaz.'

Five minutes later and Tomaz, his wallet now fattened by the money given to him by James, was stamping passports. He didn't even look at their gear. They could have brought their own weapons in after all.

'Okay, Mr. Walker. You have someone picking you up?'

'We do.'

'Then please call them and I will let them through the gate. They know where to come?

'They do.'

'Fine. Have a great time in Slovenia.'

And, he was gone. Jake got on the phone and they were rolling out of the gates twenty minutes later. Tony drove the front vehicle with Stefan in the passenger seat and Nikki and Jake in the back. Andy drove the other vehicle, with Eddie next to him, while Andy dozed in the back seat.

The first objective for Jake was a safe place where they could inventory everything and commence a plan. His first instinct was to head to the Fortress now, but he knew that was not a good idea.

Nikki told him of a small warehouse on the outskirts of Portorož, which belonged to an importer friend, who was out of the country and she'd got the key from his son. With Nikki directing the way, Tony drove through the dark, deserted streets. Jake checked his Seamaster, 03:27.

Chapter 41

Granite Falls, Washington State

Iain sat on his sofa trying to focus on a new novel he'd picked up when he'd last been into a shopping mall. A cup of Bill's coffee sat cooling on the coffee table and Iain had wished him a good night half an hour ago. The book was a thriller, but he felt no thrill tonight, only dread that what he'd put in place could all turn to shit. Pat, a man he'd hired in a business relationship was now in danger. Their relationship had turned to friendship and his heart had plummeted at Nikki's phone call less than twenty-four hours ago. Now that he was in danger, he knew that he would abandon his mission to see Danielle's killer brought to justice.

He heard his cell phone buzzing away over on the bureau and got up and took the call, a blocked number. 'Yes?'

'Iain Fisher?'

'Who is this?'

'Sorry, Mr. Fisher. This is Agent George Simmons.'

'From the FBI?'

'Yes.'

'How can I help you Agent Simmons?'

'Well, you are not going to believe this, but I am down in Vegas and I have just come away from the Sherriff's office where I have taken a statement from a young Slovenian man, Miroslav Christophe Juricic. You remember that name?'

Iain's mouth went dry. First Pat and the preparations to get Jake and his team over there, now this. 'Tell me everything, please George. What's happened?'

George went over his own investigation, his interview with Cathy Dickson in Baltimore and the Federal watch that had been logged in a number of databases in the hope that something would break. Their luck at how Juricic had been caught red handed and the leverage this had given them. He then took him through Miro's version of events that night and Iain again felt the deep hurt and anger at what these men had done to his daughter.

'The thing that struck me with Miro, Iain, is that Marko disgusts him. If I didn't have that, I wouldn't have a sworn statement from him. He's afraid, but deep down, the young man has some ethics and I think he has the determination to do this. Most people in his shoes would've said fuck you and gone to jail on the drugs charge. His statement and willingness to testify gives us a case. I can now go to a Federal Judge and obtain a warrant for Marko Kovak's arrest.'

'Not much use if he stays in Slovenia though is it?'

'No, I agree with you there. We don't have an extradition treaty with Slovenia and neither Cathy nor Juricic would be willing to testify in Slovenia. And, no court there would convict Kovak, I am certain. But, there are plenty of countries where we do treaties. So we'll be watching and waiting.'

Iain didn't respond and George said: 'Are you still there, Iain?'

'Yes, still here. George. I think I need to tell you what I've been doing.'

Iain told him about the plans he'd put in place and their hope that they would get sufficient evidence to bring Marko back to justice in the States. And now, how it had all turned when Pat was taken and

Nikki almost killed. How Jake was on his way there, solely with a mission to rescue the detective that had made everything possible and restore the status quo.

'So, you've been planning your own black op?'

'I guess you could call it that, yes, and the op is now in the trash. No different from what the US Government does every single week. Now however, Jake's only objective is to get on the ground and rescue Mr. Davis.'

'And if your Russians object?'

'Hey, they started things George. Jake will defend himself and his team and do whatever he needs to do to succeed. You don't know him.'

'Okay, point taken. Anyway, I've got to contact Hank Grady and move this forward. At some point, Zoran and Marko will find out about the arrest warrant and Miro Juricic's intention to give evidence. I want him and his father in a place of safety well before that happens.'

'Well he won't hear it from me.'

'I know that. Please keep me informed about how Jake and the team go, will you do that?'

'Of course. And I thank you for obtaining Juricic's statement. That must have taken a lot of persuasion.'

'You've got no idea, Iain. But, we've been lucky too. Let's hope it stays that way for us. Good night.'

Chapter 42

Portorož

Eddie closed the roller door to the small warehouse and Nikki went to turn on the lights. The men got out of the SUVs. It was quiet and the engines ticked as they cooled.

'Spider, Sensei. How are the vehicles?'

The men looked at each other and Tony spoke. 'They're good Luke, as we expected, full tanks of gas. We'll get seven-hundred kilometers out of them, five if we're forced to push it.'

'Okay, get the gear sorted, checked and distributed. You too Frog. I'll just have a chat to Nikki.'

Nikki and Stefan sat on packing crates. Jake regarded the pair, the older man and his niece. It had taken some guts to jump from a balcony and escape armed men. Jake admired the way that she'd stuck out her assignment, picking up the vehicles, purchasing weapons and now this. 'Hey,' he said, 'sorry if our introductions were a bit hurried back there. The boys all have call signs and I hope you don't mind addressing us on that basis. When we leave here, we don't want our identities known by Zoran and his men.' Jake explained the Special Forces call signs and their origins.

'Sure, no problems, Luke,' said Stefan. 'We'll use your tags from here on.'

Over near the vehicles, the men had the gear on the ground and they moved quickly to clean, check and load the weapons. 'Eddie was holding up a rifle and a machine pistol. 'You're the weps guy, Spider, what're these?'

'The stubby one is a PP-19 Vitzaz submachine gun. Simple weapon, cock and fire, 30 round magazine, standard 9x19mm parabellum round. Good for about 30 meters. How many you got there?

'Four, with about a dozen clips,' said Tony.

Andy picked up one of the rifles and brought it to his shoulder. 'Optical scope, integrated silencer. This is an AS Val rifle, or carbine. Russian Special Forces issue, only good for about two-hundred meters as it uses these,' he held up a round, '9x39mm round, sub atomic, but will still kill you. A good weapon. Four as well, Sens.?'

'Yes, four.' He held up a pistol. 'Seen this handgun before?'

Andy put down the rifle and took the pistol, looking at it closely. 'Nah, never seen one, but I'm sure it's a Pistol Yary something or other. PYa it's more commonly known as, named after its designer, Yary dot dot,' he smiled. 'Same ammo as the submachine gun, seventeen round magazine, eighteen if you load one in the chamber. Used by elite Russian police and the Army.' He put down the pistol and picked up a case, inside of which was a sniper rifle. He handed it to Eddie. 'Yours, I think, Frog.'

Eddie took the rifle out of the case. 'Wasn't planning to do any sniping on this trip, but you never know.' He pulled back the bolt and looked in. 'Chambered for a fifty cal. round, been used before too. In good hands, it's capable of hitting a target over a mile away.'

'It's an M93, the Black Arrow,' said Andy. 'Yugoslavian Armed Forces.'

On the other side of the vehicles, Jake peered at a rough drawn map. Nikki had told him about the three GPS devices, how the cars had travelled the short distance to Divača airstrip and then returned yesterday afternoon. 'So this is where Pat is?'

'We can't be sure, but yes, that's our destination,' replied Nikki.

'They could have left the device there and gone somewhere. They may also have returned.'

'I guess you'll find out when you get there. But, I can also call each of these and they activate and transmit sound. All I heard overnight, was someone sleeping. It sounds like Patrick.'

'Alright, you can drop all of us on the road here,' Jake indicated a point on the road nearest the Fortress. 'We'll walk in. Then you and Stephan take the SUVs and hide them off the road somewhere. Keep your cell phone on and we'll call okay?'

'Roger that, Mr. Luke,' said Nikki.

'Just Luke is fine, Nikki,' he smiled and she brought her hand up to her head in a mock salute.

'You two have any weapons?'

'Not yet,' said Stefan. 'We hadn't planned on being part of your team.'

'No. I guess the attempt on Nikki's life yesterday changed things and we're glad to have you with us. Come over and we should be able to give you both something to defend yourselves with.'

They moved over to the vehicles where the men were finishing sorting the gear and ditching the stuff they wouldn't need into a couple of the bags and filling four with the stuff they were taking. 'What you got, guys?'

Tony spoke. 'Silenced automatic rifles with scope, Russian Special Forces issue, plus machine guns and pistols, both taking nine millimeter rounds. Also, Frog has a fifty cal. sniper rifle with optical scope. Not too happy that we're going in without zeroing the weapons. But they've been used and better than having new ones where you have to clean off all the machine grease.'

'Box of twelve RGO hand grenades,' added Andy holding one

up. 'One to two second fuse, so throw them before you let the fuse go. Also one RPG-29 Vampir.' He held up a rocket launcher. 'This sucker saw service in the nineties and our own boys were fired on in Iraq by towel-heads carrying one of these. Load, aim and squeeze the trigger. Duck down as it goes as the rockets only have the one type of propellant in them and exit the tube quickly heading toward a top speed of around eight-hundred feet per second. Definitely good for a car or light plane, or for taking out a room full of people.'

'Point taken about zeroing the weapons,' said Jake. 'Much of what we are doing is on the run, I know. We'll try and minimize the risks by scoping out this place properly when we arrive. It's less than half an hour from here.'

He dropped his own bag and opened it, passing out boxes. 'Short wave communications, one for you too Nikki, I bought five. Place it in your ear, turn it on. We'll use frequency number three, just select it on the dial here. Voice activated transmitter, good for five hundred yards, less in built up areas. Put them on now. Turn them on when we get there.'

He reached in again and pulled out what looked like a pistol with a screen on top and a cable of sorts. 'Inspection camera. Used by mechanics and a variety of people to look under doors and around corners.' He tossed it to Andy who examined it. 'Also in the bag are two NVGs,' he pulled one out and passed it to Eddie. 'I'll take the other set as we might need them when driving and can't use our lights.'

He looked in the bag and said, 'I also have a number of movement detectors.' He pulled one out, and they saw what looked like a solar powered light. 'Infra-red, wireless, range of about twenty yards. We'll use these as we head up to the Fortress, push them into the ground, turn them on here. I have a device in the bag that can receive the transmissions. They'll give us early warning of anyone approaching. Finally, I have an assortment of detonators and det. cord for the C4.'

'What's our plan?' asked Tony.

Jake laid a small hand drawn map on the bonnet of the nearest

SUV and they gathered around him. 'This twisty little road leads to this small village here, called Dolnja Košana and the Fortress is here. The small town of Betanya is here, with the Divača airstrip here. As we travel along the road, we'll each drop off. Each of you, take a pistol and rifle, and two of the motion detectors. Nikki and Stef, you two take one of these,' he handed them a Vitzaz machine pistol and addressed his men. 'When you are dropped off, get up to the perimeter of the property as quickly as you can and report in. Nikki tells me it's pine forest to the south and west of the property, a steep ravine to a river below the escarpment provides a natural barrier for the property to the north and east.'

Each of them was dressed in boots, black pants and t-shirt. Jake handed around tubes of cam cream. 'Put this on as well. He looked at his Seamaster. 'Let's synchronize for 04:22 in twenty seconds...now.'

Each man made adjustments to their own wrist watches so that they all had roughly the same time.

Jake looked at the faces around him. 'Let's go and get Pat Davis back.'

Chapter 43

The Fortress

Jake exited the SUV first and started running through the pine forest using what little moonlight filtering through the trees above him. The evenly-spaced trees suggested plantation timber and it was well kept judging by the lack of smaller trees and limbs on the forest floor. That said, Jake kept one eye on the deck looking for anything that would trip his progress. Andy had been next, then Tony and Eddie. The rough plan was to surround the south and east sides of the house and watch. Nikki and Stefan were then to drive away and find a track off the road to hide up until needed.

Jake estimated about two miles from the road to the Fortress and he'd given himself the longest route to the northern-most tip of the property boundary. It was not surprising, therefore, that he heard, 'Sensei in position, over.' Followed by, 'Spider in position, over.' Jake could see the silhouette of the house through the tree line and he was approaching his own surveillance point when he heard, 'Frogman in position, over.'

'Luke in position, Roger all, watch your fronts, out.'

The sky started to lighten to the east and Jake and the others focused on using their hearing and sight to detect any guards, inside or outside, as well as looking for ways to get in. Eddie and Jake had the NVGs, which they used to scan the iron and brick wall to their front and the house and grounds beyond.

Jake detected cameras on the wall, three on the nearest side, including one to his front. It hadn't moved which suggested either it hadn't detected him, or was fixed in position. Or it was movable, and that person wasn't watching...

Similarly, the house had several cameras on the roof and walls, giving the place full coverage of the grounds and approaches. He couldn't see any motion detectors, but these could be buried under the ground, so he drew nothing from this either way. To the rear of the house he could see a heli-pad and a pathway to the house and then a wide row of stone steps leading to a terraced area. To the left of the heli-pad and toward the ravine was what looked like an orchard. It was autumn and he could see apples and pears in the trees.

He reported his findings and Eddie gave him a similar report of cameras from his vantage point. He could also see one small light coming from a room half way down the East side of the house on the ground floor. Apart from that, they could detect no other signs of life or guards on the property. 'Okay, move forward until you are inside the perimeter,' said Jake. 'Contact when in position, out.'

The perimeter consisted of ten foot pillars of brickwork, between which were iron railings to the same height. Jake assessed that he could climb the railings, but they were tricky and the brickwork could be embedded with broken glass on top, so he looked down into the ravine and saw a steep slope leading to a small stream, about eighty feet or so below. The railings continued out into the void and he climbed on the lower rail and gingerly stepped out to the end. The construction swayed a bit, but held and he crept around the end, avoiding the razor wire which had been placed to deter people. It was not a wall for stopping anyone determined.

'Luke in place, over.' One by one the others called it in. 'Okay, Spider, with me to the rear patio doors. Sensei, do you have a target, over?'

'Roger that, there is an entrance door half way along the West side,' replied Tony.

'What about the front door?' asked Jake. 'It could be open.'

'Okay, Frog and I will check out the front door.'

Andy heard it first, a vehicle starting and he reported it in as he watched the light from inside the basement garage slowly get brighter as a motorized garage door rolled upward. 'Wait all, a vehicle or vehicles are coming from the garage, over.'

'Roger that, everyone stay down and watch, out' said Jake.

Chapter 44

The Fortress

Petr waited for the garage door to clear and then gave the Mercedes SUV a little gas to take it out. Beside him in the passenger seat sat Francesca, a passionate seventeen year old he'd been 'seeing' for several weeks. Once he'd passed the door and onto the concrete drive which led up to the ground level, he pressed the remote to close the door and squeezed her knee as he drove up and onto the forecourt. She'd been drinking, they both had, and she giggled and gave him a playful slap on his wrist. He focused on his front, feeling happy after finally screwing her in a proper bed. Until last night, their love making had been outdoors in the fields or in Marko's SUV, as the men were not allowed visitors and she still lived with her parents. He was expecting a phone call from Marko soon as he knew they would be shortly returning to the airstrip, assuming everything went right with the Croatians.

Vlad and Sasha had looked the other way, content to share a three man watch of the American. With Zoran, Marko and Valery out of the frame, it was a very rare opportunity to have a few beers, watch the Italian soccer, the *Serie A*, and relax. Apart from the American, there was no one to guard. Petr knew the American was thirsty, fearful, angry, hungry, uncomfortable and tired. But, they'd stuck to their instructions, part of them anyway, and the American had not complained, had even managed to sleep with his arms cuffed behind him.

He pressed the remote on the dash to operate the gates. It was early and he saw nothing out of the ordinary and wasn't really expecting anything in any event. He didn't see Andy sprint across the gap to the house, down the sloping driveway and duck under the garage door before it closed.

As the SUV disappeared from view and the front gates closed, three men hugged the ground next to the perimeter, watched their front and waited for the man inside to give them the nod to go.

45

Airstrip near Brežice

The Mercedes saloon pulled into the hangar at Cerklje airstrip. Marko was in the front, Valery drove and Boris and Zoran sat in the back. Behind them, a Mercedes Vito held the balance of their team, the men who'd participated in the surprise massacre of the eight Croatians they'd come to kill. They'd loaded the stolen cocaine into the rear of the truck trailer, leaving broken statues littering the warehouse. Two of the men, Kostya and Ziv had left to drive the truck back to Portorož, where Zoran had several warehouses. The cocaine would then be repacked for the journey north.

Boris had been full of himself on the short drive from Brežice, regaling Zoran of other times he'd killed. 'There's time when you have to show everyone who's king. If you don't act quickly and decisively, everyone will take advantage…'

On the airport apron, they exited the vehicles and stood before the Antonov. 'So back home, Zoran.' He proceeded to walk around the plane, doing some visual checks, before they would take off for the twenty minute flight to Divača. They didn't need fuel; it was only one-hundred-and-fifty kilometers. The men were passing around a bottle of vodka, having stowed their gear in the baggage hold.

'Yes, thanks for everything, Boris. That Radic cunt will think twice about stealing from us again,' said Zoran.

'I've got a surprise for you too, my friend.'

'A surprise?'

'The dog will get more than a surprise. I've brought down a helicopter for you, Zoran. Going to teach you how to fly it too. Then we'll fly over to his home and put a cruise missile down his fucking chimney. Ha!'

'A helicopter?' Zoran smiled too, his friend was a bit mad, he was sure.

'Anyway, get this lot aboard while I go and look after the Captain over there,' he pointed to an air force officer who sat in a lit office in the corner of the administration block. 'This is Slovene air force, they are good friends of us Russians.' He reached for his wallet and walked away.

Zoran recalled the one image from the morning that played over and over in his head. The look on Marko's face once they'd dealt with the men who'd shown the courage to resist them. How much he'd wanted it, the chance to hurt them. He turned to look and saw that his son stood to one side of the others. A loner, always had been. 'Marko,' his son turned and Zoran beckoned him over.

'Yes Papa,' he said as he walked over.

'We're only twenty minutes flying time from home.'

Marko pulled out his phone. 'I'll call the men; get the cars to meet us.'

'Don't worry,' Marko raised his eyes, 'Boris has a helicopter coming to meet us. Says, he is going to teach me how to fly, can you believe it?'

Boris walked back from his short meeting with the officer, his phone to his ear. He ended his call. 'My helicopter has experienced a mechanical problem, Zoran, probably dirty, Slovenian fuel. That was my pilot; we'll have to wait about an hour before he gets to Divača. Still over Poland, but she is quick machine, you will see.' He shouted out.

'Hey you lot, get in. We're going.'

Zoran turned to his son, could see what he wanted. 'Call Petr, okay? He can meet you when we land, take you home to start questioning the American.'

'Thanks Papa.' Marko pulled out his phone and brought up Petr's cell number.

Chapter 46

The Fortress

After they could no longer hear the SUV, a further minute or two passed and Andy's voice came over their earpieces, 'Frog and Sens, take the front door, come in now it's unlocked, over.' The two men acknowledged. 'Luke, come through the side entrance, over.'

'Roger that, out.'

Jake ran quickly to the door on the West wing of the house, turned the handle on the big old door and pushed it slowly. It was well oiled and he found Andy inside and closed it behind him. Jake spoke into his throat mike so that the others could hear. 'Frog and Sens, go up to the first and second floors and hold position, okay? We'll clear the ground floor and be with you soon, over.' Eddie and Tony acknowledged.

'What you got, Spider?'

'Frog was right, one light on in the whole joint. In the room, across from us.' Jake could just make out a small crack of light at floor level. Also, Zoran's car is here, plus two more, late model BMWs. You got the inspection cam?'

'Sure, in my pack.'

Andy reached into Jake's pack and pulled the device out. He held the pistol grip display and turned the unit on. The display illuminated and the camera came on, the white led lights at its tip, harsh and bright. Jake grabbed the camera tip. 'I'll turn that off,' said Andy, 'how's it now?'

Jake opened his hand slowly and saw that the lights were off. 'Let's see what we can through the keyhole, okay?'

'I'll cover you,' said Jake and he checked his rifle for the sixth time since they'd left the safety of the cars, round in chamber, safety off. They crept down the narrow corridor, which opened into a larger one. Jake looked to the right and saw the front door beyond a large foyer. To their left, the corridor led to a larger room which overlooked the terrace at the rear of the house. There were other rooms and doors too, but he was getting the basic layout of the place. He knelt down opposite the door, a double affair with a large keyhole in the right door, built into a brass plate.

Andy knelt down and listened. The house was dead quiet and he couldn't figure out why there was such a lack of security. He bent the tip of the cam and slid it gently through the keyhole, peering intently at the screen. He turned the device left and right to ensure he'd seen everything, pulled it out carefully and crawled over the Jake, who remained focused on the door.

Andy whispered into his throat mike, 'Frog and Sens. Everything quiet up there, over?' Two Rogers came back. 'Okay, remain alert while we take out one of the guards; be prepared to act if we set off an alarm, out.' He looked at Jake. 'Pat's definitely inside the room, directly to the left of the door, about ten feet away, lying on a couch, probably tied up. The room is a library. There is a floor lamp on over near the window and a man is sitting in an armchair. About one o'clock. He looks like he's dozing.'

'What you thinking?' said Jake, still aiming for the door opposite. 'You open the door and I take him out?'

'I'll do him,' said Andy, 'I know where he is.' He took up position several feet from the door, checked his rifle and sighted along the barrel.

Jake moved over to the door and took hold of the handle. He looked back to Andy, who nodded.

Jake turned the handle and pushed it quickly open. Andy's rifle coughed twice. The sudden noise sounded very loud, despite the suppressor. Jake saw two holes in the man's head. The window remained intact, probably the low velocity rounds, but then he didn't care and was through the door and by Pat's side.

Pat was instantly awake and then alarmed at the sight of armed men dressed in black and covered in cam cream. He thought his time had come and then he registered a voice he knew.

'Pat, it's alright. It's me, Jake.'

'Oh, thank God,' he managed.

Andy stood at the door, listening to the conversation and keeping an eye out. Jake scoped out the chain and the handcuffs behind his friend's back. 'I'll deal with the cuffs soon, Pat. Need you to tell me who else is here.'

'Only two others. The boy and his father left on business yesterday afternoon. They left three goons to guard me, one of which brought a woman in last night. I could hear them.'

'We saw a man drive out of here with a woman in Marko's SUV, about fifteen minutes ago.' He pointed over his shoulder. 'He's dead, that leaves one. Any idea where?'

'Not really.'

'Okay, stay here and we'll go and find him.'

'It'd be top floor if I was a gambling man, Jake.'

'Why's that?'

'Didn't hear any footsteps on the floorboards above. Heard them cooking in the kitchen behind me; think the dining room's at the end, plus a television. They were watching the soccer, I think. The guy over there came in just before midnight. The top floor, Jake. Not here or the first. His name's Sasha.'

Jake put his hand on his shoulder. 'Whose is'

'The last one. If Petr took his girl home, Sasha is still here asleep somewhere.' He shrugged.

'Right. Spider, let's go up. Oh yes, Pat?'

'What?'

'Call me Luke from now on,' Jake went on to explain the four call-signs of his team.

At the first floor landing, Tony crouched in the shadows covering the corridor which led toward the rear of the house. Jake quickly filled him in and he elected to remain and cover the corridor. 'I'll stay here, in case. You two go.'

Jake and Andy mounted the final flight and crouched down next to Eddie. 'Anything?' said Jake.

'Nothing, no light or noise. Could hear you two though.'

'Still quieter than an M4,' said Andy.

'Spider, you stay here and cover us. Frog, let's go and see if this guy snores.'

Eddie took the right side of the corridor, Jake the left. Some of the doors were open and, from a glance into the rooms, it confirmed the floor as the one with the bedrooms. Most looked unused, or were storing furniture and other household items.

Fourth doorway down on the left and Jake heard a sound, someone moving. He pressed close to the wall and signaled to Eddie, who came over. He signaled inside and they both heard movement. Jake pulled the NVGs down onto his face and watched the darkness turn to green. He held up three fingers and moved in front of the door, taking a shooting stance. Eddie held the door handle and Jake nodded. Eddie turned the handle, it was locked, but he'd made a noise. Jake signaled with his foot for Eddie to kick the door.

Eddie stood back and kicked the door near the handle. It flew open to the left and Jake quickly moved into the door frame. His eyes registered a man moving to his right, from a bed toward the window, he instinctively fired at the man's center of mass, once, twice, and the man went down. He pulled up the goggles as Eddie hit the light switch. A man wearing just undershorts lay on the floor. Two rounds had hit him in the middle of his back and a large pool of blood already pooled around him. His legs twitched as the life poured out of him.

Jake spoke into his throat mike. 'Okay everyone, second man down. Stay alert, but Pat thinks there were only two guards on the property, three if we count the one who left in Marko's car earlier. Meet on the ground floor, in the library, out.' He turned to Eddie, 'Frogman?'

'Luke.'

'Find me some water for Pat, okay?'

He nodded.

As they went down the stairs, Jake punched Nikki's number into his cell phone. Nikki answered straight away. 'All good, Nik, bring up the cars now.' He hung up.

'Spider?'

'Luke.'

'You know where the garage is. Get the remote controls out of one of the cars down there, open the garage and then the gate so that Nikki can bring the cars right in. Leave the remotes in one the cars and then bring Nikki and her Uncle upstairs. See you in the library.'

'You sure you want the Bimmers in here when Zoran or Marko come back.'

'Not going to hang around, Spider. We've got what we came for, remember?'

Chapter 47

Granite Falls

Iain checked the time in Slovenia, just after six in the morning, eight hours ahead of his ten in the evening. He lifted the receiver, checked the international dialing codes and punched in Jake's cell number.

'Yes?'

'Jake, it's Iain.'

'Iain, hi, we have him.' Jake headed back to the library and kept speaking as he went. 'All's good. Couple of Zoran's men were killed in the process. We were lucky. Zoran and Marko went out on a business trip yesterday, left the place virtually unguarded. We're just waiting for our vehicles to arrive and then we'll be on our way.'

'How's Pat?'

'Hey, he's okay, shaken, dehydrated. He's lucky, feels he was in for a spot of torture from our boy. Here, I'll put you on speaker.'

Jake headed for the couch, where Pat sat, drinking his second glass of water. 'It's Iain, everyone.'

They all gathered around and introduced themselves, like they were on a conference call.

'Andy's outside waiting for the cars to come up. What's up

Iain?'

Iain quickly told them about the work of the Vegas cops, the DEA and the FBI in arresting Miro and, particularly, the skill and persistence of George Simmons in obtaining Miro's witness statement. 'So, there it is, we now have the capacity to go for Danielle's killer.'

The men looked at each other. 'That's great Iain,' said Pat.

'But you know what boys, getting Pat back has scared me plenty. I'm not sure I want, or indeed have the right to ask, for you to go through with the original mission. Why don't you just drive out of there and come home?'

A full ten seconds went by. Jake was about to offer his views when Eddie beat him to it. 'Eddie here, Mr. Fisher. I'm only speakin' for myself, but I want to go all the way here. I came here for the money and to get out of the personal hellhole that I'd climbed into, I'll grant you that. But, we trained hard for this and now that we're here, we are ready to prosecute this boy.'

Jake looked at Tony and indicated he should talk. 'This is Tony Mr. Fisher. I expected a fight with these Russians. I know I've been trainin' for one. The mission's been easy for us so far. But, I'm with Eddie. We can't leave here knowing we could've taken that boy back to the States. You know, to face his accusers. We're here for you Iain and every other father who lost a daughter to murderers like Kovak. I say we go through with it.'

'Pat here, Iain. Sorry buddy, I was careless, put the whole mission at risk, but you know you want this and were prepared to walk away if we couldn't get the evidence. Hey, now you have it, I'm with the boys here. We are right here. They don't know we're here. We have the element of surprise, we have the better ground, and we have the better men. If he drives up that track, I say we take him.'

It was quiet for several seconds. 'We were ready to go, Iain. We are now ready to stay and do the job,' said Jake.

Iain thought their responses through for a few seconds. 'The

FBI came to my house. I told them what you are doing.'

'And?' said Jake.

'They're going to turn a blind eye I think. The Special Agent In Charge just told me to tip them off where and when. He said they were going to see a Judge for a Federal Arrest Warrant using the evidence from Cathy Dickson and now from Juricic. He told the Feds he couldn't go through with rape and that it was Marko who gave Danielle the fatal shot of heroin. Simmons said he believed him and it was consistent with his decision to give evidence against Kovak. Also, it was difficult for him as he will probably have to leave Slovenia. Then again, he has enough money...'

Jake heard the garage door motor. 'Iain, get some sleep. I will call or text you with any news we have, okay?'

'Okay. Thanks everyone.'

Jake ended the call. 'Right, I'll go brief Nikki, Spider and Stefan. Let's inventory every last inch of this joint. As well as knowing just what we have here to support us, I want to know the best fields of fire, how it might be attacked and defended. Frog, you start looking at how we might blow this place. It all feels dirty to me and the style is all wrong. Be doin' Zoran a favor in my humble opinion.'

Chapter 48

Gračišče, Slovenia

Petr and Francesca were enjoying a cigarette, parked near a lookout high above the small town of Gračišče, where the girl lived, and not far south from his own home, if you could call it that.

She was examining the intricate tattoos on his hand and knuckles and saw a serpent, flowers and strange symbols. She'd never known anyone like Petr. He was over thirty and her parents would not approve. Not let her out ever again, if they knew. She didn't know what he did in that big house; protect its owner she thought. The sex had been good…

Petr's phone buzzed in his pocket. He pulled it out and saw that it was Marko. He took his hand away from the girl and signaled her to be quiet. She focused on her cigarette and looked away while Petr answered.

'Marko.'

'Petr, hi, how are things there?'

'Very quiet, I'm just doing a walk around the grounds. How was your trip?'

'Fine. How is the American? Is he angry yet?'

'He is going to be tough one.'

'Good. We're just about to get back on the aircraft. Pick me up at the airstrip. About thirty minutes.'

'I'll be there.'

Chapter 49

Divača Airport

Zoran dozed on the short flight back as did most of the others. It had been a long night. They'd hardly reached cruising altitude before Boris throttled back the engines and the aircraft commenced its descent. On the ground, he taxied to the apron next the two hangars and, once the props stopped turning, one of Boris' men, Alek, cranked the handle to the forward door, opened it and lowered the steps. He stepped out and, soon, everyone was out on the grass enjoying the fresh air. The airstrip was otherwise deserted.

Zoran was talking to Valery when he saw Marko's SUV drive down the approach road. 'Why don't we all go with Marko?' suggested Valery.

'You know how Boris is, Val. A stubborn Russian. He make big effort for me. He's coming now.'

Boris lumbered over, a captain's cap on his head. 'You ever rode in a smoother plane, Zoran, with a better pilot? Ha! My helicopter is thirty minutes out. Wait till you see it, your face will go like this.' He opened his eyes wide and dropped his jaw wide, revealing a mouth full of gold. His men laughed and Zoran thought it funny too. 'Where is the fucking vodka? Alek, Yuri. Find me a bottle, I need a drink.'

'Papa.'

Zoran turned to his son. 'You're going?'

'Yes. I'll see you back there.'

'Don't fucking kill him or hurt him too bad, you hear? I want to hear what he has to say as well.'

'Don't worry. I'll just soften him up a bit.'

Zoran looked into his son's eyes until Marko blinked. 'I know you, boy. No fucking tin snips, okay?'

Marko headed to the SUV and got into the passenger seat.

Chapter 50

The Fortress

Jake could not believe his eyes. A corner room in the basement, designed as storage, a workshop perhaps, although there was another room clearly used as such. From his tour of the house, there was little of the original structure left and most of the new was concrete with exterior and interior finishes a mix of the modern and the old. To Jake, the house was hideous, from the gold plated taps and black marble of Zoran's bathroom in the North-East corner, to the paneling and chandeliers of the more formal areas. And now this. Jake couldn't see how large the room was from the inside, he had to guess from looking at the possible dimensions from the outside. One side of the room, they simply couldn't tell. It could go back thirty or a hundred feet.

'Just a simple lock on the door, boss,' said Eddie. 'How much is here?'

Jake ran his hands up and down the stacked bills, stacks which went to the ceiling. Mostly Euros, but some Greenbacks as well, all in hundreds as far as they could tell. They must have started stacking in one corner and kept going. Only a narrow corridor which led from the door remained.

'Who knows Frog. I guess they stopped filling the place when they reached the light bulb. It's stored down here because of its weight. Each note weighs about a gram. So, a thousand c-notes, ten grand and you have a kilogram, just over two pounds. There must be tons and tons of it here. The floors above us wouldn't take such a weight upon them.'

'You'd think they'd keep it more secure, even the help, you know.'

Jake went out of the room. 'I think the help don't need money like you and I do Frog. They're in a brotherhood, remember? A *vory*. Lifelong allegiance and all that shit. Can't marry, can't leave. Hey, come out of there, so I can take a picture.'

Eddie came past and Jake took a few photos with his cell phone, before hitting the light and closing the door.

'You know one of the reasons I like you so much, Frog?'

'Who me?'

'You haven't asked about taking some of what's in there.'

Eddie chuckled. 'I may be an alcoholic, boss, but I ain't never stole in my life. Anyways, that there's tainted money. I spend any of that, I bring bad luck on myself and my family. Forever.'

'Looks like old Zoran has been skimming though, don't it?'

'Not so sure, maybe they don't trust the banks.'

'What's that?'

'You're only as rich as the amount of liquid assets you can carry with you. Governments can always take your wealth, even in so called safe havens, proceeds of crime. This is more likely to belong to the *vory*. Zoran's insurance is more likely to be the thousands of uncut diamonds upstairs in his safe.'

It hadn't taken long to find Zoran's safe in his bedroom. Once they'd blown it with an ounce of C4, it revealed a small satchel of papers, including a will, stock certificates and some gold, but the most valuable thing was the stash of uncut diamonds, tray after tray. Andy reckoned the whole lot would weigh at least ten pounds.

'I want you to start figuring out a way to blow this joint, I want an inferno, Froggie. Hot enough to melt diamonds. You think you can do that?'

Eddie had already spotted some gas cylinders and was figuring out how he could place C4 in the right spots. There was plenty of timber and other flammables in the place. Set some fuses... 'Sure, I'll get to work on it.'

Jake headed back upstairs. The two BMWs sat in the garage. They just needed an extra passenger and they were out of there.

He checked the charge on his phone as he went up the stairs to the floor above, coming out into the corridor where he'd met up with Andy hours earlier. He needed to get his phone charged up, but could also do it in one of the vehicles. Their comms gear was being recharged in the kitchen and he headed down to his left and entered the well-equipped room.

Andy and Pat were in there, making some basic sandwiches using the remains of a cooked chicken they'd found.

'You know there are enough guns in here to arm a fucking African uprising,' said Andy.

'Anything we can use?' said Jake moving over and grabbing a drum stick.

'Rifles of every sort. Machine Pistols, a Luger. Knives and revolvers, knuckle dusters, coshes... The one thing I thought would be useful is that,' he pointed to the corner, where a light machine gun on folding bipod legs rested, a box of linked ammunition next to it.

Jake was about to answer when his phone buzzed. He looked at the screen, it was James. 'James, hi.'

'Luke, we've been given half an hour to leave.'

'By who?'

Nikki and Stefan came into the kitchen, looking worried.

'The Police. They're here in my hotel room now.'

'Why?'

'Doesn't matter why, Luke. Visa irregularities, I think he said. The gun at his hip and 'Leave the country now' said the rest. Are you coming?'

'No James, we'll have to rendezvous another way. Initial objective attained. We have a new one now. The boy. Lodge a flight plan to Italy and wait for us there. I have a backup plan being formed and I'll call you and tell you as soon as I can.'

'Okay, keep in touch.'

Jake ended the call. 'That was James. The local police have tracked them down and they've been asked to leave. Which means someone knows we're in the country. Even if they don't know why.'

Nikki came over, showing her cell phone. 'Marko is coming look.'

On the small screen, Jake saw a map of the area and could make out a blue pin on a road.

'That's the road which leads from the highway to here,' explained Nikki.

'Okay, grab the comms pieces guys and switch them on. Use frequency 3. Spider, go find Sensei and establish two OPs looking south and west, take the GPMG and the belt ammunition. Pat, you find a weapon?'

He held up a Colt Revolver. 'Would you look at this thing, one of Zoran's?'

Jake took the revolver and noted the mother of pearl inlay in the grip and the shiny nickel plating. 'Not my type.' He handed it back and Pat checked the safety before tucking it into the waistband of his shorts.

'Okay, come with me. Nikki and Stefan, stay put for the time being. If you could find or make us some food to take and some water, that would be great.'

Chapter 51

Divača Airport

They sat on the ground, back to back, passing around a bottle of Vodka, nearly empty. Boris was alright, Zoran decided. A good man to have at your back. He was looking forward to getting home. Fuck the American. He didn't care one way or the other. He would go home and kill the fucker. No-one could touch him here. Boris nudged him with his elbow.

'You hear that?'

Zoran strained to listen. Most of the men were lying against their luggage, catching some sun, while a few dozed or drank vodka. After a few seconds, he could hear something, a whump whump.

'There!' Boris stood up, pointing toward the range of hills to their north. Isn't she a beauty? MI-24 made by Russians, my friend. In Moscow, no less, in the MIL Helicopter Factory.' He slapped Zoran on the back. 'My, just look at her.'

As the helicopter came closer, Zoran could see what it really was, a genuine, Russian attack helicopter. He laughed. 'Oh Boris, you are so funny. How in God's name did you manage to get that? Do the missiles work? They've flown it from Poland?'

'Zoran, Zoran. With money, we can buy anyone and anything. And, there are plenty of these in mothballs right now. It was hard to register. Needed to get the right paperwork, that the armaments and so on don't work. Looks good painted black, No?'

'Do the armaments work?'

'Hell, yes, but you think we would fly it all this way with eighty mil rockets in the launch tubes?' He smiled at his friend and tapped his head. 'I didn't get to be what I am, thinking like a peasant, no…'

The roar got louder as the helicopter, known in the west as a Hind Gunship, came in and hovered, before gently descending onto the pad marked out in the grass, about a hundred feet away.

Zoran felt the vibration of his phone, which sat in his shirt pocket. He looked at it and walked away to answer it.

'Zoran?'

'Who is this?'

'What the fuck you been doing, Zoran? A fucking law of your own. How do I explain the fucking carnage you left up at Brežice this morning?'

Zoran finally recognized the police chief. 'It was business, Pavel.'

'Don't you fucking Pavel me! The fucking press is all over this. Some children found your mess, for fuck's sake. They are calling it a war, Zoran, a drug war. Ministers are calling me. What am I doing about it?'

'Pavel, Pavel. Come now. They are Croatians. And, your Ministers get a cut of our business.'

'You think that makes it any better. You said you would take care of it across the border.'

'I had to make an example, Pavel. If I didn't do it there, I was going to lose another shipment.'

'How much is enough for you, Zoran? I want nothing more to do with it. Any more civilian deaths, I will have you, you understand?'

'Don't you give me shit, you little cunt! You take my money

and now you think you can just walk away. It's not just you. We own the generals, ministers, judges, customs. You can't fucking stop me. Expose me and everything is exposed. Your trips to Brussels, the two-point-six-five million Euros you have in your so-called secret account. Gone, if I say so, you hear me? You too and your whole fucking family.'

'Zoran, this morning's mess. I don't know what to do.'

'Do what you always do, Pavel. Watch my fucking back and you might get to spend the money I pay you.'

Zoran could hear the man thinking. 'We understand each other, Pavel?'

'The American sent in a team of men.'

'Which American?'

'The father of the woman who was killed. I told you about the private detective, asking questions…'

'What about him?'

'A private jet landed this morning. As soon as I found out, I deported the pilots. I will do the same for the four men that were on the plane when I find them.'

He waited for Zoran to respond. 'Is that what you call watching your back, Zoran?'

But, Zoran had hung up.

Pavel Novak closed down his cell phone and took another deep lungful of smoke. He really didn't want to go back into his office this morning.

Chapter 52

The Fortress

Petr approached the gate, pressed the remote button on his dashboard and it slid to the side on rails. He was glad to have Marko and the others back. It would be useful to see what this American was going to say for himself. He drove through the gates. He knew Marko was tired after the trip. He would talk to the others later.

As they approached the side of the house and the garage, Petr, pushed the other remote and he drove part way down the curved concrete driveway toward the door.

Marko's phone rang and he answered. 'Papa?'

'Where are you? Everything okay?'

'Yes, we are fine. Here now. No, everything is good.'

Petr turned his head and looked at the young man. He saw the two BMWs inside. They looked out of place but he couldn't work it out. He didn't see Eddie come up and strike his window with his pistol grip, shattering glass all over the two men. Before he could turn, the pistol was touching his left ear.

'Move an inch and you are dead.' Petr believed him and allowed the man to reach in and take the key from the ignition.

Marko had just told his Father that everything was fine. As his door was wrenched open and a second man brought a pistol up to his face, he said, 'sorry, Papa, they are here.'

His pistol didn't move and neither did his eyes as Jake took Marko's phone and ended the call, slipping it into his pants pocket. 'Shut the fuck up and get out of the car.'

Marko got out of the car and Jake shut the door. He stood back. 'Put your hands on the roof and spread your legs.'

Marko slowly reached up and Pat came over from behind Jake and slammed his right fist hard into the young man's kidney region. His legs buckled and he cried out. As he fell and turned to look upward, Pat saw the holster under his jacket and quickly relieved him of his pistol. Despite the tears which welled into Marko's eyes, he clearly recognized Pat and remembered. The tables had turned.

'Get the fuck up,' said Pat.

Marko could feel the bruise welling in his back. He got slowly to his feet. Pat expertly turned him around and frisked him, taking his cosh, a knife and the laser attachment for the Strike One pistol.

He held the fancy pistol in front of him. 'Very nice, Marko. Now move into the garage.'

On the other side of the SUV, Eddie had not moved, not even blinked, and Petr still had his hands on the steering wheel. Jake came around and they quickly disarmed him and took him into the garage. Eddie got into the vehicle and parked it. He stayed behind to clean up the glass while the two Russians were taken upstairs into the library.

Chapter 53

Divača Airstrip

'Fuck, fuck, fuck!' Zoran roared.

Valery rushed over to his boss's side. 'Zoran, tell me.'

'There are men, Americans, friends of our detective. They are in our house and they have Marko.' He told him about the phone call from the policeman, Novak, and the one he'd just made to his son.

Boris came over, quiet for once.

'Tell Boris exactly what Marko said again,' said Valery.

Zoran quickly retold his conversation with Novak, about the American pilots at Portorož, that Novak had said there were more Americans. 'I was worried, so I called my son. He said he was there, at the house, it all looked okay. Then, I heard a window being smashed and an American voice, and Marko said: 'sorry Father, they are here.''

Boris turned and whistled, whirling his right arm above his head. 'Get the weapons and get aboard!' he shouted. The men had already sensed something was wrong and they quickly gathered their gear and hurried over to the helicopter.

Valery went to get their own bags, which contained two Heckler and Koch Machine Pistols and a selection of pistols. Boris led Zoran over to the Hind as its rotors started to spin.

Chapter 54

The Fortress

Andy had found the key to Pat's handcuffs on the first guard they'd killed and Pat took pleasure in snapping them on Marko and a second set from Marko's bedroom secured Petr, each of them back to back attached by chain to one of the radiators in the library. 'See how that feels. Asshole,' he spat.

Marko looked across at Vlad in the armchair, still in the same position he'd died in several hours earlier. The woman they'd missed at the Kempinski and an older man he didn't know, sat across from them, pistols in their hands, vigilant, watchful.

Pat left the room and walked to the kitchen, where Jake and his team stood around a large stainless island bench. He placed the nickel-plated revolver on the bench and tucked Marko's Strike One pistol into the waistband of his shorts. He said, 'Why don't we just get in the cars now and drive, before they know what to do.'

'I agree,' said Andy. 'Every second we wait, gives them time to get here.'

'I think they're already within seconds of being here,' said Jake.

As the whump whump of the Hind's rotors became more loud, Tony remarked, 'That's a chopper.'

'And it's getting closer,' agreed Jake.

'What would you do, Luke, if you were Zoran?' asked Pat.

'He doesn't know who we are, how many, or what capabilities we have. His tactics will depend on how many men he has with him. One helicopter, perhaps only five men? We'll soon find out.'

At that moment, the Hind roared into view. The windows shook as it flew past the kitchen window and did a circuit of the house.

'Was that a fucking Hind Gunship?' asked Tony rhetorically.

'You know what kind of chopper that is?' said Eddie, impressed.

'Russian,' said Andy. 'Well armored, eighty mil rockets, large caliber forward mounted electric guns.'

'No match for a Stinger, though,' said Tony.

'Thanks for the intel, boys,' said Jake. 'We still have surprise on our side. They don't know what they're up against. Let's show them. The worst thing we can do now is let them into the perimeter until we are ready.

'Pat, go and look after our rear,' he handed him one of the rifles to augment Marko's pistol. 'Frog, stay here and watch the West. Sens., head to a room upstairs looking East, wherever you can get a good view. If that thing lands in the perimeter, we all head over to that side of the house ready to protect our position. Meanwhile, just watch your front and keep listening,' he tapped his headset. 'Sorry Pat; should have given you the one that Nikki has, no time now. Spider, come with me to the South. You placed the light machine gun up there?'

'Yes.'

'Let's go then.'

Chapter 55

The Fortress

Zoran counted heads in the cabin and was glad to see Marin, Tosya and Valery, his boys. His other men Petr, Vlad and Sasha, were captured or dead. Boris had Gregor, Alek and Yuri. His other two, Kostya and Ziv, were driving back to Koper. Eight men, against four, six if you included the American detective and the woman he'd recruited.

As they sped towards his home, a few minutes flying time, he took out his cell phone, called one of his warehouses down near Koper and received a commitment for two trucks, the largest prime movers he had, to drive up to his property. 'I want you there in five fucking minutes, you hear,' he shouted, struggling to hear over the noise in the cabin.

Boris also spoke into his cell phone to his number two, Igor, who was protecting his home in Gdansk, in Poland. His personal jet was a converted Ilyushin IL-62 and Igor said that he could bring another three men to Ljubljana in about five hours, assuming they moved now and he could find the pilot. 'Hire some vehicles at the airport; some fast Audis,' Boris insisted.

He ended the call and looked out as they swept over the forest toward the property. He stood up and reached for an overhead strap and looked around. Gregor and Yuri didn't look too good, he needed them ready to fight; on the ground they'd soon be themselves. Zoran joined him and they watched as the Hind swung past the east wing of the property.

'I've got another four men coming,' said Boris. 'But will be six hours before they are here.'

Zoran moved closer and shouted above the noise. 'Looks fine, no sight of anyone.'

'You think they've gone?'

'Only one way to find out.'

'The heli-pad?'

'No, too close,' said Zoran. 'If they plan to leave via vehicle, there is only one way out. Drop her down on this side of the gate.'

Boris moved forward to the cockpit. They were on the second sweep and Boris conferred with the pilot and pointed back where they'd just come. He turned back to the cabin, shouting to be heard above the roar of the engine. 'Get your weapons ready men, we're landing.'

A palpable sigh of relief could be heard, even over the din of the rotors.

Chapter 56

The Fortress

'There's no missiles in those tubes, Luke,' said Andy as they peered through the French doors in the first floor drawing room at the front of the house.

'Yes, it's just transport at the moment. Quick transport, however.'

He checked the time on his Seamaster: 10:11. He thought about whether they should've just gone for it. The call from James had stopped him. They no longer had a plan and needed some time for one to formulate. The one exit road worried him, but he had a very capable team. They needed time to prepare and to plan and they needed darkness.

The Hind came around a second time and Jake checked the belt feed from the box he held in his hand. 'You got the safety off on this thing?'

'I'm ready.'

Jake reached forward and opened the door outward onto the balcony. He saw that the pilot was hovering this side of the gate. 'We can't let them land inside the perimeter. That's our first line of defense. We can hold here all day with two people. Unless they bring an army,' he added.

As the Hind descended, Jake said, 'Fire about twenty rounds, Spider.'

Andy squeezed the trigger and they watched as the 7.62mm rounds peppered the armored glass and panels of the Helicopter. The pilot immediately brought on the power, heading back up.

'Give him another burst.'

Spider still had his cam cream on and he was well-muscled from their recent training. It wasn't an M60 in his hands, but the long hair, black t-shirt and everything else had Jake thinking back to Sly Stallone and his portrayal of David Morrell's Rambo character.

'Go Sylvester,' he whispered to himself.

They watched as the helicopter disappeared back over the tree line toward the road.

'What did you say?'

'Nothing Spider, just a flashback.'

Andy stayed to set up a proper firing post, one that would give him a field of fire extending right across the southern fence line. Jake left him to go talk with the others.

He met Eddie and Tony in the foyer. 'They gone, Luke?' asked Tony.

'Yes, but they'll be back.'

'Why don't we get out now?' said Eddie.

'We have no plan,' replied Jake. 'Fail to plan, plan to fail. Not going to try that now. I know the one road in and out is a choke point, a risk for us, but if we surprise them and flank them at the time we move, I think we can bust through whatever they put in place to stop us, get on the road and disappear.'

'What do you want us to do?' asked Tony.

He turned to Eddie, 'Frog, Spider's going to cover the front, our South flank, with the light machine gun we found. I don't think the helicopter will be back, unless it arms up. Find a good spot to cover the perimeter to the West. Take the sniper rifle and keep listening in, okay?'

Eddie was already moving and he turned to Tony. 'Come with me, Sensei. I want you to research a route out of here, including contingencies if we need to deviate. There's an airbase in Italy, American controlled, called Aviano. I need you and Spider to drive us there. Use the lap top we saw up in Zoran's study.'

'What are you going to do?'

'I've got some phone calls to make. I think it's time to call in some favors...'

Chapter 57

Gorice-Košana Road

They'd landed on a field close to the road and, once out of the helicopter, the men gathered around Zoran, who held his machine pistol at his side. The Russian looked at his friend. 'Sorry, Boris I think that was my Kalashnikov machine gun firing at us.'

'Hey, is okay, Zoran.' He turned to the helicopter. 'Is Russian gunship, armor-plated.' He forced a smile.

Zoran looked through the glass at the pilots. They were young. Boris had probably recruited them from the air force. Money always attracted some. They looked plenty scared. He turned around and saw that Val had gather the men together. 'Alright, I've got some trucks coming up from Koper to create a road block so they can't escape via the road there. Boris has some of his men flying in from Poland and they'll be with us later today. You know my son is important to me and it appears that the Americans have come for him, but they have underestimated me and the power of our *vory*. Am I right?'

The men nodded. 'Now, let's get up that road and we'll wait outside the fence line until we have the ability to take them on.'

Chapter 58

The Fortress

Jake entered the library and saw that things were unchanged. He'd strapped his Vitzaz machine gun to his right shoulder using the gun sling and carried two mugs of coffee, which he set down on the coffee table for Nikki and Stefan. 'They been quiet?'

'The young one is really, really pissed,' said Stefan pointing toward Marko. 'The older one? He's embarrassed, let the team down.'

Jake looked at the two. They couldn't hide their discomfort, leaning against each other and their feet up on the sofa. Jake stood in front of them, hands on his hips. 'So, Marko, you know why we're here?'

Marko looked at him like his eyes could burn him up. Jake walked closer, returning the gaze. He put his hands up, mocking him. 'Shit Marko, I can almost feel your hatred.' He chuckled and looked at the other guy. 'What's your name, pal?'

Petr thought about it for a few seconds, looked over at Vlad's body in the armchair. 'Petr.'

Jake didn't miss Marko clenching at Petr's response. He pointed at him. 'Marko. You really are antsy aren't you? Just mind your manners okay?'

He addressed the older man. 'Petr. My name's Luke and we are not here for you, only the boy. You just happened to be caught up. We're not murderers, and we're sorry about your buddy over there. But, we will defend ourselves and kill as many of your Russian pals as we have to in order to get out of here and take Marko with us. If you do what you're told, you should come out of this alive. Resist, put me or my men at risk and I will shoot you dead. Like a dog. We understand each other?'

Petr nodded.

He noted their heads were about the same height and turned around. 'Nikki, come outside for a second.'

Jake shut the door. 'Go up to Marko's room on the top floor, Eddie knows where. Get a couple of Marko's shirts, preferably the same or similar.'

'Sure, no problems.'

'Get a couple of pillow cases as well. Take them down to the cars then come back to the Library. You and Stefan alright?'

'Bit worried about what will happen when you go, Luke. Is all.'

'Don't worry about that now. We aren't going to leave you to Zoran. Anyway, Zoran and I are going to have it out before this is over. I can feel it.'

Jake re-entered the library, checked his Seamaster: 11:17. He studied the large wooden coffee table and figured it would take his weight. He sat on its edge, about ten feet from the two men. 'So, Marko. You figured it out yet?'

When Marko didn't respond, he added, 'Not happy enough fucking the girls who wanted to be with you, to feel your power, your money? Had to taste something a bit more dangerous, no?'

'I don't know what you've been told, Mr. Luke, or whatever your name is. But, you are making big mistake.'

'Tell me, Marko. What is my mistake?'

'Even if what you've been told is true, and I assure you it isn't.

Taking me anywhere isn't going to solve your problems or those of the people who have sent you here.'

'Marko?'

He looked at Jake. 'We have proof.'

'Proof of what?'

'Proof of you, Marko. Proof that you drugged, raped and then killed a young American woman on May 18th this year. Here, in Portorož.'

'Bullshit.'

'No bullshit, Marko. As we speak, agents from the FBI are applying for an arrest warrant, which we will use when we fly you to the States.'

'You won't get out of here alive, let alone take me to the United States.'

'Been in a lot trickier places than this one, Marko. You think you Russian dogs are good? Not nearly good enough. You'll see.' He stood up.

'Why don't you untie me? I'll call my Father. We'll forget all about this. A million Euros, no five million, for you and your men.'

'Marko, we've seen your money downstairs. It's dirty money. I would feel all the pain and suffering your drugs have created if I spent just one dollar of it. No, we will burn it all and everything else here in your house when we go.'

'Luke, please. There must be some way to work this out. You know that isn't my father's money. It belongs to our *vory*.'

'I don't care who it belongs to, pal. They won't get to spend it either.' He turned and left the room to find Tony.

Chapter 59

The Fortress

Despite having twenty-five years on the younger men, Valery was first to the top of the road. Nothing seemed to have changed and he kept to the tree line as the others slowly made it to the top. Alek, Tosya, Marin, Yuri and Gregor came in one by one, clearly out of shape, sweating despite the coolness of the day. Valery called each of them over and gave them positions to take up, just inside the tree-line.

Finally, twenty-five minutes after they'd started up the two mile climb, Zoran and Boris, both red faced, sweating and out of breath came into view. Valery called them over and they sat down gratefully. It took a couple of minutes before they got their breath back. They all heard the trucks coming up the road.

'Should have waited for a lift,' said Boris with a grin.

'Got a plan, boss?' said Valery.

'We'll put the trucks on the roadway over there,' replied Zoran. 'Find out what we're up against. Negotiate. Then we'll kill the fuckers.'

Valery thought his boss underestimated things, but he could also see that they held the upper hand as long as they could prevent the Americans from leaving. He went away to supervise how the trucks were positioned; he figured about twenty yards back down toward the main road would keep them out of sight from their guns.

'What we up against, Zoran? What did the policeman say?'

'Four men. Only four, plus the American detective and the local woman he recruited.'

'What's he done, Zoran, your Marko? Why are they here, risking so much?'

'Marko killed an American woman, a doctor here in Portorož. Her Father. He wants his revenge. They're not here to kill Marko; I'm sure they're here to take him away. If they'd come to kill him, it would've already happened.'

'So, why haven't they gone already?'

'I guess we got here pretty quickly, before they could get ready. You wait. They'll try to talk their way out of this…'

'And, then we'll kill them,' finished Boris.

Chapter 60

The Fortress

Jake retrieved his phone from the charger in the kitchen. The charger was Marko's, whose own iPhone sat in his pocket. He'd keep it for the moment, as he was sure Zoran would call at some point. He looked up his own contacts, reflecting how much information, photos and music was stored on the hand held device. Among the numbers it stored was one under the contact Bill, his code for the personal cell phone of the former US President, Bill Parker.

The clock on the phone was local time and showed 13:05, just after five in the morning Houston time. He pressed 'call'.

One, two... at the sixth ring, Jake was about to end the call, when he heard 'Yes, who is it?'

'Bill, it's me Jake Walker.'

'Jake who?'

'Sorry about the time, Bill. It's Jake Walker, helped your daughter out a while back. I need your help. It's important, or I wouldn't have called you.'

In Houston, at his ranch, Bill Parker searched for his dressing gown and fumbled for a light switch on the standard lamp near the window. His wife, Delia, stirred in the bed. 'Who's calling at this hour, dear? Tell them to call back.'

'It's Jake, Jake Walker, honey. Needs my help.' He found the light and sat down near the window in a favorite armchair.

'Okay, Jake, I'm awake now.'

Jake began at the beginning, with Iain and Pat and their story about the murder of Danielle Fisher and what they knew and, now, what they were able to prove. How they'd come to Slovenia to rescue Pat Davis and now their plans to make a dash to Italy in order to bring the man to justice.'

Bill listened, asked a few questions here and there, and chuckled at the end. 'What you're doin, Jakey my boy, plain old-fashioned rendition. Ah should know, coz ah invented it.'

Jake didn't want to tell him different. 'Yes Bill, agreed, but we wouldn't be here if we didn't have the proof and the FBI promising to make an application for a Federal Arrest Warrant.'

'Okay, so your motives are pure, dear Jake. Sorry for the diversion. What can I do? I'm sure you're not callin' for any other reason than you need my help. And you got it; you know that, so ask.'

'Well, the main thing is that I think we can make it to an American airbase in northern Italy, called Aviano. Udine would be the closest large city, about thirty miles to the east of the airbase. It's an old world war two base. NATO got it in the fifties I believe and it's currently under our administration.'

'Okay, what do you need from me?'

'If you have any contacts, Bill, I have a jet sitting on the tarmac in Rome. It was here in Slovenia, but the local Police have sent my pilots out of the country. When we make a dash for it tonight, I'd like to know that our Cessna was going to be at Aviano, fueled and waiting for me. I'd like to know that, when we arrive there in the next twenty-four hours, the troops on the gate and those in charge know that we are coming and allow us to get aboard that Cessna and fly away, no questions. No Sir, never saw them. That's what I need.'

'You think I still have that sort of influence after all these years,

Jakey?'

    'I was kinda' hopin''

    'Okay, what number you got?'

    Jake gave it to him.

    'I'll call you as soon as I can.'

    'Thanks Bill. Sorry to bother. Regards to Delia, for me, will'ya? Oh yes, and Emily too.'

Chapter 61

Houston, Texas

Bill Parker knew he wouldn't sleep after the call with Jake, the man who had personally pursued a gang of narcotics traffickers into Colombia so as to rescue his daughter. Emily was their youngest child and he owed Jake big time. He washed, shaved carefully, dressed in chinos and a favorite sweater and took his two Jack Russell Terriers outside for a run. He loved the mornings and the walk would give him some time to think, even with Oscar, one his Secret Service Agents, following at a respectful distance. Jake's request was a tricky one. He was on one of those missions where the mission-giver tells the agent they will be disavowed if caught. It didn't matter if Jake was 'right'. He was still trying to take a foreign national by force and against his will and, as such, those that helped him and condoned his actions would want to keep their distance. It was the nature of so called 'black ops'.

When he returned home, he brewed a coffee and went into his study. His first call was to the President's Chief of Staff, Bob Perry, who was always up early at his office on the Hill, five newspapers already consumed.

'Bob, its Bill Parker.'

'Hi Bill. How are you?' said Perry, turning down the volume on CNN.

Despite the proximity of his boss's reelection, Bob had time to talk for almost ten minutes about the goings on around the House and some of the pressures they were all feeling as the election got nearer.

'Anyway, what are you doing up so early?'

'Remember our Jake Walker guy?'

'Sure I do, Bill. How is Emily doing these days?'

'She'll get her pilot's wings soon...'

Bill told him the gist of his phone call with Jake.

'So, how can I help, Bill?'

'I just want you to talk to the President. Brief him. I'm going to call in my markers with Woods and King. With Charlie, he probably isn't even aware of this Russian guy and the lengths his own Agency has taken to gather evidence of his guilt. I'm just going to ask him to give whatever support is reasonable, so that Jake and his team can deliver this boy onto our soil.'

'Okay, that seems reasonable...' Bob wasn't sure it was, but why should he care?

'With King, I am simply going to ask that he gives all reasonable support to some US heroes who need to get a lift home. I don't think he'll have a problem with that, do you Bob?'

'No Bill. I'm on your page.'

'So, nothing to bother the President about, Bob. But all the same, I think you should let him know that we had this call.'

'Sure, Bill, I will.'

They ended their call and Bill Parker proceeded to call General David King, the Chief of the Air Force and Charlie Woods, the Director of the FBI. Both men had strong allegiances to Bill Parker and he got a promise that permission would be given for Fisher's Cessna to fly to Aviano base and the Air Force guard would be briefed to allow Mr. Walker and his team onto the base to 'rejoin' their flight.

Bill Parker never forgot favors owed or owing, and he always got his way. Except where his own women were concerned.

Chapter 62

The Fortress

Jake spent the afternoon talking with the men, getting their views on the escape and evasion plan forming in his head. He left Stefan to look after the Russians and took Nikki to the rear of the house to watch the approach route the Russians were least likely to use. This gave him Pat to relieve Eddie who went off with half their C4 and a roll of detonator cord to implement a plan he'd discussed with Jake to take the building down. When Eddie finished the preparations, he asked him to write down how it was to go.

'Why?'

'Because I'll have another job for you when we drive out of here. Someone else is going to have to set the charges.'

Sometime around mid-afternoon, Bill Parker came good on his promise and sent through a short message to Jake's cell phone:

Aviano all good. God's speed, dear Luke

Jake smiled, there were some good memories in the message and it was a highlight of the last twenty four hours, that and finding Pat safe and well. He now had a destination, if not a firm plan, and Jake used the time to refine his thoughts, talking with the team. He also took the opportunity to take each of them water and food and to look at what the small group of men were up to on the other side of the fence.

'Waiting,' said Andy.

'I know, for reinforcements.'

'Fucking Amateurs, Luke.'

Jake lined up his rifle's scope one of the Russians opposite, who sat with his back against a tree.

'We could have taken them out hours ago and been out of here.'

'I know Andy, but we had no plan. Now, we do. An hour after the Sun goes down, about seven pm, we are driving through that gate for a quick dash to Italy and our plane.'

'And how do we get past them, the trucks blocking the road and any other men they bring up in the interim?'

Jake told him.

Chapter 63

Las Vegas, Nevada

A loud banging on his door woke George Simmons from a deep sleep. By the time he'd taken a proper statement from Miro Juricic, it had been well after one in the morning and he was asleep as soon as his head hit the pillow. Two cops had taken him to the *Platinum*, saying it had a good rep, but they could have taken him anywhere, he was that tired.

He looked at the clock next to the bed: 08.25. The banging continued and he was thankful he hadn't touched the mini bar when he got in.

'Alright, alright. Take it easy, I'm coming.'

From habit, he picked up his Sig Sauer pistol and peered through the peep hole in the door. Two men, military. He put the chain on and opened the door. 'Id please.'

A hand came round the door. Standard US Government issue, but it looked real. 'Staff Sergeant John Williams and Airman Dean Steinwick, Sir. Are you Special Agent George Simmons?'

George took the chain off and let the two in, aware that he'd slept on top of the bed in his pants and shirt. Managed to take the shoes off, but the tie was still on. *So sad.* 'Come in. I'm sorry. Late night. Not expecting visitors.'

The two airmen came in and George shut the door.

It was a basic room and he gestured to the two chairs flanking the small round table and sat on the bed.

Williams spoke. 'Agent Simmons, we've…'

'Call me George, please.'

He began again. 'Sorry, George. We have orders for you to come with us. Metro cops told us you were here.'

'Orders. From whom?'

'From my boss, George. You know how this works. Call your own boss if you want.'

'I will.'

He found his cell and called Hank.

'Go with them George. This has come down from the big man himself.'

'Woods?'

'Is there another? Call me when you get there.'

'Where?' but Hank had gone.

'Okay, Sergeant Williams, where we going?'

'To Nellis airbase, Sir. A fast jet is fueled and waiting for you.'

Chapter 64

The Fortress

Valery came up from the rear after distributing the bread, cheese, apples and water to the men who'd watched and waited throughout the day. Zoran noted his presence and reflected on how unprepared they'd been. The route up from the road had surprised them all, how unfit they were and then they'd been forced to wait, without water, for so long. Zoran knew they'd been at their most vulnerable and he wondered why the Americans hadn't taken their chance. They had firepower and transport, but the day passed and they saw nothing from the house opposite.

Boris felt the strain too and, as soon as the trucks arrived, without water or food because Zoran hadn't thought of it, he called the pilot sitting in the Hind and told them to get some food and water. The pilot had replied, 'Where?' and Boris nearly exploded, explained that the man had a helicopter that could fly to anywhere in the entire fucking country. Could he not use some fucking initiative before they died of fucking thirst?

They sent the truck drivers down on foot to the road to pick up what the pilots managed to buy from a nearby supermarket, after landing the Hind on a soccer pitch. The lack of vehicles and the other failures of the day weighed on them all, buoyed only when they'd taken some food and water.

The men opposite seemed to have the upper hand. They had his house and had his son. Now, as the day grew to a close, Zoran knew that they'd see action soon. Boris joined them opposite the gate and sat down. 'What a fucking day, eh Zoran?

'Sorry about everything, Boris. My son, our… sorry, my lack of preparation. A big balls-up all day long. I am fortunate to have you here, my friend.'

Boris was tired and dirty, but he kept up the spirits of all around him, he enjoyed this role and slapped his hand down on Zoran's thigh. 'Zoran, we will laugh about this you will see.'

'I've just been talking to Igor, my number two. They just left the airport, two Audis, a BMW and a Mercedes, fast machines. Four fresh men, here in about forty-five minutes. We have weapons, transport.' He spread his arms. 'We hold the only way in or out. It will give us leverage and we can negotiate; call these men on the phone. If that doesn't work, I think we should go in, take them in their beds. Early in the morning is the best time. We saw that last night. It will be the same here, you'll see.'

Chapter 65

Las Vegas, Nevada

George Simmons arrived at Nellis Air Force base in the back of an Air Force sedan. The two men who picked him up from the hotel had been quiet on the journey, content to let George wake up and get to grips that he was going somewhere. It was all very clandestine, but he trusted Hank and felt somehow pleased that the work he'd done had somehow reached the lofty heights of the Director himself.

They stopped outside of an administration block and Sergeant Williams turned in his seat. 'This is your stop George.'

Airman Steinwick held open his door and held his overnight bag.

'Thanks John.'

Thirty minutes later and he was kitted out in a flight suit and ascending a ladder which led into the cockpit of a B-2 Stealth Bomber. The sharp angular lines were familiar to him, but the experience of getting inside and hearing the thunk and lack of noise as the glass cockpit closed took his breath away. He was in a state of shock.

Next to him in the Pilot's seat sat Captain Simon Rush, who helped him with his harness and plugged George's suit into the aircraft's comms and oxygen systems. 'Hi, I'm Simon.'

George shook the man's hand. 'George.'

'Where can I take you George?'

'You don't know.'

'Just kidding,' he smiled and continued with his flight preparation. 'Must have a pretty urgent appointment to get a ride in one of these.'

'You could say that.'

'Well, sit back and enjoy the ride. We're going up to forty-thousand feet and while we don't exceed Mach one, she's still pretty fast for a two-billion dollar bird.'

'You're kidding?'

'Not this time, but you wouldn't know it to look at the facilities aboard. No bar, no in-flight entertainment, just me. Flight time to Italy is twelve-hours, all on one, very big tank of fuel.'

Chapter 66

The Fortress

The sun was setting and his preparations were just about complete. Jake went down to the garage and saw the two Russians, each sitting in separate vehicles, belted into a rear seat, arms still cuffed, heads covered by pillow cases, still able to breathe freely through slits that Nikki had cut into the fabric. Stefan and Nikki continued to watch while Pat came over to the door.

'Trouble?' said Jake.

'From these two? No, kittens both of them. They're weak, no food or water all day. It gets to you quick. I felt it last night. Marko gave me some cheek, but he's just talk. Like many bullies, he's a man of straw and is afraid right now. Petr's a tough man, but even he can't fight us when he's cuffed behind his back. And, he knows who you are and believes that you'll let him go at some point.'

'He's a part of their brotherhood, a *vor*. The fact that he was overpowered by a superior force; will that save his life once we've gone?'

Pat shrugged. 'Who knows? I don't really care. He would've killed me without blinking if told to do so and then gone out to screw his girlfriend. Anyway, this place gives me the creeps. We all set to go?'

'Almost. Stay here. When we go, you get in with Marko; Stefan can go in the back with Petr, Nikki in the passenger seat. Keep your heads down. When we get going, put your belt on, we'll be moving quickly.'

Jake went up the internal stairs and talked into his throat mike. 'Sensei, you all set, over?'

'All ready to go, Luke. You?'

Jake checked his Seamaster: 18:11. 'All good. We go in fifteen minutes. The garage will open at 18:26. Spider, Frogman, you got that, over?'

Two Rogers came through his earpiece. *As one.*

The phone in Jake's pants pocket vibrated, Marko's iPhone, its ring tone loud and shrill inside the empty corridor. He pulled it out and looked at the screen. *'Papa' Fucking Papa, isn't that just too fucking cute?*

Jake slid his finger across the screen and put the phone to his ear. 'Yes Zoran, this is Luke.'

A slight pause. *That threw him.*

'Luke is it? Yes, this is Zoran, Marko's Father.'

'What do you want, Zoran? I haven't got much time.'

'I am sitting in a car at the gate. I would like to drive into the compound so we can talk.'

'Okay, I'll let you in. Don't come armed.'

Jake hung up.

'Was that wise?' said Pat.

'We have his son. Time for me to face this guy anyway.'

Jake spoke briefly to his men, to let them know what was happening, and then headed down to the garage. He'd taken a pistol and sub-machine gun with him. He picked up the gate remote from where it lay and went outside via the side entrance. He opened the gate and an Audi 8 series coupe rumbled through and into the courtyard. Jake closed the gate and then moved to a position where he could see into the car.

He'd seen photos of the man in the vehicle. It was Zoran. 'Keep both your hands on the steering wheel. Try anything and I will shoot you, okay? If your men attempt to shoot me. We will kill you and your son.'

Zoran's eyes were locked onto Jakes. 'I want to apologize, Luke. To say sorry. Sorry for Marko's behavior.'

Jake left him hanging. 'Is that all you've got Zoran?'

'I would like to let you go now. I have lots of money. Just name your price. I am sure I can provide a big multiple on what your employer is paying you. Set you all up for life. Your pilots have gone. I'm sorry about that; I had no say in it. I can fly you anywhere, or just let you drive away. What do you say? We can make a deal here, no?

Jake didn't reply, so Zoran continued, 'You have children Luke?'

'No.'

'Family is important to me Luke. You Americans understand family. I can't let you just take him out of here. You know that. My only son. I'm being reasonable here, you can see that.'

'You know who my employer is Zoran?'

'I assume it is the woman's father?'

'That's right Zoran and the woman's name was Danielle. She was an only and much loved child, like your Marko. Your money is no good. I haven't come here for money. I've come here to take your boy. Danielle's father lost his only child to the evil little cunt you spawned from a Russian whore. So, don't talk to me about fucking reasonable. I am not a reasonable person when I deal with cunts like you.'

Jake could almost see the steam coming out of the man's ears, but Zoran composed himself and controlled his anger. 'You leave me no choice, Luke.'

'That's fine with me, Zoran. Come and get me.' Jake opened

the gate. 'Time for you to go.'

Zoran had enough room to turn around and he drove back through the gate and into the tree line. As he reached the gate he called back: 'You are making a big mistake!'

No, buddy, you are.

As he reentered the house, Jake's cell phone buzzed in his shirt pocket. He pulled it out, 'Blocked Number'. 'Yes?'

'Luke, it's James.'

'Hi buddy, you in Rome, everything okay?'

'Yes, how are you?'

'We're all set, James, a tough day, but all on track.' He checked his watch. 'Have to go in sixty seconds. You alright to fly to Aviano?'

'You know already?'

'Sure I know, I set it up. Don't know what time we'll get there; could be eight hours or twenty, but we'll see you there, I promise. May have some extra passengers too.'

'Okay, Luke. Good luck.'

Jake ended the call as Andy came down the hallway. 'Go start the cars, Spider, and ask the others to get ready to go.' He spoke into his throat mike. 'Sensei?'

'Luke.'

'Time to go, man.'

'Doing it now, Luke. That Zoran's going to be one pissed off Russian.'

'Froggie, you good?'

'As gold, Luke.'

Chapter 67

The Fortress

Zoran got out of the Audi and punched in a redial, to call Luke back, see if he could convince him one more time. It went straight to message. He'd turned the phone off.

He threw his phone down and immediately regretted the action as the screen cracked. He'd already ruined the expensive Italian loafers on his feet, but he didn't care. He wanted to kill this 'Luke' so very much, he was hurting, a rage he hadn't felt since the *gulag*. He picked up the phone and saw that it was still working.

Valery took his boss by the arms and forced him to look at his face. 'Zoran, we are right behind you. The others are only twenty minutes out. I know you are angry, but it is time to act, to direct your anger to defeat these daring Americans. They have not negotiated. We will win this. We may not get Marko back, but these fuckers will die. You know that.'

'Valery is smart man, Zoran,' said Boris. 'Look what your anger has done. That was nice phone.'

Zoran shrugged off Valery. 'Thanks Val, I'm okay now.'

'Look,' said Boris.

The house was dark, no light shone, yet they could see the house against the night sky and could just make out two vehicles approaching the gate, having emerged from the garage. Despite the low light, neither vehicle had side or headlights on, but the rear windows of the SUVs were down and he could see two hooded figures in each of the vehicles.

'Hold your fire!' shouted Zoran.

The gate slid open and the cars came closer and closer, until they were only twenty yards from the gate. Gregor and Tosya, closest to the vehicles on the southern perimeter, approached the fence railings, their machine pistols drawn. Zoran, Valery and Boris also drew closer and closer to the area around the gate…

Then everything turned upside down.

♦

Earlier in the afternoon, Jake had walked through the large rear doors and headed toward the northern perimeter of the property. He carried a small pack, his PYa pistol and one of the AS-Val silenced rifles, strapped to his back. He'd just spoken with Nikki, who pointed out the three men monitoring the East perimeter. Nikki hadn't seen them move since someone had brought them some food and drink mid afternoon. Andy was about right in his assessment: 'fucking amateurs'. Yet, he understood their complacency, as they held the only way in or out.

He moved quietly and quickly through the small orchard he'd seen earlier. The trees were still full of fruit; apples, pears and nectarines and he wondered who among Zoran's men had tended to it and nurtured the trees. Probably the same person who'd made the jams and preserves they'd found in the kitchen. Beyond the orchard, there was a chain link fence, perhaps eight foot in height with barbed wire on top. He selected a spot next to one of the pine uprights, climbed to the top and jumped down heading to the edge of the ravine.

He looked over the edge and judged perhaps a hundred feet to the bottom. The whole property sat on the slopes of a ridge of hills to the North and he considered the small stream below probably carried water off the hills. The sides of the ravine sloped down precipitously and he contemplated moving down, traversing across and then up once he'd gone far enough, but the loose rocks and shale suggested a better plan would be to climb all the way down, which he did. The stream at the bottom was just a trickle, but the size of the ravine told him how large it would get during wet weather. He walked downstream about one hundred and fifty yards before he found a good route back to the top.

It was hard going climbing to the top, but he took his time and said a silent thank you to Joe Grant for the extra fitness he'd gained from the four weeks in Montana. At the top, he moved quickly through the forest and could just make out the Fortress to his left. He was watchful, but not too concerned. His team knew how many they faced and where they were, but he kept several hundred feet between himself and the perimeter to his left as he came around and toward the two trucks that blocked their passage to the road beyond.

At the road, he waited for several minutes, watching the two trucks parked one behind the other, each blocking one side of the road, the roadway not wide enough to park them side by side. Andy told him he was certain the truck drivers were in the cabins, perhaps asleep, but he couldn't count on it and was watching for any movement which might signal a sentry. His actions would need to be quiet and stealthy, so he went further south before dashing across the road. Once across and hidden behind the trees, he dropped to a crouch before crawling the last one-hundred feet to the front-most truck and underneath it.

He lay under the machine for several minutes, listening and watching. There was almost no vegetation at ground level and he could see Zoran and two other men some sixty feet away opposite the gate. Any of his team could have shot them all easily; they had no idea of who they faced, who had taken them on. The truck shifted slightly and he detected movement in the cabin, but whoever it was remained inside, a decision the driver would regret, thought Jake.

C4. He'd used the secondary, high explosive many times before. He knew how much to blow a lock, cut down a tree or power pole, blow up a car and put a hole in a wall. However, he'd never needed to move a ten ton truck before. Moreover, he needed to shift it off the road and at a specific time.

As well as the C4, Nikki had sourced an assortment of detonators, which are made of primary explosive and will explode and create heat and shockwave once detonated by heat or via an electrical current. Jake knew secondary explosive, such as C4, doesn't explode in a fire, or by use of an electrical current, it requires the heat and the shockwave of a primary explosive, such as that within a detonator, in order to explode. What Jake didn't have was a detonator connected to a clock, an item that had been readily available to him in the Special Forces. Film goers are familiar with Tom Cruise and other action heroes pulling out a time pencil, setting the digital display and boom. Life in the real world is very different from Hollywood and such items are very tightly controlled within the military and intelligence services. Jake didn't have one or anything like it, just the C4 and detonators.

However, USSF personnel are trained to be innovative, to use whatever resources are at hand to survive and a smoke alarm provided a nine volt battery, a wiring harness and, once cleared of the circuit board and detector, it also provided him a platform to mount one of Zoran's treasured wrist watches.

Zoran owned perhaps a hundred watches, all mounted in a special glass and wood display cabinet in a room off his bedroom, a dressing room which also housed his clothes. Rolex, Tag Heuer, Omega, Patek Philippe... Jake had only heard of some of them and selected a mechanical watch, a Breitling, which he wound up before setting the time to match that of his Seamaster. He then removed the face glass and mounted it to the base of the smoke alarm using cable ties. Without a soldering iron, his task would have been difficult but a small workshop off the garage provided one as well as a workbench and lighting to mount some contacts. When the watch's hour hand reached half the distance between the six and the seven, it would touch a contact he'd soldered into the watch face. This would complete an electrical circuit and the resulting electrical current from the battery would heat the detonator and cause it to explode. So that the second and minute hands would not touch the contact, he'd carefully cut them at their bases.

They would continue to go around the face, but not touch the contact reserved for the hour hand.

Jake wiped his eyes with his sleeve and peered up at the underside of the truck.

The detonator sat on the underside of the smoke alarm platform, held in place with a cable tie. His task now was to mount a quantity of C4 against the truck body and press the detonator assembly into the malleable C4, where it would sit until the watch reached the appointed time and the hour hand completed the electrical circuit. The circuit was low voltage, so the probability of a spark and early detonation was low, but he knew there existed a margin for error given he was using an hour hand on a wrist watch. It was the best he could do.

Still watchful, Jake pulled the components out of his pack. He'd guessed on the amount of C4 to use. Eddie had done a special course when he was in the army, but even his experience had not given him a simple formula for estimating the amount they needed. In the end, Eddie handed over a good fist-sized piece and, as Jake went to go, he added half as much again. He pressed this into one of the main chassis rails behind the cabin, a place hidden from view by one of the two fuel tanks. The placement would direct much of the explosive force and shock wave away from the thick iron rail and push the prime mover up and into the tree line. That was Jake's theory anyway.

He pressed the crude detonation device into the C4 and then the nine volt battery its terminals outermost. He didn't like explosives and held his breath as he connected the battery up. He noted the time: 17:32. *Time to get back.*

♦

Approximately fifty-eight minutes later, as the hour hand on the watch mechanism touched the contact, there was a blinding flash as the C4 underwent a chemical reaction resulting in its explosion and an enormous shockwave pulsed up and out, blowing through the fuel tank and igniting the fuel inside.

Zoran, Valery and Boris were closest to the blast and the shock wave flung each of them like rag dolls about thirty feet beyond the gate, end over end. The prime mover lifted fifteen feet into the air, slammed into the trees lining the roadway and flattened dozens more within a forty foot radius.

As the truck crashed down to the ground, Andy and Tony floored the accelerators and the two SUVs speared through the gates, the gap in the roadway and past the cordon of trucks. Zoran, Boris and Valery were in no condition to see this happen.

The blast also stunned Gregor, but he raised his machine gun as the vehicles started to move. There was a loud crack as a super-sonic fifty caliber bullet entered Gregor's head behind his right ear and, packing an enormous amount of kinetic energy, it exploded his head like a ripe melon. Tosya came running up from the east fence line and aimed his pistol down the road. He never got to fire it as a second fifty caliber bullet entered his body just under his left armpit and blew his heart and lungs through a football-size exit wound on his right side of his body.

Boris was first to his feet. He couldn't hear anything, but somehow managed to pull out his cell phone and told his pilot to fly up to the house quickly, not knowing if he'd heard him or not. He helped Zoran to his feet and saw that the man was bleeding from multiple cuts on his face and from his right ear. He brought his own hand to his face and saw that he was also bleeding. Valery just sat on the ground shaking his head.

Marin, Alek and Yuri had just gathered with them, when the first of seven large explosions rocked the air and they took to the ground to avoid the blast and debris which rained upon them. Zoran held his head up to see as each successive explosion destroyed more of the house he'd called home for all these years. *Our money, my diamonds, personal papers, my cars, watch collection, clothes... My fucking son...*

He stood up as pieces of concrete, brickwork, wood and tiles flew about him. He shouted, 'Cunts!' several times before Valery pulled him down as another explosion shook the earth. Then night turned to day as a huge fire, fueled by liquefied petroleum gas and gasoline that Eddie had siphoned from the other vehicles, hungrily commenced to consume the house and everything within.

Chapter 68

The Fortress

Once clear of the trucks, Tony and Andy put on their NVGs enabling them to see the road as the devices enhanced the low light levels and revealed their front through a green glow. Tony reached speeds of almost one-eighty kph as he pushed the SUV to its limits along the gravel roadway.

Without night vision or headlights showing the way ahead, Jake in the passenger seat was on his own private terror ride and hung on tight to the hand hold above him. 'Easy Sens, they can't follow and we have to wait for the Frog at the bottom.'

'Still want to get down there, Luke. Until we are down there, we are still at risk of being blocked. I'm not walking out of here.'

'I'm right with you, Sens,' said Andy behind them.

Jake accepted their viewpoint and held on and watched as the Hind helicopter flew over their heads toward the Fortress.

'How long before they can get that airborne and after us?' asked Nikki.

'We have about five, maybe ten minutes and they'll be coming,' said Jake.

It was only two miles to the road and the tee intersection quickly approached. Tony seemed to leave the braking to the very last second before pushing the brake pedal hard and the massive anti-skid brake calipers pressed the huge brake pads hard against the rotors dropping the four ton vehicle's speed rapidly. Tony twitched the wheel to the right and, as the rear came around, planted his foot, putting the steering into opposite lock, the rear wheels scrabbling for traction. In a flash they were back on bitumen and Tony drove two hundred yards before pulling over to the shoulder. He put on his sidelights and removed the NVGs. Andy pulled in right behind them.

'You didn't even look,' chastised Jake.

'Didn't need to,' said Tony, tapping the NVGs on his head. 'These would've told me if anyone was on the road, assuming they had their lights on of course.' He smiled.

Jake turned round. 'Sorry you didn't get to see that, Marko. Quite a sight. You also missed the big bang as we blew the shit out of your Father's home and everything in it. All that money...'

Marko laughed, 'You made an incorrect assumption, Jake. One you will pay for. You'll see.'

'I don't think so, Marko.'

'The money. It wasn't my Father's. It belonged to everyone in the *vory*. You will find they have long memories.'

Jake looked at Tony, 'Whatever. We're a match for a bunch of old Russians, Marko, you will see.'

Tony saw movement in his mirror; a figure emerged from the trees, crossed to Andy's vehicle and climbed into the back seat through a rear door.

'Luke, we're all here. Let's go,' said Andy.

Tony hit a switch and twin xenon lights illuminated the road before them. He put the car in drive, pressed the 'M' button and accelerated down the road, building speed quickly and taking the first bend at 100 kph, fifty ks more than the advisory speed.

Jake had worked with the car's complicated Sat Nav. system for several weeks and spent a good part of their day going over the route to Aviano as well as contingencies. He omitted entering their destination into the system, feeling the computer voice would distract them and the system wouldn't always give them the best route. He intended to use a combination of the vehicle's system and the one on his cell phone to to get them to Aviano.

In the rear vehicle, Andy focused on keeping up with Tony. The Sat Nav. was on, but it simply tracked their progress toward Italy. He hoped he wouldn't need it.

Chapter 69

The Fortress

As the two BMWs disappeared from view, two Audi A8s appeared from the other direction leading to Pivka closely followed by a BMW 330i and a Mercedes CLK500. The lead driver and Boris' right-hand man, Igor, watched his Sat Nav. as the hidden intersection came up quickly. He stood on the brakes hard and the large Audi sedan pulled rapidly to a stop, kicking up gravel in a dramatic display of driving. The other three drivers that accompanied him on their dash from Gdansk were attentive and pulled their own cars up behind him. As he looked right, he could see a huge glow on the horizon. He planted his foot down on the gas rapidly accelerating up the narrow road which led up to the Fortress.

◆

The Hind helicopter hovered about one-hundred feet above the gate to the property. Boris raised his eyebrows at Zoran, who looked tired and defeated, a factor which would spread to them all if he didn't move to reverse it. He spoke into his cell phone, communicating with his helicopter pilot, 'Look,' he said, 'all the explosions have happened already.'

He heard the pilot and said, 'It's not too hot. I'm going to go in and stand where I want you to land okay?'

He ended the phone call just as Igor's vehicle came into view, followed by the three others. 'Zoran, come with me. Valery, organize the others, distribute the weapons and ammunition. We must get going, or we'll lose them.'

Boris walked through the gates looking up at the Hind gun ship and waving his arms. Zoran followed him. 'You got a plan. Boris?'

'First thing is to get rid of these fucking pilots. Piss weak cunts.' He smiled upwards and pointed to a suitable spot on the ground, about a hundred feet from the corner of what remained of the house. 'That's right, down here.'

The Hind flew over the fence line, about one-hundred feet up and descended into the area suggested by Boris, who opened the door to the cabin and went inside.

Zoran looked at his house and felt something he hadn't felt in a very long time, fear. A clenching in his gut. He checked his watch, one of his favorites, a Tissot. Perhaps only five minutes since his son had been driven away. He looked up to see one of the pilots being kicked out of the helicopter's cabin, literally.

'And give me that fucking helmet, you useless fuck.'

The second pilot opened the front cockpit hatch and jumped out before Boris could get there. He walked up and handed Boris his helmet, who said, 'Don't let me see you two again, you hear me?' He jumped down to the ground. 'Come Zoran, time for you to tell us what to do.'

They walked back through the gate and gathered the group of men. Zoran recognized Igor, a huge Belarusian with a large handlebar mustache, deep black eyes and a snake tattoo that curled around his face and culminated with the snake's open mouth right in the middle of his forehead. Zoran drew in a deep breath and spoke to them.

'Men, you see what has been done to us, to our *vory*. Americans have done this. Apart from my personal shame and the kidnapping of my son, these cunts have destroyed about ten billion Euros of our wealth. We cannot fail in this. We must catch them and we must kill them. If my Marko dies, then that is God's will. His return to me is now secondary to the death of the people who did this.

'Igor, thanks for coming so fast, you and one of the other cars head west into Italy along the toll road, the other two cars head North toward Ljubljana. Boris and I will head into the air and will give you further instructions once we determine where they are. Their plane flew to Rome, so I am assuming they will be heading across the border and we must be ready to intercept them as it will only become more difficult the further they travel.' He looked at his lieutenant. 'Have you sorted things out?'

'We are good,' said Valery, 'but we have lost Gregor and Tosya, a sniper they left behind to cover their escape, now long gone.' He looked at his boss. 'These men are ex-military, Zoran. Are you sure we can do this? I know this is your son, but we have lost so much already...'

'Bullshit, military or not, we go,' said Zoran, his eyes blazed with fury. 'With or without you, we will make these men pay. Igor, you go with Valery here. Alek, you will go in the other Audi with Roman driving. Yuri, you go with Hans in the BMW. Marin will go with Jorge in the Mercedes.'

'Okay,' said Boris, 'you all have my cell phone number, no?' The men nodded. 'I'll give you further details as soon as we spot them. Zoran, let's go.'

Chapter 70

Slovenia, heading west

About ten kilometers away from the Russians, the two BMWs hammered along the twisty road, lights ablaze. 'How far to the highway?' asked Tony.

'Roughly seven,' replied Jake, referring to kilometers, the unit of measure in most of Europe. The BMWs measured speed and distance used Kilometers and they had trained in Montana to dismiss their thoughts about miles, even the temptation to convert, so they could focus on the task.

The passengers hung on as Tony drove through the twists and turns, accelerating flat out from the exits of each corner then putting all his skill into selecting his braking point and then driving smoothly through and out of each bend. Marko struggled to stay upright with his hands cuffed behind him and only a simple rear seat belt to hold him in place.

Jake found the gray plastic duct tape from where he'd placed it in the glove box and passed it to Pat. He turned on his throat mike so they could all hear. 'Sens., slow down a touch, we need to tape Marko to the seat, stop him moving so much, same for the other Russian with Spider. Bad for him and for us. Pat can you do this?'

'Sure,' said Pat as Tony eased off the accelerator.

'Spider, you copy?'

'Loud and clear, Luke.'

'Frogman, you got tape there?'

'Sure, Luke. Was goin' to ask about it. Man's flappin' about all over the place. None too good for me in the back, either.'

'We'll be on a smoother track soon, the highway North and then a toll road West into Italy.'

A few minutes passed and they saw the glow of the lamps which illuminated the highway ahead. To their left they saw the small town of Divača and they could see no people out and only a few cars on the road. 'Okay, Tony, head under the highway and take the first left. Slow down as we head through here as we don't want to attract attention.'

Once on the other side of the highway, they could see more of Divača and skirted along its eastern boundary heading for the loop that would gain them entrance to the highway and the route north.

Jake looked around and saw Andy, fifty yards back, maintaining a constant distance. Tony found the loop, following the signs to Ljubljana, and they were soon up on the highway, travelling North.

'Coming up is an off ramp, should say Sežana, about five hundred out.'

Tony saw the Hind helicopter first, hovering a few feet above the roadway, blocking their exit. Then, they could all see it and Zoran, framed in the doorway, a machine pistol in his hands, which was pointed in their direction.

Tony noted the guard rails either side of the two lane road and, although he saw a small gap they could have taken around the Hind gunship to get onto the off ramp, he floored the accelerator and Andy followed suit.

Tony spoke, 'Why didn't he fire?'

'Doesn't want to hit his Precious,' replied Jake.

'Fuck you,' said Marko.

'At some point he's going to have to,' said Tony.

'What's our contingency, Luke?' asked Andy.

'Working on it buddy.'

Chapter 71

Slovenia

Zoran jumped down to the roadway as Boris touched the Hind's undercarriage onto the bitumen and closed the main door to the cabin. Two cars stopped unable to exit the highway and a man emerged from the front vehicle. Despite seeing Zoran's weapon, he shouted in Slovenian, 'Get out of the way. What are you doing?'

In reply, Zoran fired several rounds from his machine pistol over the man's head and he quickly got back into his car.

Boris cracked open a window. 'Zoran, forget them, come, we have to go.'

Zoran moved to the front of the Hind, opened the gunner's door on the port-side of the machine and got in. Boris started to bring the rotors up to speed as Zoran buckled himself in and closed the door. He pulled on his helmet, a size too big for him, but it had the comms connections and enabled them both to talk over the noise of the engines.

'Boris, let's go.'

Boris brought up the speed of the main rotor until the machine roared and the twin Isotov turbine engines took them quickly upwards into the night sky, Boris kept a careful watch for power lines until they gained altitude and then took off after the two BMWs.

'We are going to leave them alone for a while, Zoran.'

'No, we need to press home an attack, before they get too far.'

'No, we need to give them some space, to relax, become complacent.'

'We should get to the next exit and make them take it.'

'Zoran, sorry my friend but I disagree. If we do that, they will remain suspicious, may even find a way to avoid the route we want them to take. No, I will gain some height, where we can watch them without being watched.'

When the time comes, we will make our move and we will do what needs to be done.'

'They have Petr too.'

'I know.'

'I couldn't tell which car contained Marko.'

'I know.'

'I think I want to kill this Luke man, more than I want Marko back.'

'That's good, my friend, let's do it. Call Igor and Valery. Make sure they know their part in this.'

Chapter 72

On highway to Ljubljana

They'd travelled a further five kilometers from the last exit ramp. The traffic was light and Tony and Andy hit speeds in excess of 180 kph. A couple of minutes had gone by since seeing the Hind gunship.

'Okay,' said Jake, 'a big intersection coming up. Our second chance to head to Sežana and link up with the main toll road.'

'Looks clear to me, Luke,' said Tony looking ahead.

'Yes, okay take the off ramp. It loops around. Take it cautiously. If we see that Hind gunship, we find cover. I think the next time we see him, he'll fire upon us, son or no son.'

The vehicles looped around and then under the highway and the two BMWs were soon able to pick up speed.

'Sens. take the next left.'

A hidden tee intersection came up and Tony turned. The road looped right toward the West and straightened.

'Three hundred meters, there's a switchback, said Jake. 'A dead-end to the left. Head up there, I want to see who's following.'

The five men stood outside the ticking BMWs, Nikki and Stefan also got out, but remained by the vehicles to keep an eye on Marko and

Petr. They were well trussed into the seats, but Jake wasn't taking any risks.

'Listen for a second,' said Jake.

The four ex Special Forces men adopted a strange pose as they remembered their training and opened their mouths to better enable sound waves to be detected.

'There,' said Eddie and he looked upward. 'Up there, I am sure of it.'

'I agree,' said Andy.

'Must've turned off his nav. lights. They're in a military helicopter, so not surprising,' said Tony.

'So, he knows where we are,' said Pat. 'No matter. We destroyed his capacity to follow us by vehicle when we blew his house to bits and all the cars in it.'

'I know,' said Jake. 'But, I want to check if he managed to bring in some reinforcements. I just don't know where the nearest chapter of his gang is, *vory*, whatever. Looks like he's by himself at the moment.'

'My research told me very little,' said Pat. 'I think his nearest pals are in Germany or Russia.'

'Okay, stay here,' said Jake. Be prepared to move quickly or defend our position. I'm just going to head up that ridge over there to get a view of what's coming. Stay alert. If there's nothing along in fifteen, we keep going. Once we cross that border, he's going to be reluctant to follow as the Italians won't like military gunships coming over the border.'

Chapter 73

Slovenia

Jake walked down off the ridge to the roadway and rejoined his men. Jake saw them look to him for direction and said, 'No cars following, nothing, just the strong feeling that Zoran is up there, watching.'

'Let's get going then,' said Pat.

'Before we do, remove the cover from Marko's head and give him some water. Let the other one, Petr, go. We don't need him anymore.'

Eddie and Pat attended to Marko and allowed him out of the vehicle still cuffed and Eddie made it clear he would pull the trigger on his pistol if he tried anything. Pat gave him some water from a flask. Through all his, Marko kept quiet, but couldn't hide the hurt and anger he felt. They sat him back in the SUV and reattached his seat belt.

Andy and Nikki attended to Petr and he stepped out of the car on unsteady legs and regarded the men with contempt.

Jake came over to him. 'You're free to go, Petr. Make your own way from here.'

Petr turned around. 'The hand cuffs?'

'They stay, I am sorry.'

Andy watched the man in his mirror as they drove away. 'Be an interesting conversation with whoever finds him.' He relaxed back into his seat, Eddie sat next to him with Nikki and Stefan in the back; they were no longer encumbered, all on the same side, at least in this vehicle. Andy visualized getting aboard the jet, just over an hour to their destination.

'So why'd you get out, Spider?' said Eddie. 'If there was one man, apart from Luke, I thought'd grow old in the life, it was you...'

'I guess I gained perspective after a while,' replied Andy after a moment.

'Perspective's a good word for it.'

'This helped guide my decision too.' Andy lifted his long hair on the right side, revealing a three inch scar behind an ear that Eddie could see was only half there. 'Fucked up my movie star looks too,' he chuckled.

Nikki was following the conversation. 'So, how'd you get hurt, Spider?'

Andy thought for a moment. 'I was coming to the end of my second tour in Afghanistan. We'd rotated back to the States at the end of '02. Lost quite a few men in that first tour, too many. Generals and politicians were still getting to grips with the enemy, fucking everyone around. We just wanted to take the fight to them, but you know how it was, never committed enough to the enemy, wanted to fight them from a distance.

Eddie nodded. 'Ain't that so true. Can't substitute men on the ground with a drone piloted by some nineteen year old kid in Utah, doing his eight hours and then back into the real world.'

'In my rotation back home, we got some rest and I met a girl, Kylie, sweet southern gal from Virginia.' He smiled. 'We were together for about three months, just started to feel like there was another life out there for me. And then we were given orders to report back to the Middle East again.

'I could've got out; hell I could've got a training role. I was super fit back then. But the call of the Corps was strong, you know that Frog, and my buddies were all going? I decided one more time.'

'I know that feeling,' said Eddie.

◆

In the front vehicle, Tony slowed to the speed limit as they approached the outskirts of Sežana.

'This road tracks around and bypasses Sežana,' said Jake. 'You can see it there on the left. Stay in this lane.'

Tony drove within the speed limit. 'No customs or border crossing?'

'No, there used to be, but all part of the Eurozone now,' said Jake. 'Ahead is a loop that will take us around and into Italy. Stay in the right lane and follow the signs for a place called Fernetti.'

As they passed a sign which signaled one-thousand meters to the toll road ahead, Jake clicked his throat mike. 'Spider?'

'Yo, Luke.'

'Come on up and take point, okay?'

'Sure thing.'

Andy pushed down on the accelerator and quickly overtook the other SUV and slotted in front, about one-hundred meters ahead.

Jake checked the time on the dash, 07:42 and checked their speed, one-twenty kph. He looked behind and saw several cars behind, but the traffic was light. They were over the speed limit, but not by much.

'Tunnel coming up,' said Andy.

'See it,' said Tony.

As he entered the tunnel, Andy noted a car in the breakdown lane on his right, flashers blinking. He was going to call it in and thought better of it. The tunnel curved around to the left, well lit from hundreds of yellow strip lights in the ceiling above. After a further three hundred meters or so, he saw another car in the breakdown lane, no flashers. Another Audi.

'Another Audi A8, Sensei, in breakdown lane, two hundred ahead.'

Just passed an A8, thought Tony. 'Caution, Spider.'

'I'm watching Sens.'

Jake was listening, but couldn't initially see as the front BMW obscured the Audi from view. Too soon however, they saw the second Audi as it quickly accelerated to match Andy's speed, still traveling in the breakdown lane.

'Time for speed, Spider,' said Tony, as he planted his foot and the BMW surged forward.

Andy responded, but the big Audi saloon matched him for pace. Jake looked over and saw they were doing one-fifty kph and rising.

Tony checked his mirror and noted the first Audi was also moving, its hazard lights still flashing. 'Other one's coming too, Luke.'

Jake quickly checked his weapons and looked up as a man's arm appeared out of the window from the passenger seat of the Audi in front. The arm held a machine pistol. 'Spider, look out,' he called.

Tony tensed and slowed. They watched as rounds struck the rear of the BMW and the Audi surged forward striking its rear left quarter. As the Audi moved over, they saw Andy's run flat tire on the rear right shred and disintegrate and sparks flew out of the rear as the wheel rim impacted the concrete roadway.

'Pat, get the rocket launcher ready,' said Jake.

Pat reached over the back seat, noting the smug satisfaction on Marko's face as he watched things play out. He grabbed the bulky launcher and one of the twelve rockets they had in a case. He quickly armed the device as Eddie had shown him earlier.

'Spider, get out of the way,' called Tony.

'Sorry, guys, I'm out of it,' came the response.

They watched as the powerful Audi surged again and Andy was powerless to prevent the left rear of the SUV being pushed forward. He turned his steering to compensate, but he suddenly reached a tipping point and speed did the rest, the left front of the SUV digging into the concrete roadway and they were airborne, their speed just shy of one-hundred-and-sixty kph – a hundred miles an hour in the imperial measure.

Jake saw this happen, but his thoughts were on their immediate threat, the Audi A8 to their rear. 'Pull over, Tony,' he said, but Tony had already planted his foot onto the brake pedal and the SUV dropped speed rapidly and they came to sudden halt, still in the right-most lane. Tony was first out of the car and, seeing the Audi still accelerating toward him, he brought his machine gun up and sighted along it. He squeezed off five rounds, noting them hit the front of the car, glancing off the bonnet. This didn't slow them so he gave it a sustained burst, noting the distance, two-hundred meters, one-fifty, one-hundred. Several of his rounds smashed through the windscreen, yet the vehicle kept coming.

Jake stood on the other side of the BMW and watched the Audi approaching rapidly. When it was only fifty meters or so away, he pressed the trigger of the RPG launcher, aiming for the roadway to the Audi's front. *Wish I'd had time to test fire this,* he thought as the rocket ignited and burst out of the tube in a blinding flash.

I'm dead, thought Tony and saw Jake's rocket explode in front of the car almost upon him or so it seemed. He brought his hand up, as though this would somehow protect him from the impact, when the Audi suddenly left the roadway and turned on its side. Tony felt the air move above him as the four ton vehicle's underside passed only feet from his body, before crashing into the wall and the guardrail behind him in a shower of sparks.

'Pat, stay in the vehicle and watch him,' said Jake, pointing to

Marko, as he turned and headed up the tunnel to attend to the other threat. He heard a screech of brakes and he saw in his periphery a mid-eighties Volvo Estate going past to his left, its wheels on full lock, its driver on daydream. The Volvo glanced off the side of the Audi which had come to rest after turning one-hundred-and-eighty degrees, and careened into the back of the other BMW which lay on its right side, some thirty meters distant.

Jake broke into a run, his PYa pistol in his right hand, his left checking his pockets for a spare clip, feeling one in his left pants pocket.

'Spider, Frog, talk to me over.'

Nothing.

Jake quickened his pace and, as he went past the crashed Audi, he noticed movement and a weapon being pointed in his direction. He knew Tony was behind him and barely registered the threat as several rounds from Tony thudded into Boris' men, Hans and Marin, in the front seats. He focused on his front and saw that two men had emerged from the first Audi which had stopped side on, perhaps fifty meters past the fallen BMW.

Rounds buzzed past Jake's head as both Valery and Igor brought up their machine-pistols and started to fire, but he managed to make the rear of the BMW and gained some cover. He looked back and saw Tony standing in the middle of the roadway firing aimed shots toward the Audi.

'Cover me, Sens.' called Jake and he walked around the BMW and started to jog towards the two men. Holding the pistol in one hand, he judged his shots and emptied the first clip in two-shot bursts, instinctively adjusting his aim as he saw the rounds strike metal and flesh. He saw rounds hit the man nearest to him, the driver, and watched him slouch forward over the Audi's front door. Igor was dead.

As the final round was fired, the pistol's slide clicked back and Jake ejected the spent magazine and brought up a full one with his left hand, sending the slide forward and inserting a round into the breach. The remaining man stood behind the Audi, on the passenger side, firing a machine pistol in his left hand, but Jake saw he'd been hit in the shoulder and the rounds were going wide. He broke into a run, firing the same two-shot burst at the man. Several struck him in the chest and, as he leaped across the Audi's bonnet, he fired two shots into the man's head.

He looked at the man on the roadway, registering muscle through a tight blue silk shirt and tattoos on his hand, neck and face. As if he needed any confirmation about who they were. Valery was now dead as well.

'Coming back, Sens. All clear.'

As Jake walked back to the wrecked BMW, he could already hear sirens. Eddie's head was visible through the passenger window and Jake saw he had a deep gash on his head. Nikki was already on the ground, stunned, but her eyes locked onto Jake's and he could see she was okay.

'Who's hurt?'

'Uncle is trapped; he's conscious, but his legs are pinned by the driver's seat. Andy's not moving. The airbags saved us, no doubt.'

'Thanks Nik. Could you go back and drive the other car over here?'

As Nikki headed away, Jake looked more closely at the BMW, but could hardly recognize it anymore. He thought back and recalled seeing it tumble once, twice and then he'd been focused on the Audis.

Tony, climbed up and went inside the cabin, he threw out some bags, their gear and weapons. He called out, 'Luke, give Frog a hand.'

Jake hoisted himself up onto the passenger side and looked through the front window frame, the glass no longer there. He saw that every airbag had deployed and Jake could see how the curtain airbags around the doors had done their job. The roof was crushed and Eddie held Andy around his chest, pushing him up toward the gap. Jake reached down and they carefully pushed and pulled until he was out of the wreckage. Jake could tell he was breathing, but his left arm was broken, his wrist hanging limply. The other BMW drew alongside and Jake carried Andy to the passenger side and opened the door.

As Jake put him inside on the passenger seat, he opened his eyes. 'Hey, Luke.'

'Hey, Spider. Everyone's fine, buddy. But we are now down to one vehicle. You stay here, okay?'

Nikki came around to the door. 'You stayin', Nik?'

'Yes, Luke. I will stay here with Uncle. We'll be okay. You finish what you started. Head back into Slovenia, go the long way round.'

'What about Zoran?'

'We'll see how this ends, first. I have an Aunt in Italy and will head there if I need to.'

'Right,' said Jake. 'Thanks for everything. Couldn't have done so much without you. Go and look after him.'

'See you, Luke.'

The sirens were getting louder now and Jake closed the rear hatch. 'Sensei and Frog, leave most of the gear, but bring the gun and belt ammo, okay?' Tony and Eddie continued to load their gear into the rear of the BMW and Jake turned as they passed the Audi, pockmarked with bullet holes. Pat was driving and pulled up alongside.

'There are too many of us now for the one car,' said Pat.

Jake looked around. Marko was still strapped into his seat trying his best to look unconcerned. Andy was sitting in the front seat of the BMW holding his arm. Blood trickled down his face. 'Good idea, Pat. Help Spider he can go with you.'

He walked to the rear of the BMW and looked in the bags until he found one of the first aid kits they'd brought with them. He addressed Tony and Eddie. We'll follow you in the Audi. Head back the way we came, the alternate route through Sežana and Branik to the border. It's longer, but I think the way forward is going to be difficult for us.'

'Okay, Luke,' said Eddie.

Jake opened the kit and extracted a field dressing before passing it to Eddie. 'Here, press this against your head, Frog. I'll clean you up a bit when we stop. Stay in the back and keep an eye on Marko.'

He walked forward and could see the tunnel exit and the blue lights of police and ambulance. *Not long to go.* 'Let's go ladies.' He climbed into the back of the Audi with Andy.

Tony started the remaining BMW and performed a quick three point turn. Dozens of cars had now formed back through the tunnel and many people stood out of their vehicles to watch the display before them.

Tony pressed the horn and lights blazing, drove back the way they'd came, along the service lane, with Pat following in the Audi. A gap formed in the traffic and Tony saw a break in the guard rail. He turned around and locked eyes with Marko. 'Nice try, Marko. We're still here.' He winked.

Back onto the east bound lane, he increased speed and rapidly took them back the way they'd come, crossing back into Slovenia, past Sežana and north.

Chapter 74

Slovenia-Italy border

Five minutes had elapsed since Luke's team had entered the tunnel and Boris took the helicopter down as Zoran tried to call Igor and Valery on their cell phones.

'No answer,' said Zoran.

'Maybe, they have no signal.'

'No, the phones ring out.'

'There!'

Zoran looked and saw one of the BMWs emerge from the entrance to the tunnel.

'Take her down, Boris. Land on the road near the western exit.'

The rotors still spinning, Zoran cracked open his hatch and climbed out onto the ground. He ran forward and negotiated his way along the embankment until he could see into the tunnel. An ambulance was parked next to one of the BMWs which lay on its side. The police and fire service had yet to arrive and he could hear more sirens coming in from Trieste.

His cell phone rang and he answered it. 'Back soon, Boris.'

'It's not Boris, Zoran. You should check out caller id.'

Zoran didn't respond.

'Good try, but not good enough. Ciao.'

Zoran put his phone in his pocket. He saw the woman, Seztac, talking to one of the emergency services workers and a plan started to form. He walked into the tunnel and noted with sadness the bodies of his men, saw the double tap to Valery's head, execution style, the roadway awash with their blood. He quickened his pace.

Chapter 75

Slovenia

In the back of the Audi, Jake cleaned up the gash on Andy's head and applied a field dressing and bandage to keep it there. Andy managed a smile. 'And I thought we were home and hosed.'

'I know. Zoran must have called in some extras; got me wondering what else is out there for us. Here, can you lift this arm?'

Andy held his broken wrist up with his good arm and winced. 'No pain like a broken bone, is there? Worse than gunshot I reckon.'

Jake made a sling out of a bandage and he placed this over Andy's head and adjusted it until it was fully supporting his broken wrist. They were going past Sežana again and he clicked his throat mike. 'Sensei, Frog, you reading me, over?'

Thirty seconds went by with no response. 'Pat, give them a flash of the lights, okay?'

Pat flashed the Audi's xenon lights, something Tony wouldn't miss. 'Roger Luke, what's up?'

'Take the next exit, Sens., and find us a place to pull over. We need to work out a route out of here, you copy?'

'Roger that.'

A few minutes went by and Tony signaled his exit. He

proceeded down the off ramp and Pat followed. A truck stop came up and the two cars went off the road and pulled up alongside each other. 'Pat, while I talk to Sens, could you get out and keep a watch?'

Pat picked up his pistol and they both got out. He went around to watch the road while Jake went over to Tony's window. 'Gorizia, Sens?'

'Yeah, thinking the same. It's longer, but the roads are all sealed. There is a road back there leading to Dutov something or other. If we head to there, we will be on a road to Branik which takes us to the border at Gorizia.'

Jake checked phone and brought up a map until he had it, 'This one?' he pointed to a town called Dutovlje. 'I think the j is silent.'

His phone rang and he looked, it was Zoran's number.

Chapter 76

Slovenia

Nikki was furious with herself. The ambulance had just arrived and one of the two paramedics was inside the BMW assessing Stefan's injuries. They were going to need the fire services to extract his feet from the seat which had collapsed on them. The other paramedic was talking to Nikki, who was explaining what had happened, but her Italian was basic and she'd resorted to English.

'So, there was gun fight?' said the man.

'Yes, there was another vehicle, a Mercedes…' she looked to her left and saw Zoran Kovak, some twenty meters away pointing a machine pistol in her direction. The paramedic followed her gaze and flinched. He raised his hands and started to edge away.

'You,' said Zoran in English. He fired a burst of rounds over Nikki's head into the tunnel wall. A number of people screamed and went down to the ground or retreated back to their cars. He walked toward her. 'Are coming with me.'

Five minutes later, and she now sat in the main cabin of the Hind as it flew over Sežana and looked across at Zoran. He was very disheveled and blood had scabbed in a number of places on his face and hands. He was dirty and no doubt tired, but his hands were steady, one holding his machine pistol in her direction, the other his cell phone. She felt the helicopter descend and, presently, they touched down in the middle of a parking lot of a small shopping center. Boris shut down the engines and as the rotors ground out their last turns, he got out of the pilot's seat and opened up the cabin door.

Nikki looked at the man as he took off his helmet. Like Zoran, his shirt was no longer tucked into his pants which were ripped in several places and he also sported a number of cuts and abrasions. He saw Nikki looking at him and attempted to pat down his hair. 'Here, give me the gun,' said Boris in Russian. 'Let's see what this Luke has to say for himself now.'

Zoran passed over the machine pistol and climbed down onto the asphalt of the parking lot. He checked his watch and saw that it was after nine pm. One or two cars were visible but it was otherwise quiet, everyone tucked away in their homes. 'Where are we?'

'A small place, not sure, just east of Sežana.'

Zoran checked his phone and brought up the number for the man he knew as Luke. He pressed call.

'Zoran?' came the man's response.

'Luke.'

'What do you want? We're kind of busy here, making plans to head north where we can catch a flight to the States.'

'Are you sure that's what you want to do?'

'Hey, if your boy had been a good citizen, none of this would've happened'

'I want him back.'

'He's non-negotiable now, Zoran. A US Federal warrant has been issued for his arrest for the murder of Danielle Fisher. You wouldn't want me to ignore my civic duty now, eh?'

'I have something to trade.' He put the phone on speaker and passed it to Nikki.

'You have nothing I want, Zoran. Hey, why don't you come

over to the States for the trial? I'm sure you'll be welcome, you and all your *vory* pals or whatever you Russians call your gang bangers.'

Nikki took a deep breath. 'Luke, it's me. I am sorry.'

Jake was silent for several seconds, thinking through the options. 'It's okay, Nik. We'll get you back. Put Zoran back on.'

She handed the cell phone over. 'I repeat, Mr. Luke. I want my son back,' said Zoran.

'Give me five minutes and I'll call you back.'

Chapter 77

Slovenia

Jake had moved away from the group to have his conversation out of earshot from Marko. He went back to the BMW and motioned Eddie out. They walked in front of the BMW until they could speak in private.

'Zoran's got Nikki.'

'At the Tunnel?'

'Looks like it, while she was waiting with her uncle. I need to find out what the others are thinking. And you.'

Eddie thought for a second and then looked at Jake. 'You know my answer, buddy. We never leave anyone behind and not for a dirt ball like that kid in there. Mr. Fisher will understand.'

'Okay. Go back and watch him while I talk to the others. Ask them to come and see me.'

When the others had gathered around, Jake took them through his conversation with Zoran.

'We should've foreseen this, Luke,' said Andy.

'Yeah, I know, but we couldn't just leave Stefan there alone and she wanted to stay. Yes, hindsight is wonderful, should've foreseen the Audis in the Tunnel too.'

'Alright, this isn't helpful,' said Pat. 'It's getting late and we have Spider to take care of. I take it we are all in agreement that we exchange Marko for Nikki?'

One by one, they signaled their agreement. Pat looked at each of them in turn. 'Okay, I'm pretty certain they don't know about the safe house. I say we head over there, get some food and rest. Jake, you call Zoran back. Tell him yes and we'll give him the time and place in the morning. I suggest you say to expect a text on his cell at three am and to plan for an exchange at six. That should give us time to formulate a plan so that we don't get our asses burned.'

Jake pulled out his cell phone and pressed call.

'Yes,' came the response.

'Okay, we'll make the exchange.'

'Good, I'll call you back soon with the details.'

'No, Zoran. That is not how this is going to work. You want your son back, we do this my way. You are in no position to dictate how this will go down.'

Several seconds passed and Jake could hear muffled conversation, Zoran's hand over the cell phone mike.

'Okay, where and when?'

'We'll send you a text at three in the morning, for a rendezvous at six. Have you hurt Ms. Seztak?'

'No, of course not.'

'Let me talk to her.'

Zoran put the cell phone on speaker and held it to Nikki so she could speak. 'Hello Luke,' she managed.

'Nikki. We'll come for you in the morning. Are you hurt?'

'No, I am fine...'

Zoran took the phone back.

'See, all is good.'

'You touch her in any way, Zoran and your boy gets the same. Tit for fucking tat. You hear me?'

'I am honorable man, Mr. Luke. You offend me.'

'You have no concept of honor. We'll be in touch.' Jake ended the call and walked back to the vehicles. Pat was sitting on the Audi's fender. 'Pat, you know the way from here to the safe house?'

'Yes, I think so.'

'Right, you lead the way.'

The men got back into the vehicles and Pat drove off, with Tony following closely in the BMW.

Chapter 78

Aviano Airbase

James and Paul had been confined in the Cessna, which was parked in one of the hangars at the airbase. Although they obtained permission to fly to and land at the former WWI airbase, the US-led NATO administration had given them a cool reception and had told them not to leave the airplane.

Paul reclined in one of the club chairs and had just called his wife in Seattle; James could tell from Paul's side of the conversation that she was not pleased at his extended absence. The money they were earning was good, very good, and they had promised each other a break from work when they got back to the States, some time they could spend with their families. James looked at the options to get home using his iPad. The distance to New York was just under seven-thousand kilometers, a full one-thousand more than the range of the business jet. They'd refueled at Rome airport, but had used some of that on the short flight north.

'I think we should aim for Dublin,' said James.

'Sounds good. They should be here by now. How far is it to Slovenia?'

'I agree. It's only an hour or so to the border.'

'Why don't you call Jake, find out what's going on?'

The two men looked up as a man came up the steps into the cabin. He was dressed in a flight suit, which suggested he was US Air Force. His longer hair suggested otherwise.

'Hi. I take it you are James Reilly and Paul Lawson?'

'That's us,' said Paul. 'And you are?'

'George Simmons, I work for the FBI.'

'You got some id?' said James.

The man put his overnight bag down and opened a side pocket from which he extracted a small leather-bound id case. He tossed it to James who opened it to reveal an official looking badge of the Federal Bureau of Investigation and an identity card which confirmed the man's status as a Special Agent.

'You here for same reason we are?' said James.

'Yes,' said George. 'Twenty four hours ago, I was in Seattle going through my case load. Next minute, I'm in Vegas. Now, I'm here, wherever here is.'

'Why don't you take a load off and tell us all about it.'

Chapter 79

Slovenia

Even though Pat was certain their location was safe, the team had agreed to a two on four off roster and Jake felt a little safer knowing that Tony was outside keeping watch and would call in if they came under any sort of threat. It was just after two and Jake sat in the kitchen with Pat going over options. Earlier, they had crudely reset Andy's arm and splinted it; he now had some pain relief and was sleeping in one of the bedrooms. Eddie reclined on the sofa in the lounge room. The team had been going for more than twenty-four hours and they'd all eaten well from the ground beef that Pat had fashioned into a pasta sauce using the tomatoes and onions they'd found in the pantry.

Earlier, Jake had called James and Paul to give them an update. They'd made it clear that they were anxious to be moving and Jake had promised that they would meet them at Aviano within twenty-four hours. The surprise had been the presence of Special Agent Simmons, who filled them in on their witness, Miroslav, and how they had caught him and persuaded him to testify. They'd all felt the pain at having detained Marko, only to face the prospect that he would soon be free and back with his father. This pain was reflected in the reactions from Simmons and the pilots when Jake told them what had happened on the border and their current plans to exchange the boy in several hours.

'As you say, Jake,' said James in closing, 'you have no choice but to exchange Marko for the woman. We'll be here, give us a call if there are further problems. We can fly at one hour's notice.'

Marko sat on a chair in the corner of the kitchen and was chained to it. Despite his discomfort, his head bobbed as he fought to stay awake.

'You know we aren't going to stop, Marko?' said Jake. 'There is nowhere in this world you can hide.'

Marko looked up and tried his best to look tough. 'My Father is very influential; it will be you who will be looking over your shoulder. They will never forgive the destruction of all that money.'

'That's bullshit Marko and you know it. The *vory* has billions more. You won't get to spend any of it and will be in a US prison within months, I guarantee it.'

'Leave him here,' said Pat. 'We need to work out a place to get Nikki back.'

The two men got up and went into the dining room. Jake got his laptop out of his gear sack and powered it up. One of Pat's people had set it up and had established the necessary connections for it to work over mobile telephony in Slovenia. He put the dongle into the usb port and waited for a few moments for the network to establish a connection. He opened a browser window and was pleased to see the familiar Google come up as a home page. 'Nice when things work properly,' he said.

'Yes, my people are good at what they do. What are you thinking?'

'Well, we need to keep that helicopter out of the loop and I'm thinking a bridge, somewhere with a natural barrier, like a river, where we can protect our side and control the exchange. The more open it is, the less chance Zoran can ambush us. It also needs to be close by.'

Pat recalled reading about the salt works south of Portorož. 'I think there is a reasonable sized river south of Portorož, where they still make salt, the traditional way.'

Jake brought up Google maps and, sure enough, there was a bridge over the Dragonja River. He did some more searching and found some photos. 'Yes, this looks like a spot we can use.' He checked his Seamaster, 02:25. 'Why don't you get some sleep? I'll relieve Sensei and call Zoran.'

Chapter 80

Divača Airstrip, Slovenia

The rented Mercedes and BMW were parked on the grass next to the Antonov. After the last call with Jake, Zoran had called in the remaining men, just Alek, Yuri, Roman and Marin, the only one of his men left he reflected sadly. They decided to spend the night aboard Boris's plane while they awaited instructions about the exchange.

He'd also had another call from the police chief, Novak, wanting to know what had gone down at Zoran's home, asking him how he was to explain the bodies found outside and give an explanation to his superiors about the fire, which was still being battled by no less than six fire service tenders. Zoran had told him to go fuck himself and to think up his own explanation. And if he didn't like that response then he would find a new Police Chief. Novak had exploded at this and reminded Zoran that it was he who personally provided protection so that he could operate. Zoran had pulled out his notebook and relayed the number of Novak's bank account in Zurich and the amount currently in his account. A simple call to a journalist, eager for a scoop and his game was over. Novak ended the call and said he would cover for him.

Nikki sat alone at the rear of the cabin. She was not tied up, but one of the Russians, a young man she'd heard addressed as Marin, sat about ten feet away and he remained vigilant while the others slept or tried to. She had contemplated escape, but there'd just been no opportunity and there were four men between her and the cabin exit at the front. She trusted that Jake Walker would come for her, but the real shame of it all was that Marko would again be free, after all their hard work. She closed her eyes and tried to get some rest.

The shrill ring tone of Zoran's cell phone stirred them all and she heard a command in Russian, followed by Zoran's voice in English. 'Yes, this is me.' He got up and went out of the cabin.

'First,' said Jake, 'if I even smell that fucking gunship of yours, I will personally put a bullet in your son's head. You got that?'

'Sure, sure, no problems. We will drive car.'

'No traps, no ambush, no bullshit, Zoran. We just want the woman and you can have your son back in exchange. Then we both walk away, agreed?'

'Yes, but same goes for you.'

'Right. There is a bridge over the Dragonja River, just South of the small village of Seca and North of the airport. I want you to arrive at the bridge at six am and drive in from the town of Sečovlje.' Jake spelled it out for him. 'You got that?'

'I think so.'

'Don't think, Zoran, know it or your boy will come with us to receive justice in America and you can do what you like with Nikki Seztac. It hurts me to even think of exchanging him, but I am a soldier, as you have witnessed, and we never leave one of our own.'

'Okay.'

'Your task is simple. We'll be on the North side of the bridge with your boy at six am. You are to arrive on the South side of the bridge dead on six o'clock and to approach from Sečovlje or the exchange won't happen. If I see anything out of the ordinary, you will not get your boy and I will hold you personally responsible for the safety of Ms. Seztac, in any event.'

'If you agree with all this, we will see you at six am shortly.'

'Okay, we'll be there,' said Zoran and he ended the call.

He walked back to the plane and went inside. Boris was sitting in the nearest seat, apparently asleep, and he tapped him on the leg. 'Boris, come outside, we need to talk.'

Zoran went out and sat on the bottom step while the older man came down and sat beside him.

'Boris, thank you.' Zoran paused for almost a minute, sharing the silence and Boris was content to let him find his words. 'I am so sorry about your men, and mine for that matter. Words are insufficient I know. I am ashamed and I grieve their loss and the circumstances around how this has happened.'

Boris turned and looked at the man he had known since their days in the Gulag. 'We all make mistakes, my friend. It is a wise man who learns from them. I know he is your son, but your love for him has blinded you, and your allegiance to our *vory*.'

'No, never. You know this.'

'No I don't. You know it is true. I have a son too, Mischa, so I know something of your own personal anguish, but Marko has cost us much. And the American...'

'Yes, there is the money.'

The older man looked up at the moon above them and paused before he spoke. 'If we put it in the banks, there is a high chance it will be stolen from us anyway. Bankers are the worst sort.' Boris cleared his throat and spat at the ground. 'At least we have allegiance to each other. Bankers would steal from their own family. So, yes, it was a lot of money, but there is always a risk, wherever we put it. We have enough money elsewhere. You know this, so you will be forgiven its loss.'

'I just spoke with the American. We will exchange the woman for Marko at six am.' Zoran looked at his watch and could discern the dial in the moonlight, showing the time to Boris. 'Just over two hours from now.'

'You know that Marko will have to answer for his actions.'

'Answer? How?'

'Not for me to say. When you return, we'll fly to Germany to meet with Andrei. We have a job for you there, but you need to know that they are not happy with how your son's behavior has been viewed.'

'Yes, I understand. I think I have known for some time that his penchence for violence would be his downfall.'

'Your time here is over, Zoran, and we are bringing in a new team to take what you have built to a new level. This American, this Luke, which I don't believe is his real name, he must be punished for the damage he has done and the good men he has killed. Take Marin with you for the exchange. I will talk to Yuri and we will see if we can't give Luke and his American colleagues a little surprise.'

Chapter 81

Droganja River

Marko felt like his head was on fire. A situation compounded by lack of food, some water, just enough, and sleep. His whole body was exhausted, from being handcuffed for almost twenty-four hours. The older one of the Americans climbed into the rear seat of the BMW, holding his Strike One pistol in a steady hand. The other American, the driver, reached in, put on Marko's seat belt and closed the door. It was an effective strategy and Marko could not even think of a counter. His thoughts turned to his father and he focused on his father's face and the thought that he would come to help him kill this man, this Luke. He shivered as the thought of putting a bullet into the man's neck ran through his head.

'Pat, if he so much as tries anything, I want you to shoot him in the leg. You got that,' said Jake as he climbed into the passenger seat.

'Spider and Frog?' asked Pat.

'Both injured and staying behind to pack for a quick rush to the border and out of here. You, you shit of a man,' he looked firmly into Marko's eyes, 'are going back to Papa.'

Tony climbed into the front seat. 'We right to go?'

'Let's roll,' said Jake.

Twenty-five minutes passed by and Tony approached the final

one-hundred meters before the bridge. No-one had spoken during the journey as Tony followed a pre-arranged route on the BMW's Sat Nav. 'Just over there,' said Jake, pointing to a parking lane in the lead up to the bridge, where they could see a lit stretch of road which went around to their front and right. Jake checked his Seamaster: 05:57, cracked open the door and listened for a minute. Dead quiet. 'Pat, you cover him until I signal, then bring him out of your door and up to me. Sensei, with me.'

The two men climbed out of the BMW and walked forward. There was a street light near the start of the bridge and several more along. 'Cover me', said Jake when he was ten meters from the bridge. Tony stood and held his rifle close to his chest and looked closely at everything around him. At this hour, there were no people and he counted seven boats anchored along the shore at the other end of the bridge, where the city fringes ended and the pristine salt flats began in the distance. Dawn approached but the sun's rays were still minutes away.

Jake watched for a sign of anything from across the bridge and a couple of minutes passed before he saw headlights and a large Mercedes saloon came down the roadway toward the bridge, coming to rest on the left shoulder of the road on the other side.

A figure got out of the car, followed by the driver, just as he'd done it himself. His phone vibrated and he saw that it was Zoran.

He accepted the call. 'You ready to do this?'

'Yes, the woman is in the back. Bring up my son.'

'You first, Zoran. Let me see her out of the car and then we'll bring your son forward.'

Zoran signaled back and the rear door of the Mercedes opened and Nikki was pushed out to the roadway, her hands bound at the wrists to her front. She gathered her footing for a second and then moved steadily forward, one of the Zoran's men holding her left arm. Jake could see she was all in one piece.

'There you are,' said Zoran into his cell.

Jake turned and gave a quick hand signal to bring Marko forward and Pat brought him out of the car and prodded him in the back with the pistol. 'Start walking,' he said.

As Marko came up, Jake pressed his hand on the young man's chest to stop him and looked across the bridge, some forty meters between the two parties. He spoke into his cell, 'Now, no tricks Zoran, my men are expert shots and we are good at what we do.'

'Is okay, I just want my son back,' said Zoran.

Pat held Marko by the arm. The young man was clearly defeated but still managed to ask about his handcuffs. Pat crushed his arm a little harder. 'The key's probably a small blob of molten metal by now, but you should find a way to get them off.' He showed him the Strike One pistol. 'Better still, shoot them off with this,' and he shoved the pistol into the front waistband of Marko's cargo pants. 'Safety's off, so walk slowly. Nice pistol, but once I knew it was yours, it lost all that shine.'

Pat gave Marko a push and he started to walk across the bridge. 'Zoran, let her go,' said Jake. He saw Nikki take a few steps and then she was walking boldly toward them. He turned to Pat, 'Get back to the car and take the wheel. Sensei has the car's remote you need to be carrying. Take it from him and push the 'Start' button. When we're all aboard, I want you in gear ready to head out of here, okay?'

'Got it,' said Pat and he turned back and palmed the remote from Tony on his way back. He'd had some experience when they'd picked the cars up from the dealer in Ljubljana and drove them into the shipping container back at the safe-house. He knew he could get them out of there, no problems.

Jake turned back and saw that Nikki was only fifteen meters from him. Further on, Marko was almost to his father. He called to her. 'Quick Nikki, we have to go.'

Nikki forced her legs to move a bit quicker and she managed a sort of run. As she reached Jake, he supported her by the shoulders and they quickly headed back to the car. Tony followed quickly. He'd only gone a few yards when two gun shots pierced the dawn silence and he knew that someone was either dying or dead.

Chapter 82

Droganja River

Three hours earlier, just after three am, Jake and Eddie drove the Audi to the bridge. Planning an exercise to retrieve Nikki safely on the basis of some tourist photos on the internet was not Jake's style and he certainly didn't trust the Russians, who he was sure would never forgive or forget the shame he had brought upon them. Russians in Jake's opinion always wanted their revenge. *Bring it on*, he thought.

Jake spent several minutes looking around the bridge and the approach roads while Eddie looked for a place where he could lay unseen, a laying up point. After several minutes, he found a suitable spot between some packing cases and the wall of an old warehouse. He crouched down and saw that his view gave him some elevation and he could see along one side of the bridge all the way to the other side.

He found some cardboard boxes which he used to cover himself and settled down to wait. Jake returned and crouched down near Eddie's hide. 'Looks effective, Frog. You got two and a half to wait. Rear left door when we go. Okay?'

'Got it. See you soon.'

Jake went over to the Audi and drove back to the safe house. Eddie settled down to wait.

An hour passed and all Eddie had seen had been one cat, a fox, two rats and a container truck. He flipped up the NVGs and peered down the optical sight of the As Val rifle. Movement always gave you away. You can develop ways of dealing with the Ss, your shine, shape, silhouette, and so on, but if you have to move, you move and Eddie saw a shape, a man, moving along the steel superstructure beneath the bridge.

He hadn't seen the guy arrive, so he must have come in on foot and Eddie was under no illusion that he was here for the six am meeting. Eddie sighted through his rifle scope and saw the man conceal himself behind some of the steelwork. The natural parking point for Jake would be clear in this man's line of sight and would place Jake and the team at great risk. Particularly once the exchange had gone down. Eddie relaxed his breathing and kept watch on his front.

As expected, the team arrived first. Eddie checked his watch as the BMW pulled up and the driver, Tony he supposed, switched off the head lights. 05:57. Three minutes to go. He rechecked his front and sighted down the telescopic sight of the As Val. The light was not good, but he could just make out the shape of the man who had not moved from his hidden position. He was looking around the large upright beam, but had not yet brought a weapon to bear on the people he protected. He held the cross of his sight on the man's head and focused on his breathing. He was aware of a second vehicle approaching from across the other side of the river, but tuned it out, focusing solely on the man in his sights.

After several minutes, he was dimly aware that the exchange was taking place and opened his left eye and saw Nikki and the boy were both crossing the bridge. He refocused again and concentrated on slowing his breathing, looking through the sight at the man he now knew to be one of the Russians. Seconds passed and the man brought a rifle up and adopted a firing position.

Eddie knew it would take several seconds for the man to get his sights locked onto his intended target and that meant his people, his team. He drew in a final, deep breath and held it, at the same time applying pressure to the trigger, remembering his training to squeeze, and not pull on the trigger, keeping the cross hairs of his sight on the man's body mass, his chest. There was less than one-hundred yards to the target, almost zero wind, and the projectile would only drop less than an inch, but Eddie was not going to chance a head shot, not on a rifle he'd not zeroed and practiced with. His rifle fired and he saw the bullet impact the man's chest within inches of his aim. Less than a second later and he saw his opponent's own rifle flash as he fell forward, about ten meters or so, into the water below. Eddie knew he'd shot the man and looked up, relieved to see Tony, Jake and Nikki unhurt and preparing to get into the BMW. He rose up to join them.

Chapter 83

Droganja River

Zoran bundled Marko into the backseat, still bound by his handcuffs, and he grunted with pain as he fell face forward into the rear seat of the Mercedes. Marin climbed into the driver's seat ready to go, the engine already ticking over.

Zoran looked up and waited for Yuri to act, to shoot and kill the American, the man called Luke. He could see the woman supported by Luke approach the BMW and noted a flash from his front and left. A second shot and, too late, he realized that the first had not been fired by Yuri. As he saw Yuri fall into the river, he felt, not for the first time, fear grip his chest. He climbed into the rear of the Mercedes. 'Drive,' he barked.

Once Marin had completed his turn, the tires spinning for traction, they were away. Zoran kept his head down waiting for another shot from the sniper who'd been waiting for the exchange all along.

Marko, still prone on the back seat, struggled to get upright and Zoran helped him, pulling his hands around from behind his back. 'Here, hold still.' He pushed a key into one of the cuffs and unlocked it. Marko had been handcuffed for almost twenty-four hours and he winced in pain as he brought his hands to his front. Zoran handed him the key and Marko undid the last cuff and dropped them to the floor.

'Thank you, Papa. I will not forget.'

Marin held the car steady, travelling fast, but not excessively. 'We are clear, boss, where do you want to go?'

'Head back to the airfield. We are heading north.'

'Where are we going?' said Marko.

Zoran looked at his son and reached out and squeezed his shoulder. 'Germany. I know of your dislike of the Germans, but our time here is over. A new guy is coming in to take over the operations here.'

Marko examined his wrists and rubbed them trying to get his circulation going. His pistol was sitting uncomfortably behind him and he pulled it out. He pulled back the slide and saw a round inside. He dropped the clip and pressed down on the bullets he could see within, noting it was full or near full, and then reinserted it, placing it on the seat space between them. 'Why don't you drop me off back at Portorož? You don't need me, Papa.' He added, 'not after all the trouble I have caused.'

Zoran didn't answer and focused on the route ahead as Marin expertly navigated the big saloon toward their destination.

'They will never forgive you for losing the money, Papa. I saw the numbers, more than ten billion.'

Zoran turned to look at his son. 'You are talking nonsense, and you know it. I've already talked with Boris. Our *vory* has many billions more. We lose money all the time. It is a cost of doing business. We'll be fine. You'll see.'

Marko looked at Marin and lowered his voice. 'I have some money put away. Some cash.'

'Yes, I know.'

'It is not much, a few million Euros, but it could buy us both a start. We could buy a boat. We could move, change our names and start afresh, take tourists out, sailing, fishing. Come on Papa, you know this would work.'

'You know we cannot leave our life.'

'It is not my life, Papa. It is your *vory*, not mine.'

'Marko, I owe my life, everything to the *vory* and pledged lifelong allegiance to them. I would have died in the Gulag without their protection. You are my only son and now belong to us. It is time you are initiated as a *vor*, just as I am. I know you will miss your life here, but it is over. You have learned a lesson, an expensive one I know. But, we will be okay. I am not without influence and we will build a new life together. Stop worrying.'

Marko looked out of the window as they sped toward their destination and his 'new life'. He was less certain than his father about their future and felt shame and regret at his actions. He was also angry at how easily the Americans had fucked them over. He cared little for the men who had died in the last couple of days, had felt nothing at their deaths, Sasha perhaps, but his hatred for the man they'd called Luke knew no bounds.

'I will kill him, Papa.'

'Who, the American?'

'Yes.'

Zoran smiled. 'Forget him. It is time for you to grow up. If it weren't for Boris, for me, you'd already be on a plane to face your accusers. The American is a soldier, or a former soldier, I am sure of it. And a good one, you know that. We're lucky he didn't kill us all. No more talk of killing, we need to look forward now, not to the past.'

Fifteen minutes later, some forty after they left the bridge, the twin hangars at Divača airport came into view and the Antonov turbo-prop sat on the apron in front of the nearest hangar. The helicopter was no longer in sight and Zoran assumed the pilots they'd ejected from it back at the Fortress had made their peace with Boris and had already flown it back to Poland.

Marin drove toward the plane and parked next to it. The sun had risen about 10 degrees above the horizon and Zoran looked at his watch; it was close to seven am. As Marin switched off the engine, Boris came down the steps of the plane and onto the concrete apron. He'd found some clean clothes and looked rested.

Marin got out of the car and came around to Zoran's door and opened it. Boris came towards them and pulled out a pistol, discharging it from a distance of ten feet into Marin's head who collapsed against the car and slid down to the ground, blood pouring from his head. Marko reached for his pistol, but Boris was quicker and fired again through the windscreen spraying both Marko and Zoran with glass shards. 'Put your hands where I can see them.'

Zoran and Marko complied. 'Climb out of the car, slowly and keep those hands up.'

Zoran climbed out unsteadily, Marko more slowly, looking for an opportunity, but there was none. Boris' was steady and kept his pistol pointed in their direction, now at the front of the Mercedes. He walked back a few steps. 'Come to the front of the car.'

'Boris, let's talk about this,' said Zoran.

'Zoran, I am sorry. Keep coming.' The men reached the front of the car and stood there, hands above their heads.

'What can we do to avoid this, Boris?'

'Nothing, you know how it is. I have my orders. Too much mess, too much loss. What can I say? Turn around.'

'No, not like this,' said Zoran.

'Turn around.' Boris fired the pistol between them.

'No,' said Zoran. 'If you are going to be my executioner, then I want to face you so that I can remember your face as the last thing...'

Chapter 84

Droganja River

As the Mercedes sped off away from them, Eddie emerged from his hiding place across the road, his rifle held in his right hand. Stiff from lying in a prone position, he walked gingerly down to the others.

'Well done,' said Jake. When did their shooter arrive?

'About 04:30 or thereabouts.'

Nikki sat in the back of the car with Tony. 'Thanks for coming to get me. It was stupid of me to get caught and ruin the mission for everyone.'

'Sorry we left you exposed,' said Tony. 'We should have foreseen that Zoran would not give up. How was Stefan when you left him?'

'I think he'll be okay. He had cuts and bruises and I suspect some broken bones in his left foot, but the paramedics were there. He'll be in good hands. What will you do now?'

Jake came to the passenger door. 'Well team that's it then.'

'Not so fast,' said Pat.

'It's over,' said Jake, pointing across the bridge. 'They have a three minute start on us.'

'No,' Pat held up his phone and passed it to Jake who could see a familiar Sat. Nav. map of the area. 'That blip there, the blue one, is Zoran's Mercedes. A dollar will get you fifty cents they are heading for the Divača airstrip West of the Fortress.' He got out of the driver's seat. 'Tony, you're driving.'

Tony climbed behind the wheel and Jake sat next to him. Eddie and Pat climbed into the back with Nikki in the middle. 'Tony,' said Pat, 'turn us around and get us to Divača as quickly as you can.'

Jake looked at Tony. 'Go Buddy.'

'Everyone fasten your seat belts,' said Tony

As the car did a U-turn and accelerated back the way they'd came, Jake turned around. 'Where is the GPS device?'

'I put it in Marko's pistol, in the clip. I emptied it and found that the device could just fit inside. Topped it up with three bullets. The gun will fire, but instead of having fifteen rounds, he'll run out after four shots and may jam after three.'

'Why don't we just follow them if we can track them?' said Eddie.

'And how do you know they are heading for the airstrip at Divača?' added Tony.

'If we follow them and they get to their plane first, they could well have taken off by the time we get there,' said Pat. 'Our route to the airstrip at Divača is about fifteen kilometers shorter, which gives us a good advantage. And, after they captured me, when I was back at the Fortress, Marko mentioned they were going to kill some Croatians and they were going to the airport. At first I thought he meant the main one at Portorož, where you entered the country. But later, I realized that they were going fully armed and the small airstrip at Divača, which is close to the Fortress, made much more sense.'

♦

Tony pushed the BMW as hard as he could and they approached the airstrip only fifteen minutes later. 'Okay, slow down Tony,' said

Jake. 'The airstrip is only a klick away. Pat, where are they?'

Pat studied his cell phone and passed it forward to Jake. 'They are still about ten minutes out, but I'm almost certain they are coming this way.'

'Okay, go past the airstrip.'

Tony continued driving and a sign displaying a plane signaled the entrance to the airstrip. 'Slow down,' said Jake, 'but keep driving.'

The Antonov was clearly visible on the apron in front of the two hangars and Jake studied Pat's cell phone again looking to match the features to what they could see. He pointed out the front windscreen. 'See that small stand of trees, about ten o'clock?'

'Got it,' said Tony.

'There should be a track coming up on the left.'

Tony kept driving and some four-hundred meters past the turnoff, Jake saw what looked like a track to their left. 'There.'

'Already seen it, Luke.' He pulled off the road, but their way was blocked by a gate.

Jake saw a padlock. 'Can you open that, Pat?'

'Should be able to. Open the rear, Tony.'

The rear tailgate swung upwards and Pat looked through his hold all in the back, emerging with his lock picker. Less than thirty seconds went by and the gate was open. Tony drove forward and Pat closed the gate behind them, before closing the tailgate and getting back into the car.

Tony took the car slowly along the track and, just as the map indicated, it took them up and into the stand of trees that Jake had spotted from the road. 'About here should do, Tony.'

Chapter 85

Divača Airstrip

Boris moved back a couple of paces so that there was a good five yards or so between him and the two men standing next to the car. 'You've had this coming Zoran. Even this morning, I give you my best man. All he had to do was place a few well aimed shots.'

Zoran interrupted, 'You weren't there, Boris. They second guessed us and had a marksman already in place.'

'It was your plan anyway,' added Marko. 'Get this over with.'

Boris lifted his pistol.

Zoran felt a wet spray across his face and saw the front of Boris's head explode. Half a second later came the sound of the bullet that he'd just seen punch its way through the man's head.

Marko reacted quickest, grabbed his father's elbow and pulled him behind the Mercedes. He activated the front door and it opened 'Get in Papa,'

Zoran crawled inside and Marko followed, keeping low until he was in the driver seat. He popped his head up and quickly determined a route to get them turned and headed back down the access road.

'Why didn't they shoot us as well?' said Zoran, still unwilling to unwind himself from the depths of the backseat.

'Want me alive, don't they? So, they can fly me to America to face their version of justice. Fucking scum!' Marko slammed the heel of his left hand against the steering wheel. 'We're fucked.'

Zoran cautiously lifted his head and looked out the back window. 'I know you're thinking of running.'

'Too right. Not hanging around here. You can do what you like.'

'No, you don't understand. If we use our heads, I think we can fall back on our family.'

'No way.'

'Hear me out.'

'As soon as they see us, they will kill us.'

'Not if we give them some vengeance to strengthen the weak hand we currently hold.'

Chapter 86

Portorož

The BMW came to a stop behind an Audi A8, which was parked in a side street near Marko's apartment in Portorož. Jake got out and walked forward so that he was level with the driver of the Audi. The driver's window came down and Andy lowered his sunglasses. 'What's the score, Spider?'

'Marko nearly clocked me. I was down there,' he pointed behind them. 'Perhaps two hundred distant on the other side of the intersection.' He looked at his watch. 'I saw him arrive twenty-six minutes ago in the Merc, his father in the back. He waited almost fifteen minutes, looking for a tail, and then decided to have one last look and drove around the block.'

'Well, they didn't see you and, assuming he hasn't found the GPS transmitter, they should still be inside. How's the arm?'

'It's paining me, but I've had worse.'

'Good man. Take Nikki to the hospital at Trieste and then meet us outside the front gates at Aviano. You got the rest of our cash?'

'It's in the sports bag behind me.'

'Give it to her when you drop her off.'

'Sure, no problems.'

Jake walked back to the BMW and got in. 'Pat, you can get us inside?'

'Sure,' he held up the lock picker.

'Okay, let's go. Frog, and Sens. bring your pistols.'

Everyone got out of the car and Jake went over to Nikki.

'Your job is over Nik.'

'No way, Jake. I want to see the end of this.'

'You've already done more than your share. If it weren't for your quick thinking and getting away when they took Pat at the hotel. Well none of this would've been possible. We'll stay in touch, okay?' Nikki nodded. 'Go with Andy. He'll take you to Trieste, where you should find your Uncle at one of the hospitals there. All the witnesses, the people who know your part in this are dead. Well apart from the Zoran and Marko, and we'll take care of them.'

She stepped forward and put her arms around him. Jake hugged her back. 'Goodbye, Jake. You are a good man.'

'Bye, Nik. Take care.'

She turned to Pat and hung on tightly when he offered her a hug. 'See you Nik,' he said. 'When this is all done, I want you to come over to the States. You need to get out of this place and come work for me.'

'Sure. Thank you Patrick. Is a good thing you have done here. Now, I must go and see Uncle Stef.' She walked to the Audi and got in the front next to Andy.

'Right,' said Jake. 'Let's go.'

At that moment, a screech of tires was heard and Zoran's Mercedes roared out of the underground garage and took off up the street.

'Not going to make it easy for us are they?' said Tony.

Chapter 87

Portorož

'Turn here,' said Zoran from his position in the passenger seat. 'And slow down, I think we have lost them.'

Marko turned the big sedan into the street and adjusted his speed. He'd been continually checking his mirrors, but had seen no pursuit, and especially no BMW SUVs. Back in his apartment, he'd just wanted to sleep. Since the other morning, when they'd flown east to kill the Croatians, he'd not slept and his tiredness was starting to set in. He shook his head to clear it.

Zoran hadn't wanted to go back to Marko's apartment, but Marko had insisted as he had money and his passports there. Five minutes in and out, he'd said and he'd been true to his word. In the back was a small suitcase which he'd filled with a few things. He'd be back later when things cooled down. They weren't going to watch his place forever, surely?

In the trunk of the car lay two large suitcases and the larger of the two contained around three-million Euros. Enough to start afresh somewhere. The money didn't belong to Marko, but it had been easy to take when no-one really knew how big the pile had been in the basement.

For as long as Marko could remember, each and every week, a courier came to their house from who knew where in Europe to drop off funds from the *vory*'s operations. Except for the cleaners and the old man who came twice a week to do the gardening, they all knew about the money in the house, but no-one thought to take any, as they were all in the tent, initiated into the group and, if anyone needed money or a holiday, there was always enough money.

Marko once asked why they didn't put it in a bank and Zoran told him a story about 500 Million US dollars they'd deposited in a Venezuelan bank, one that had subsequently been 'nationalized' by the government. He remembered his father's wisdom: 'Saddam Hussein had plenty of money too, but when his time came, all the so-called secret bank accounts in the world couldn't help him. At the end of the day, the only money you have is what you can take with you.'

It was why his Father converted so much of his own wealth into diamonds; they were very transportable and Marko was sure that there were safety deposit boxes around containing diamonds. They had enough to make a new start. But where?

Marko was not a *vor* and, though he was certain that his Father had been planning to initiate him, it hadn't happened and now it never would. His Father had given him his apartment and money to furnish it and a cash allowance of five-hundred Euros a week. He'd never opened a bank account, but had a legitimate Russian passport and Slovenian driver's license, both identifying him as Marko Kovak. Perhaps he'd foreseen all this, as he'd only started to amass his own secret stash of cash some six months earlier, taking fifty thousand or so, usually five bundles of fifty one-hundred Euros.

◆

Zoran indeed had diamonds and cash stashed in his boat, safety deposit boxes in banks and he even had a numbered account in a Swiss bank. But his mind was on other things, at how things had turned out. Marko was a product of him, of his lifestyle as a successful criminal. There'd been plenty of killings over the years, but the dead were just part of the business they were in and were usually other criminals or the corrupted. Killing such people had never troubled him.

But killing tourists for sex; raping unconscious girls? Of course that was going to get him in trouble at some point. Zoran's problem had been his own ego he now realized. He should have just let them have Marko from the get go. However, that would have been seen as a big loss of face. And, who knew what Marko would've told the authorities if they'd been able to take him back to the States.

'Take the next right,' he said.

'I thought we were going to take the boat?'

'We are. I need to go to my lock up to get some gear that we are going to need on the boat. Over there,' Zoran pointed at a large metal shed. 'Pull up out the front and I'll open the roller door.'

Marko pulled up and Zoran got out of the car. A key fob on his belt was produced, a door unlocked and Zoran went inside. Marko briefly thought about taking off and then the large door was opening upward and he turned into the warehouse.

Zoran hit the lights and the door was closed behind him. Marko turned off the engine, got out of the Mercedes and looked around. About ten sea containers and one of Zoran's prime movers. An office in the far corner.

'Come Marko,' said Zoran as he headed over to the office. 'Something I want to show you.'

As Marko reached the office area, Zoran emerged. He was holding a revolver and it was pointed at his son. Marko held up his hands. 'Papa, no.'

Zoran moved the revolver and pointed it to the rear wall of the warehouse 'Move over to the wall over there.'

'Killing me is not going to solve anything.'

'Killing you is my only hope.'

Marko had reached the wall. 'How'd you work that out?'

Zoran held his revolver in two hands and stood about ten feet away. 'Now reach behind you, slowly pull out the pistol from your waistband and drop it behind you.'

Marko held his hands up, the gesture of surrender. He'd hoped his pistol hadn't been seen. 'Why Papa?'

'Just do it or I will shoot you now.'

Marko reached around with his right hand and held the grip of the Strike One pistol. He contemplated his options but he could see how focused his father was. He pulled it out of his waistband and dropped it behind him onto the concrete floor.

'You must see how this ends now, Marko? You have left me no choice. The only way I get to live, is to kill you.'

'Sure, Papa. Andrei is still going to kill you whatever happens.'

The pedestrian door opened inward and Zoran turned quickly at the sound. He could see into the street, but could see no-one.

'Zoran,' came a familiar voice. 'This is Luke. We have you surrounded.'

'Fuck you,' said Zoran and he fired two shots at the wall near the door. The gunshots were loud in the confined space.

'Here me out,' replied Jake looking at a fresh bullet hole in the metal sheet two feet from him. 'We just want your son, Zoran. He's no use to you now. That's why you've brought him here anyway, to kill him in the hope that you can stay pals with your vory mates.

'I'm right, aren't I?' continued Jake when Zoran didn't respond.

'I will say this just once, American,' shouted Zoran, keeping an eye on his son and one on the door. 'No-one is taking my son.'

'In that case, both of you are going to die. You shoot your son and we will shoot you, Zoran. Hand him over and you will live. I guarantee that.'

Zoran brought up his revolver and pointed it at Marko. He took pressure on the trigger.

Jake stepped into the door space and brought up his pistol.

'Drop it, Zoran.'

Zoran didn't move and Jake took in distance factors and the likely kickback of the pistol he held. 'I am going to count to five. When I reach five, I am going to shoot,' said Jake.

'One.

'Two.

'Three.'

On three, Jake placed a well aimed shot through the back of Zoran's head and the man slid to the floor, his revolver still held in his right hand, blood rapidly pooling on the concrete

Jake was already moving, but Marko had picked up his pistol and was firing at him. Jake rolled as the second of two shots came his way and he dived behind the Mercedes. He looked over the top and saw that Marko had retreated to the corner office.

'I thought you were going to give him to five?' said Marko.

'Nah, I knew if I got further than three, he was going to shoot you.'

'Perhaps that would have been the better outcome.'

'No, this is way better. Come on out of there. There's four of us here. You don't stand a chance.'

By way of answer, Marko's hand snaked around the door and a third shot was fired hitting the Mercedes in the rear window.

Jake moved away from the car and stood facing the office, perhaps thirty yards away. 'Come on Marko, you can do better than that. Here, have a free shot at me.'

Marko risked a look and saw his opponent, arms by his sides. He brought the pistol up, took aim and squeezed off a shot. Two things then happened. Firstly his shot missed, but only by a few inches. But as the slide of his pistol commenced going forward to pick up the next round in the clip, the gun jammed on the GPS device inside.

Marko looked at his pistol and couldn't explain it.

'It's a GPS transmitter,' said Jake, walking forward his pistol pointed at Marko's center mass. 'Hidden inside the clip. We knew where you were all the time.'

Marko's shoulder slumped. 'Okay, so you take me to the States. Then what, Mr. Luke? No-one is going to send me to jail. There's no evidence, there were no witnesses. You have nothing.'

'That is where you are wrong,' said Eddie, who was now standing by Tony next to the Mercedes.

'Remember Miro?' said Tony.

Marko didn't answer.

'He flew into Las Vegas with a bad gambling habit and a taste for coke,' said Jake now only ten feet away. 'One you probably helped him to acquire. Anyway, Miro was picked up by the Vegas cops, a fluke really, but when told he might spend five to ten years in prison for cocaine trafficking, he said that he would rather give evidence against you. Who'd have thought that such a thing could happen, huh?'

Pat came through the door and walked over toward the others 'Miro. Yes, quite a surprise that one. Without him, we probably wouldn't have a case.'

Jake stopped in front of the man. 'Miro's testimony was sufficient for the FBI to get a Federal Arrest warrant issue, Marko.' He reached out and took the pistol out of Marko's hand. 'You're coming with us, we have a plane to catch.' He looked down at Zoran's body. 'Sorry about your father. He left me no choice.'

Marko looked at the man he'd once cared about. 'Fuck him, he wasn't much of a father.'

Epilogue

Waikiki, Honolulu, Hawaii

Jake cracked open his second bottle of Heineken lager and took an appreciative sip, staring at the ocean from his balcony on the 10th floor of the Halekulani Hotel on Waikiki's famous beach. Three weeks had gone by since their dash to Aviano with Marko Kovak. After flying to Dublin to refuel, the FBI had directed them to fly to JFK where a large reception committee was waiting for Kovak. Agent Simmons escorted him off the plane and, once he touched US soil, he was read his rights and arrested for the murder of Danielle Fisher.

Simmons wanted to play down any official role they'd played in bringing Marko back. And publicity of any sort was something none of them needed. So, Jake, the pilots and his men remained on the plane while Marko was taken away and then they refueled and flew to Seattle. As far as he was aware, there was no record of them ever landing in New York that day.

In Seattle, Pat headed for home and Andy went to hospital to have his arm x-rayed and properly set. Jake and the others were exhausted from their journey, so Iain booked them into the Hilton, where they rested for three days, before taking off in separate directions. There were no big celebrations and even Eddie seemed content to drink cola, rest and recuperate and plan for a new life.

Iain had been effusive in his praise for the team's efforts, in rescuing Pat and getting Marko into a Federal prison, where he awaited a future trial date. The team had also brought Marko's money back on the plane with them and they spent a whole morning at the Hilton selecting several worthwhile charities that would benefit from an 'anonymous donor'. They were all in complete agreement when Jake suggested giving a large part to Medicine Sans Frontiers, the charity that Danielle had been working for in Armenia.

Andy was the first to go. With a couple of mil in his bank account, he was soon talking to his contacts in the film industry with the aim of establishing his own stunt business and being his own boss. He'd also been missing his woman and, after two nights in Seattle, he hugged his mates and got on a jet back to his home in Atlanta. Jake missed him already.

Similarly, Tony knew where he wanted to go and it wasn't long before he was looking online to see about getting a better, albeit second-hand, race car and talked incessantly about the team that would take him to Daytona. Despite Jake's own reservations about how successful he would be, he wished the man well when he flew back to his home in Kentucky. He knew if he ever needed a good wheelman, he'd be calling on him.

Eddie and he were the odd pair. Neither of them had a past they wanted to go back to, nor could they come up with firm plans for the future. In the end, Eddie decided that he would go to California, where his only sister operated a small fruit farm and needed some help. Jake knew that he would help her financially as well, but at least he'd set some short term goals and was resolutely taking each day at a time, something that all recovering alcoholics experience.

On the same day that Eddie flew to California, Jake went with him as he wanted to spend some time with his Father, who was in a nursing home in Los Angeles following a recent stroke. The reunion turned out be be just what he needed and he'd been pleased to see that his dad was making slow, but gradual improvements to his health.

As he'd leased out his own apartment in LA, he no longer had a home and he decided it was time for him to see some of the world he hadn't seen, and as a tourist and not a soldier. His travel plans had brought him to Hawaii, where he intended to do some sight seeing and just relax for a few weeks, talk to the locals...

Nonetheless, something had stuck with him on the flight over to the States with Marko. 'Hey, Mr. Luke,' he opened with as Jake had sat opposite him at one point in time. 'The *vory*, Mr. Luke.'

'What about them?'

'They won't forgive. And, they won't forget. Too much money and you killed some senior guys they were solid with, especially Boris and my father.'

'You think I'm scared of some old Russians?' had been his glib response at the time.

He knew they'd taken some good precautions, but he couldn't rule out that the remaining members of the gang wouldn't find out the identity of him or members of his team and act on it. There were too many people who knew, too easy to connect the dots.

Eliminating that risk would involve him finding and then killing all the other *vory* members and that certainly wasn't going to happen.

Whatever, he wasn't going to look over his shoulder for the rest of his life. If the Russians wanted to bring a battle to him, or to other members of his team, or family for that matter, they'd better bring the best they had as he'd give them a fight they would never forget.

THE END

AFTER WORD

Dear reader,

I hope you read it all, are not starting here at the end. In production is Jake's third adventure, *Meltdown*. I already think it will be his best adventure yet and hope that you will buy a copy.

Someone asked me how I come up with the ideas, the inspiration, for my novels. That answer was easy. Just look around at what we are seeing now in the world. I don't have to make anything up. Sad but true.

If you liked reading *Rendition*, please go back to where you bought it and give me a review, or even just a star rating. The new publishing paradigm is great for readers and for authors. You get more choice (most authors only have an online presence) and I get the capacity to self publish a quality product for a good price.

However, one of the consequences of not having space in a bricks and mortar store, means that I'm a tiny target, hard for interested consumers to find. Pass the word if you can.

And please, if you want to contact me, go to my website:

www.jakewalkerussf.com

With my thanks and regards

Chris December 2017

www.ingramcontent.com/pod-product-compliance
Lightning Source LLC
Chambersburg PA
CBHW071447110726
47908CB00003B/541